Knobbe Cove

Knobbe Cove

Phyllis W. Fravel

Author Representative
Kathy Wall Etheridge
473 Marshalls Beach Rd.
Heathsville, VA 22473
USA

Production: Fourth Lloyd Productions, LLC.

ISBN: 978-1-7350341-2-6

Printed in the USA

*For my family, with a special
thanks to my dear friends
Ginny Arrington and Marion Wall*

Contents

PROLOGUE

*E*ARLY *A*UGUST RAIN, STEAMING ON GREY MACADAM, SIZZLED ON the hood of a speeding car. Raucous rap in mega decibels blared from the radio of the sleek red vintage ragtop, it's driver loudly rapping along, a beer can in his right hand, the rest of the empty six-pack littered on the floor under the glove compartment. Winding mountain lanes curled out before him, his headlights dimly cutting into the view. Twilight had slipped into early night.

Angelic childish voices ignored the fast-moving storm as a father and his two young children, on their way home from church camp, excitedly told of new friends, songs learned, and games played. As the white pickup truck rounded a steep curve, it was met by headlights streaking towards them on the wrong side of the slippery road.

The head-on collision shrieked throughout the pines and maples and resounded from the rocks. In a few seconds people lost their lives. The truck, upside down partway down the mountainside, gave off the last sound, wheels slowly turning in the air, unable to get purchase of hardtop.

For a few short moments, silence lay heavy on the world and then the crickets and katydids took up their interrupted mating chirr. Somewhere an owl, perched high in a tree, asked the question, "Whooo?"

The scream began in her toes, rising, seeming to strip her flesh of life's blood, coursing its way through her belly, leaving it cold and wretched. Shriek-filled lungs left no room for air, strangling, pushing tears ahead of sound. Robey Layne never knew whether she uttered a sound for musty velvet darkness wrapped around her and she slowly floated into welcoming oblivion. There, in unconscious coolness, she was momentarily freed from the horror. The respite lasted only a short time and as awareness returned, so did the excruciating pain.

Someone was stroking her auburn hair and wiping her forehead with a soft, damp cloth, and Robey vaguely realized she was on the sofa, her head cradled in Sarah's broad lap. Looking up, she focuses her eyes on the police officer's brown uniform and her mind cruelly told her what she already knew...but had to ask again.

"I'm sorry Mrs. Layne...so very sorry, but it's true." The soft voice, full of compassion, tried to be soothing, but the message still jangled in Robey's ears. "There were no survivors, but neither your husband...nor the two children...suffered. It...it was instant.

The trooper, with a boyish blond cowlick dropping down upon his forehead, stood twisting his hat in his hands, his words low and sympathetic. "It wasn't your husband's fault. Another vehicle crossed the center median at high speed. That driver didn't survive, either. Reeked of liquor...and we found an empty six-pack in the wreckage.

With Sarah's help Robey struggled to her feet, tears streaking her cheeks as she battled with herself for control. She began to numb her mind and body and for this she was thankful. She felt near to hysterics and the constriction in her chest wouldn't allow her to straighten her shoulders. She found her legs rubbery, so she sat on the arm of the sofa, her head handging low, defeated and miserable. Sarah circled her slim shoulders with her arm giving her support, handing her the box of tissues from the end table.

"Is there anything I can do Ma'am?" The officer crouched in front of Robey, putting his hand over hers and looking up into her distraught face.

"Let me help her get settled," Sarah almost whispered, "and

we'll call you later. Leave your name and badge number over there on the desk. There's a notepad somewhere there, I'm sure."

"I have a card with that information," he handed one to Sarah, stood and swiftly strode across the room, obviously anxious to be gone. The door closed quietly behind him, and the silence was broken only by the motor revving as the black and white backed out of the driveway.

"Cry and let it out honey. Kick, yell and scream if you want... you've a right."

Robey stood shakily, blowing her nose, and walked slowly to the window seat and sat there looking far beyond the windowpane.

"I'll be fine Sarah. I've just got to think a bit." Her hands trembled and she began weeping quietly. "I'm exhausted. My bones ache. I'm going to go up and lie down a bit... just for a little while... don't leave me... Please?"

"I'll be here. Are there any calls you want me to make?"

"Call anyone you like, but I don't want to see anyone yet. Call Larry. Tell him to begin making arrangements. This sounds so cold and business-like. Does everyone accept death like this so early? Why can't we fight to bring them back? Have things the way they were a few minutes ago? That's what I want to do. I don't like being told all I have left is making arrangements."

Upstairs, Robey stretched out on the tan flowered satin comforter and stared at the ceiling. Roger... Bud... Sally. She recalled each face vividly... each detail as though they were pasted up on the ceiling—the flecked blue of their eyes, the russet curls around Sally's face that would never stay in a ribbon, and Bud's freckle and blond shock of hair that had never been tamed by a comb. Mentally she told them there were things yet for them to do... camp for Bud next week, the beach weekend before school started up again,

Roger's Chamber of Commerce dinner...he was to be installed as President. So many things undone. They couldn't be gone...but they were.

The faces began to fade into the wallpaper and Robey couldn't bring them back. She frantically wracked her brain trying to recall, but no matter how hard she tried, the images refused to return. Then came the awful realization she would never see them again and the scream, now a desperate wail, escaped from her throat and the mournful sound reached out to every corner of the house. Downstairs, Sarah, the phone in her hand, looked up, undecided whether to go to Robey or leave her alone with her anguish. She replaced the phone in its cradle and sat down, abandoning herself for the first time to sobs of grief for her beloved neighbor and her lost family.

1

ROBEY PACED THE UPSTAIRS HALLWAY AND HESITANTLY opened the door to her bedroom where lilac scent from her recent bath still clung to the air. She stood there quietly, her hand caressing the cool brass knob, not wishing to disturb the ghosts lying abed, beneath silken sheets entwined in each other's arms, making love, whispering endearments, enfolding each other with warmth, nuzzling the curves of their necks. She heaved a deep sigh, closed the door softly behind her and stepped back into the dark hallway where the mirror on the wall reflected puffy eyelids and a red nose. She hated the way she looked when she cried. Why couldn't she cry like actresses do, without shiny noses and bloated faces? Dabbing at her eyes with a tissue, she patted a wisp of wavy hair back into place and checked her clothes. Presentable, just barely, but it would have to do. Denims and a light gray sweatshirt, socks and tennies were good for travelling.

"Robey, where are you?" Sarah's cheerful contralto boomed from somewhere below.

"Up here, coming right down." Robey almost ran down the carpeted stairs. Thank God for Sarah she thought. How often she remembered how it was Sarah's strength that had sustained her through that terrible night in August and the horrors of the funeral. Thanksgiving, Christmas, and New Year's had all passed in a haze with Sarah trying to do her best to keep her occupied and reasonably busy and content. Sarah had failed in her mission, but Robey had tried her best not to let her know.

More than a year had passed, wide-awake hideous days and trouble-some nights. Sleeping pills had failed to obliterate the nightmares where policemen in brown uniforms had pointed finger at her and shouted "They're dead! They're dead!" And then the screams would come that left her sitting bolt upright, cold perspiration trickling over the curve of her breast. Days had not been much better with so many reminders of Roger and the children in the house. She still listened for the grating squeak of the screen door at half past three o'clock when Bud and Sally used to rush in from school full of tales of teachers and playmates, hungry for cookies or pudding. Then she would listen for the car to pull up in the driveway when she prepared dinner in the kitchen and tried to wish into existence Roger's footsteps on the back stairs to the porch.

But no more. Robey was determined to change the situation, this being a helpless pawn of memories. It was all going to change. She was leaving agony behind in this house. Ghosts could make love behind the closed door of the bedroom all they wanted. Robey did not intend being there to watch.

"Isn't it past time for you to go if you're to make only two motel stops before getting to Knobbe Cove?" Sarah lit a cigarette and picked up a small glass ashtray from the marble topped table, flicking ashes into it. "I still wish I could talk you into reconsidering...and staying. It'll be so terribly lonesome here and who knows what sort of neighbors I'll have to put up with when you rent or sell."

"You won't be lonesome. You have Jack and your boys. Besides, you'd make friends with and reform the Devil himself if he moved in." Robey pulled the curtains aside and sat down in the window seat. "Perhaps one day I'll be able to come back. Right now, I just don't know."

"Honey, you've never really told me why you feel you must go. I've only known of your decision for a couple of weeks. If I've done something, or not done something, I wish you'd tell me."

"You?" Robey almost laughed. "God knows you've been the only real friend I've had, besides Larry. No, it's so many things, honey...like hearing Meg tell Mrs. Whitman they should include 'poor Robey' in the plans for the skiing weekend." Robey's voice couldn't mask its bitterness, "Or Robert Caulfield suggesting 'since I now have the time' I should do more volunteer work at the hospital. Lots of things like that, they've all added up."

Sarah could only shake her head in agreement, wishing she could have done something-anything-to have erased the hurt caused by other people. She truly loved this woman who had shared cups of coffee and recipes for over ten years.

A sigh escaped Robey from the depth of her being and she threw back her shoulders to straighten the slump she felt in her back. "I've become a bitter person, Sarah, and I don't like that. I sometimes think I'm losing my sanity. I want to keep on yelling and kicking and screaming—and it's been too long now. Not a bit of it will bring Roger and the children back and I know it. And I want to scream about that, too."

Robey looked out into a bright March morning where gusts of wind fanned dry, crusty snow out of the grey barren treetops, making a sheer white curtain briefly in the front yard.

"Where's Lawrence, I wonder? He should have been here long ago." She felt frustrated and wanted to be away...far away. The parting was taking far too long. Sarah leaned against the edge of the sofa and watched out the bowed bay window with Robey, feelings of helplessness making her sad.

"I don't want to let you go. Somehow I feel you're making an unwise step, but I don't know how to help you. I've never felt a loss like yours."

"That's another point, Sarah." Robey turned to look at her friend. "I can hardly bear to see Jack drive up to your house and hear the boys yell at him from the yard and know he'll be in your arms as soon as he gets to the other side of your door. If I stayed here, I might end up hating you for what you have and I haven't. I wouldn't want to hate you." She whispered, looking down at her wedding ring, "but maybe I would."

Somewhere beyond the pine tree towering above the small house a car door slammed, and Lawrence LaPorte came into view across the snow-covered lawn. His galoshes flapped open at each step, a plaid woolen scarf covered his slight jaw and his hands were shoved deep into the pockets of his greatcoat. Lawrence, scowling, obviously did not enjoy winter weather. Icicles, dripping from the iron railing by the steps, sparkled in the sun's piercing rays, but they looked warmer than Lawrence. Odd, Robey thought, how irritated she felt at the sight of him. It was a physical repulsion, she knew. The horn-rimmed glasses, so out of style… his face, pocked from teenage acne, and those tight, thin, unsmiling lips. Even his mincing effeminate step.

How much a pillar of strength he had been during the past months. He had dealt with the funeral director and done all those mundane but necessary deeds. An efficient attorney, Roger had leaned on Lawrence heavily and his advice now made her extremely wealthy. She would have given it all for one hug from Bud and Sally and Roger's usual passionate embrace. The unwelcome memories began surging in upon her and Robey was grateful when Lawrence's lean form came through the door.

"Sorry I'm late," he mumbled as he pried off the boots and left them outside on the stoop and flopped his coat over the back of a chair. He held out his hands to Robey and she allowed him to encircle her shoulders in a friendly squeeze. Her nose crinkled in distaste at the bouquet of his cologne and she tried to pull away, but he held her, his voice pleading. "Please don't go. It's selfish, you know. You're not only changing your life, you're changing mine! You and Roger have been a big part of my existence for a long, long time."

Robey deftly twisted out of his grasp, smoothed her shirt where his hands had been, and turned to face him. "My mind's made up," she stated flatly.

Lawrence turned to Sarah. "Can't you convince her to stay?"

"I've tried. I really have tried." Sarah started out the front door and called back over her shoulder. "I know you two have to talk business. I have a couple of things to do. See you both outside."

Robey moved over to the window, pushed the curtain aside, holding it with slim fingers, and watched Sarah enter her own home. She waited until the door shut behind her before she again turned to face Lawrence.

"Believe me, I'll always be indebted to you and I know I'm leaving you with an enormous task ahead. Taking care of the estate won't be easy, I'm sure, and having to represent me in the court suit on the accident…well, that can't be helped. It just can't be helped."

"You realize you're running away, don't you?" Lawrence sat on the arm of the sofa, his slender hands stuffed into his pants pockets, his legs, crossed at the ankles, sticking out halfway to the desk. He spoke softly, as always, carefully selecting each word and watching for its impact. Robey felt she was on the witness stand each time she had a conversation with him. "You can't run forever," he continued, "You can't just leave all your bad memories locked up here in this house...or this town. It just doesn't work that way."

Robey fitted brown leather gloves over trembling fingers. Now that the time had come, she felt more nervous about going than she imagined possible.

"Yes, I know. But, honestly, I'm not a coward. It's not that kind of running. I hope I'm running toward something better. Only time will prove me right or wrong. When you have a contract on the house, let me know...rent with an option. Store all my stuff at the warehouse for the time being. Perhaps I'll want them shipped to me later, to my new home."

Lawrence stood up and stepped quickly toward her and Robey took a few evasive steps but bumped into the glove table behind the sofa. She didn't know why, but she felt uneasy, almost threatened. Her mind told her it was only Lawrence she was alone with in her own living room, but the instinct was there, and she was very uncomfortable with him so close. Foolish! Ridiculous! Lawrence was a dear and caring friend. "Maybe I'm losing my sanity at that," she muttered to herself.

"Robey," he was now right beside her and there was no escape beyond physically pushing him away. His hands grasped her shoulders and turned her toward him. His words tumbled out. "When you come back, and you will, perhaps then you'll let me tell you how I feel. I know now is too soon, but I can't let you go without letting you know how much I love you. All these years I've watched you from the sidelines...how you smile...how you brush a curl from your forehead ...and I've been unable to put my true feelings into words because of Roger." The last few words barely made it past his lips, fading away into less than a whisper. Ignoring the look of astonishment on her face, he tried to pull Robey into and embrace. Robey shivered at his touch and a gasp tore from her throat. She pushed him away with such force he stumbled backwards almost tripping over a footstool beside the sofa. She quickly stepped around him, achieving the center of the room before she whirled to look into his pale grey eyes, anger sparking from hers.

"How dare you talk to me like that? How dare you?" She almost screamed in indignation.

"I'm sorry Robey," Lawrence's face reddened. "I shouldn't have said that... not yet."

"Not ever!" Robey fought back the urge to tell him to leave and not come back, but she knew doing so would delay her leaving. She still had to depend upon his legal expertise. She couldn't go hunting lawyers at this late date.

"Robey, I said I'm sorry. Forgive me. Please?" his eyes pleaded like a schoolboy scared of being punished by his teacher. He started to reach for her again but thought better of it and let his arms fall to his sides, standing chagrined and embarrassed.

A long silence prevailed before Robey, gathering her emotions with a deep shrug of her shoulders, spoke. "Alright. Forgiven." She turned back to the large oak desk once cluttered with work Roger brought home from the office. It now looked neat and sterile. Robey picked up a large manila envelope and handed it to Lawrence, holding on to one side as though reluctant to let it go.

"My instructions are all in here. I'll get in touch with you by phone to let you know where to forward mail. I'll call soon after I get to Knobbe Cove."

"Robey, why Knobbe Cove? You've never explained that to me, although I guess it's none of my business, really."

"Of course, it's your business," Robey softened her voice, anxious to be back on an even keel with him. She leaned on the edge of the desk and straightened her sweatshirt, pulling it down over her hips. "I just didn't want to leave—going off into a complete

unknown, and I have a friend in Knobbe Cove. As you know, I
have no family. No home to go to but...there's a friend, Amelia
Wentworth, who lives in Knobbe Cove. She left here many years
ago."

Robey smiled at the recollection. "She was young, in love, and
full of dreams. Amelia left on her wedding day with her new husband, David. They settled in Knobbe Cove. He was from there,
I think. I haven't heard from her in over five years, but somehow,
I feel she's just the one I need to talk to. We used to share all our
secrets when we were kids."

"Might do you good at that," Lawrence sounded resigned. He
loped over to the suitcases stacked in the hallway, bent down and
picked up all four, two under each arm. "Time's come."

Robey opened the door, trying not to meet his eyes. She put
her carcoat on, tucked her purse under her arm and reluctantly
turned back to the room, her eyes stinging with tears. It was almost as if Roger and the children were seated there, waving goodbye. Everything looked so warm and cozy, and outside, although
the sun was melting what was probably the last snow of the year, it
was chillingly cold.

'I'm crazy' Robey thought to herself. 'But to stay now would
really be an admission of cowardice and defeat.' Nevertheless, she
realized she was terrified at the possibility of staying and going
through life doing battle with phantoms.

Sarah joined the two on the path through the front yard bor-
dered with small mounds of grey sooty snow. She handed Robey a
hamper heavy with food and a thermos of steaming coffee. Robey
put them in the back seat of the car while Lawrence placed the luggage in the trunk.

"I'll not be able to return them soon, Sarah." Robey nodded her
head toward the food basket, then embraced Sarah's ample form.

"You bring them back someday. Don't put them on an UPS truck. I'll hold you to that."

The two friends hugged again, and Sarah wiped her eyes on the sleeve of her jacket. Robey tried to be matter of fact, but her chin fought back a sob as she took one last look at the low brick rambler. Through misty tears she imagined she saw Roger running around the house, laughing and taunting, Bud chasing him, tossing a snowball that exploded and disintegrated in the air. Sally raced shakily after them, screaming in childish delight. She tripped and fell just as the ghostly scene faded, leaving a bleak, cheerless yard.

A hard, chill wind slapped Robey's face and she clutched her coat collar around her throat. She quickly slid into the front seat of the red car and slammed the door beside her.

"Is something wrong?" Sarah sounded alarmed. Lawrence pecked at the closed window with one long bony finger. Robey rolled the pane down.

"No, I'm alright. Nothing wrong. Now stop worrying about me, you two. I'll write often...I promise."

Turning the key in the ignition, she put the car in reverse and backed out of the driveway without even glancing at them or the house.

Sarah and Lawrence watched silently as the car turned the corner and disappeared. Sarah was the first to break the silence.

"Do you think she'll be back?"

"I don't know, but I certainly will do everything in my power to get her back. I intend to marry her one day."

With this declaration, the lanky attorney stepped to his car, opened the door and got in, not waiting for Sarah's reply. He sped off, leaving her open-mouthed, uneasy and disturbed. Roger Layne had been an athletic and virile man, use to hard, outdoor work and he had played as hard as he had labored. Lawrence LaPorte was a milquetoast of a man with soft white hands and the smell of too much self-indulgence about him.

"No," Sarah said aloud, "Lawrence is not for Robey. I wonder why he thinks he is?"

She turned to back into her home and paused to look at the Layne house. She, too, had experienced a few bad nights because of the accident. Remembering that night, she recalled how she had been putting the boys to bed when the young officer had knocked at the door asking if she knew her neighbor, and when he found she did, asked her to go with him to tell Robey the terrible news. She had fought her own shock, the feeling of bloodless legs and buckling knees, to go with him. Sarah slowly entered her own home now, counting her blessings.

At dinner, Jack watched Sarah over the rim of his coffee cup. He reached into his pocket and withdrew a copper coin and put it in front of his wife's plate.

"You've been unusually quiet tonight. There's the proverbial penny," he smiled, pointing to the coin. "Where're your thoughts?"

Sarah savagely stabbed at the butter dish with her knife. "Lawrence LaPorte doesn't need to think he's going to marry Robey. I'll do my best to stop him."

"With a butter knife?" Jack laughed. "I'm properly mystified, my love. How about telling me what this is all about?"

Sarah poured fresh coffee and related Robey's leaving and Lawrence's remarks. Jack listened intently, but silently, his puckered brow the only outward sign of his own disapproval of Robey's attorney.

2

BEYOND FINDING AMELIA, ROBEY REALIZED SHE HAD no definite plans. A hesitant adventurer, she laughed to herself remembering her words to Lawrence that she didn't want to go off into the unknown. Now, as she drove along, the unwelcome idea nagged her that maybe she wouldn't find Amelia. She had felt relief when Lawrence hadn't asked if she had contacted her friend before foisting herself on her hospitality. How foolish she would have felt to explain she had not. Proper upbringing, of which Robey had received and ample Victorian dose, dictated no one shows up on someone's doorstep without invitation and expect to be welcome. Robey knew all this and yet she had consciously pushed reasonable arguments out of thought. Childishly, she supposed, she had feared rejection from Amelia, so she had not written her of her intention to show up in Knobbe Cove. Stubbornly, Robey had wanted nothing to convince her to stay in Chandor instead of traveling hundreds of miles alone to a town where she had never been.

Avoiding the busy and often frantic North-South traffic corridor, Robey entered the small town of Whitney on a quiet two-lane road and easily found a motel with a vacancy. The Triple A had either ignored or flunked it. A red-faced man barely looked up from the police gazette he was reading to take her money and toss her a key.

It felt strange to be unknown by anyone, driving down roads she had never driven before. Now, entering a disinfectant-stenched room she wondered how traveling salesmen ever made it in life. What a lonely existence they must have, she mused.

After taking her small bag in from the car she locked the door behind her and pushed a chair in front of it. Removing her robe, gown, and slippers from the travel case placed on the caddy, she tossed them on the bed. Inspecting the bathtub, she found it was not too scroungy, so she luxuriated in the perfumed suds bubbling from the lavender scented soap she had brought along. Stress slipped from her body and she almost slept in the warm water. Pulling herself from euphoria, she dried and stood in front of the mirror, looking at her nakedness. Seeing the curve of her hips and flatness of her stomach, she felt an aching forced to the back of her memory the past long months. Feeling betrayed by her very being, she quickly turned her back on her reflection, donned the soft peach colored silk gown, and sat on the side of the bed viciously brushing her hair. Thoughts of Roger's nearness crept into her mind and she tried to eradicate them with each angry stroke. He had no right to inflict this torture on her… he had left her in the accident on the mountain. Back home in Chandor she could understand it because that was his home…their home…but here in a motel hundreds of miles South where he had never been—that was unfair. And then guilt at being angry with Roger gripped her heart. Contrite tears washed her eyes and it was a long time before she took control of her feelings and lay down on the too soft bed. She prayed Lawrence wasn't right. She would stop grieving if she left Chandor—she must.

Her eyes swept over the unfamiliar cubicle just before she

turned out the light. With the light out she noticed a soft glow radiating from a neon sign out on the highway. As her eyes got used to the darkness within the room, the neon glow seemed to fill every nook and cranny. Robey could hear trucks passing a few hundred feet away, noisily changing gears on the steep incline of the mountainside. Uneasy, she had the sensation of being out in the middle of the highway and promised herself to be more particular in finding a place to stay in Knobbe Cove... or wherever she was the next night.

Knobbe Cove... Robey tried to imagine what it would be like. Amelia had been swallowed up in Knobbe Cove. She and David probably had a couple of kids by now. Robey didn't know. She had received two letters years ago and knew only that David owned a bookstore in what was a sleepy university town and Robey envisioned green manicured campus lawns and tree-lined streets with small shops and restaurants.

Robey and Amelia had grown up together in Chandor just a couple of city blocks apart. Their birthdays were separated by exactly one week, Robey being the older and much more aggressive, always exploring and investigating the unknown. Amelia would trail behind when Robey wanted to go into apartment building lobbies or even sneak around the yards of old, deserted houses. As the two girls rushed from childhood to teenagers, they kept the closeness of their friendship, double-dating and working together at summer jobs. When Robey married, Amelia had been her Maid of Honor and when, four years later, Amelia met and married David, Robey, obviously pregnant with her second child, stood beside Amelia as Matron of Honor. Robey recalled the tears that flowed freely when the couple left the day of their wedding.

Amelia's promise to keep in touch had been short lived. She had answered only two of Robey's letters. Robey drifted off to sleep still questioning why.

Rain was pelting the motel roof when Robey awakened. For a few seconds she was disoriented, not aware of where she was, but Sarah's food hamper sitting on the one lone hardbacked chair in the starkly furnished room quickly jarred her back to reality. She reached for the bed lamp switch and turned it on. The light it emitted through a ruffled plastic shade was a dull pink glow that did nothing to raise her spirits, and it was with great effort she did not turn over and try to go back to sleep in hope the sun would be shining when she woke again.

"If I don't get up now," she scolded aloud, "I'll not get to Knobbe Cove until tomorrow...and Heaven forbid I have to stay in another motel like this for an extra night." Vigorously tossing back the covers, Robey dove into the bath again, this time showering to wake herself fully. In a short time, she was again ready for travel. Breakfast was a hurried Danish and coffee at the Whitney Diner where Robey remembered to refill Sarah's thermos. By the time she turned the key in the ignition, she felt renewed both in body and spirit.

The day's drive passed uneventfully and pleasantly, the scenery on Highway 95 sometimes a boring sameness and sometimes colorful enough with the onset of Spring to be beautiful. She stopped only once to finish the sandwiches in the hamper and to eat a quick, early dinner at a fast-food drive-in in North Carolina. Robey became aware of less dirty snow lying beside the road or clumped on the ground among trees. Knobbe Cove was so much further South from Chandor it would probably be like a new world. Robey wondered if it snowed there and guessed not. Leaden skies, which had been threatening all day, now poured a steady rain. Through sheets of water on the windshield, road signs finally announced Knobbe Cove as thirty miles in the distance, and Robey felt a thrill of expectancy. The rain lessened to a mist at the top of a steep hill, and then there was Knobbe Cove nestled at the bottom. No cars were following her, so Robey pulled off to the shoulder of the wide road and sat looking down on the panorama of her destination. The town appeared tinier than she had imagined. Two church spires poked above the trees framing the back streets and the University peeked from behind huge Georgia pines partially obstructing her view. To the right she could just barely discern the glitter of a body of water with boats lined up along a pier.

Robey smiled broadly, put the car in drive and exclaimed aloud, "I'm here, ready or not!" and swept down the hill to Knobbe Cove.

Slowly traversing the main thoroughfare, she passed houses squatting on sidewalks amid small patches of lawn. Shaded white-railed porches wrapped themselves around clapboard house fronts stained with rust from tin guttering. Bushy spiraeas hugged front steps and clumps of hydrangea spilled into weed-edged sidewalks. This, the sign on the corner proclaimed, was Broad Street. Residences dwindled into a few storefronts and flickering lights blinked their way around a movie theater marquee. The hotel sign, outlined in blue neon, glowed just beyond and Robey, remembering last night's motel on the busy highway, decided to discover what the back streets of Knobbe Cove had to offer before deciding on a room at the hotel.

A right turn brought Robey to a waterfront just one block away where piers, dimly lit by gracefully arched streetlights, jutted out into the black water rippling with raindrops. Canvas-hooded boats of various sizes nudged the pilings, gently rocking with the occasional breeze blowing down the hill into the cove. Rising majestically out of the water at the further end of the Bay was the rock formation Robey was certain gave the town its name. Dark and ominous in the dusk, it looked not unlike an enormous doorknob.

Little imagination was needed to envision a giant hand reaching down, twisting and opening the earth's portal to whatever mysteries lay buried below. The cove looked desolate, the water dark and forbidding, and Robey could not help but give a slight shudder as a rat scurried between two barrels standing by a boarded-up seafood sidewalk eatery.

Wheeling the car around, Robey realized night had almost descended while she had taken the time to look over the bay. Ominous clouds atop the hill threatened resumption of the earlier downpour. Water stood in puddles in the street, colorfully reflecting lights from the restaurant and hotel. Broad Street was deserted except for a couple huddled together under a navy-blue golf umbrella. They turned onto the front walk of one of the houses with small shrubs guarding the steps.

At the stop sign, Robey halted the car and looked both directions, her eyes searching for signs of David's bookstore, but she found none. Edging forward, she turned left at the next intersection and found vast lawns aproning two- and three-story homes where lights glowed cheerily through tall curtained windows. On the corner a brownstone church dominated a small graveyard spread out beside it, and across the street a dark brick house peeked from behind rhododendrons and straggling wisteria. Beside the porch stood a large linden tree, its branches twisted and bare. Gingerbread carving hung from under the roof and porch ceiling, back-to-back wooden curlicues decorated eaves and posts. Robey liked what she saw and the uneasiness she had felt at the cove disappeared in the comfort of knowing Knobbe Cove, though smaller, was just as she had imagined it would be.

Two more right turns found Robey on Railroad Street where her address book told her Amelia and David lived. She squinted through the rain-bleared windshield trying to see house numbers, but night had settled down in earnest, starless...heavy and black, making it impossible to find a number without getting out of the car.

Returning to the immediate problem of finding a place to stay, Robey looked for another hotel or motel but saw nothing but residences on the back streets. She concluded that the hotel on Broad Street was the only haven for rest this first night in Knobbe Cove.

Several elderly people sat on plum colored velvet divans in the brightly lit hotel lobby and watched, openly curious, as Robey carried her bags in and registered.

"Visiting the University?" the pleasant young man behind the desk inquired.

"NO...friends," Robey smiled, not revealing who. She was too tired to get into a long conversation...time enough for that later, but she was thankful the clerk had a warmer greeting than her host of yester eve in Whitney. After she signed her name, he turned the book around to face himself.

"Hope your stay is comfortable, Mrs. Layne." He pocketed the key and stepped around the counter to pick up her baggage. "I'd ring for the bellboy, but I'm it," he grinned. The warmth of his smile and the twinkle of his light brown eyes made Robey feel more assured about her decision to visit Amelia.

The elevator was ancient, a brass grid door unfolding inside the outer ones that laboriously slip shut. It jerked suddenly upon starting and again when reaching the third floor. Robey wondered if it was really all that safe and expressed the thought to her new companion.

"Not only safe, ma'am, but it's inspected at least once a day by a State Inspector. He lives on the fourth floor."

When he opened the door to her room, she found it was small

with massive mahogany furniture filling most of the space. Two portraits in oval mats framed by ornate gold leafed wood confronted Robey from the wall above the bed. The man and woman, whoever they were, stared blankly but sternly, as though disapproving of her being there. Robey wondered why early pictures were always of unsmiling people. Tipping the young man, she shut the door behind him.

A thin telephone book lay on the nightstand beside the bed, but no phone was visible. Robey recalled passing a payphone in the lobby and decided to call Amelia in the morning as soon as she finished breakfast. Quickly dressing for sleep, she noticed an extra comforter at the foot of the brass bed. The chill dampness of the night caught up with her and she involuntarily shivered. The one lone radiator in the room was only slightly warm, but Robey was too tired to care. She wrapped the bedcovers tightly around her and reached out to turn off the lamp when the phone book again caught her eye. She opened it and thumbed through, stopping at the W's.

"Wentworth...Wentworth," Robey muttered to herself, bringing her well-manicured finger down the short W list. She was both surprised and alarmed to find no Wentworth listed. It was conceivable David and Amelia had an unlisted number, but the book shop would surely have been there. "Of course," she reconciled her thoughts, " they probably don't call it Wentworth's Books. Maybe they call it The Corner Library, or Book Nook, or something," Robey reasoned, trying to quell the uneasy feeling that perhaps, after all, Amelia wasn't in Knobbe Cove and tomorrow she would have to face the possibility of being a stranger without a purpose in a strange town. She would have to go back to Chandor or move on...but to where?

"How stupid of me for not writing Amelia that I was coming," she scolded herself. Sleep, once already on her eyelids, retreated and Robey's mind raced with unwelcome thoughts and worry. It was past midnight before repose crept back, and Robey slept uneasy and dreaming.

3

WHEN ROBEY AWAKENED FROM TROUBLED SLEEP THE rain had ceased and a brilliant light blazed through the Chantilly lace panels at the window and lifted her spirits. Rain depressed Robey. She felt immature being so affected by the weather but, the fact remained, she could cope much better in the sunshine. Even the faces of the couple in the oval frames took on a less stern countenance in cheerful sunlight.

Eager to begin the day, Robey showered and dressed in a dark brown pantsuit with a canary yellow scarf flounced under her chin. She stepped out into the hallway and, foregoing the doubtful elevator, descended the rubber-treaded stairs to the lobby. Breakfast was served in the quaint Tea Room and Robey sat down at one of the small round tables covered with white linen enhanced by a Nobbed milk glass vase containing a single red silk rose.

"Pardon me," she smiled at the waitress when she refilled her coffee cup. "I'm here to visit a friend whose husband runs a bookstore here in town. Could you possibly help me?"

"Sure, that is, if I can. What's the name of the store?"

"I don't know the name of the store, but the owners are David and Amelia Wentworth."

"They run a bookshop?" The girl's forehead wrinkled into a deep thoughtful frown. "No, there's not a bookstore here owned by a Wentworth that I know anything about. I'm a student at the University and from out of town, so I really don't know too many people, but I've been in and out of all the bookstores—like most students—and the three shops here aren't run by anyone named Wentworth."

"You're certain?" Robey was alarmed, beginning to discover she was not really at all adventurous and being at loose ends was a most apprehensive an unpleasant feeling. She didn't like it in the least bit.

"Perhaps you should talk to Reverend Hill. He's the pastor of the church on the back street, just two blocks over. I understand he was born here. He must know just about everybody."

"Thank you, I will." Robey Anxiously grasped at any thin thread of hope. If Amelia and David had left Knobbe Cove, perhaps this Pastor Hill would know where they had gone. She paid her tab and decided to visit the church at once.

Outside, the air was crisp, but the sun warmed her back as she unhurriedly strolled, looking long at the houses one by one, making herself familiar with as much of the small town as she could. Sparrows flitted among the trees, swooping down to peck at the ground. The aroma of wet earth wafted up and Robey couldn't help but smile at the thought that spring had truly arrived. In Chandor, perhaps another snow or two would still be expected before the ground thawed and the birds returned. Chandor seemed so very far away and up 'til now, Robey realized, she hadn't thought of home all morning. Was it so easy to forget?

The church, when she came in sight of it, seemed even larger than her first impression of the night before. Stained glass windows sparkled in the freshly washed air, lending an aura of quickness to the scene. The black iron-spiked fence seemed to grow out of the sidewalk and the gate hinge creaked in protest as she pushed it open. A crumbling concrete path snaked its way to the massive arched doors at the front of the edifice, but along the side another path led to a smaller door with a pearl button doorbell in its jamb. Robey pushed it several times and could hear a melodic chime respond deep within, but no one answered. Retracing her steps, she paused a bit to admire the English boxwood hedges that framed the front of the building, their dark glossy leaves full of tiny buds. She hesitated at the gate, wondering when Pastor Hill would be in his office. Just as an impulse urged her to knock on the door of the large brick house across the street to see if it was the Manse, the quiet of the morning was split by the warning shrill of a train whistle in the distance and Robey remembered Railroad Street was only a couple of blocks further and maybe she would find Amelia there after all.

Several people strolled past her on the sidewalk and while most glanced at her, none even said "hello" in response to her smile. "I thought all small towns were friendly," Robey muttered, "these people don't even seem to see me." She put more purpose in her stride, passing the graveyard on First Avenue beside the church. Some tombstones towered over others, wreaths of plastic flowers adorned a few, and several looked as though they were old enough to date back to the American Revolution. Here and there scraggly morning glory vines entwined themselves around obelisks, further binding the dead to their final resting place. Beyond the graveyard the streets intersected, and Robey stood, momentarily unsure of which way to go.

"Now, to find number 121," she said aloud, but as she walked past most houses, she discovered that many were so far back from the street and the doors were so obliterated by tall shrubs, that it was almost impossible to read any house numbers, if, indeed, there were any. In the next block Robey noticed each house had a stone set out by the curb and on each stone a number was chiseled. Crossing over and stopping to look at the one on the corner lot, a thrill of relief enveloped her. It bore the number "121".

"What luck," she gasped. "So, this is where David and Amelia live—or lived." She stretched to see over the tall hedge that surrounded the lot, but it was too high even when she rose up on tip toes. A grey flagstone path led under a rose trellis to the front door and Robey gingerly stepped over the low grass clumps grown between them. Surely this unkempt place couldn't belong to the meticulous Wentworths.

Halfway up the path Robey hesitated a moment as she though she saw the curtains move in the narrow window beside the door. All the other windows were shuttered, and she wondered if winters were severe enough in Knobbe Cove to necessitate closing a house so snugly as this. A large brass knocker poked out of the oak-stippled door, it's clump of metal grapes tarnished dark with neglect. Robey lifted and dropped the knocker twice onto its sounding block and heard footsteps inside scurry away. She knocked again, becoming irritated at the thought someone inside was going to ignore her. And then the footsteps came slowly toward the door, the knob turned and there was Amelia peeking through the small opening.

"Amelia is that you?" Robey laughed. "Come on, open up it's me, Robey."

"Robey? Oh, Robey!" Amelia burst into laughter and swung the door wide, her arms open to welcome her dearest friend. They hugged each other, looked into each other's face, kissed cheeks, hugged again, all the time muttering "I can't believe it's you" and "you've not changed a bit. Robey felt tears of joy fill her heart. At last! Someone to talk to. Someone who would understand. Coming to Knobbe Cove was right after all.

Arm-in-arm they strolled into the living room where a small fire smoldered in the fireplace. Amelia fixed tea in a blue Spode teapot, poured it into ceramic mugs, and then the two women sat facing each other across a low coffee table. Amelia still wore her long ash blonde hair parted in the middle with a band of bright ribbon tying the straight tresses at the nape of her neck. Her blue flashing eyes, which always looked too big for her small heart shaped face, sparkled. She didn't look older to Robey, but she did have an aura about her...as though life had been a bit more than she had been able to handle. The self-assuredness Robey had remembered in Amelia was gone.

"Of course, we've changed," Robey said quietly, "so much has happened to me I couldn't possibly not have changed." She told Amelia briefly about Roger and the children. Bud had been but a toddler when Amelia married David and left Chandor seven years ago, and she had never seen Sally. For a few minutes neither said anything, staring into the fire, hearing the turpentine in the pine logs crackle until Robey, visibly pulling herself from her reverie asked, "Now tell me all about yourself. Why didn't you answer my last letters?"

Amelia didn't answer immediately, making much of pouring some more tea, carefully spooning in sugar and squeezing a wedge of lemon into the amber liquid. When she did speak, she pointedly changed the subject.

"What do you plan to do, Robey? How long are you going to stay in Knobbe Cove?"

Robey had a sinking feeling and tried to shrug off unwelcome thoughts. She realized she had hoped Amelia would ask her to stay here in the house, at least for a little while, but now she sensed no invitation of any kind would be forthcoming.

"I don't have any plans, Amelia. I needed someone to talk too and thought of you. I know I should have written first, but well, I had to get away from Chandor. There were too many 'poor Robey' looks when I went to church or shopping—too many reminders inside the house."

"Whose fault was the accident?"

"It wasn't Roger's. The man driving the car that crossed the median strip had enough alcohol in his blood to make him totally incapable of controlling a vehicle on the road. And that's another thing Amelia, there is a big hassle about the insurance. Seems the car didn't belong to the driver. It was stolen. Lawrence LaPorte...he's Roger's...was...his attorney, is taking care of the matter for me. I don't want to be there. All at once everything became hostile, the house, the stores, church. Everything. Nothing was going right, absolutely nothing. I prayed about it, but if God answered, I guess I didn't want to listen. That's when I decided to leave. Running away, Lawrence calls it. I suppose he's right."

"I wish I could ask you to stay with us—David and me—but I can't. Amelia stood up, walked over to the hearth and picked up the black poker, jabbing angrily at the remainder of the burnt log, making embers spark up the chimney. "I just can't."

"I don't mean to pry, Amelia, but I couldn't find the bookshop listed in the phone book. Haven't things been going well for you?"

Amelia turned around and leaned against the brick side of the fireplace, a grim and resigned smile turning up the corners of her mouth, but tears rimmed her eyes.

"We have enough Robey, don't worry about me. Someday, maybe, I'll tell you all about it. But right now, well"...her voice trailed off and when she again turned back to Robey, an emotionless mask had replaced the young, eager face Robey had always known.

Perhaps she was mistaken, but Robey had the premonition her

friend really wished she would leave, as if something dire would happen if she stayed. Frustration swept over her as she realized the anchor that she had hoped for in Amelia had disappeared in a sea of unanswered and apparently unaskable questions.

"I'm going to apply for a position somewhere." Robey helped herself to more tea from the coffee table. "That's what I had planned to do, and I suppose in the back of my mind I pictured myself working for David in the bookstore if there were an opening." Her voice trailed off and then softened as she saw an immense hurt in Amelia's eyes. "I'm sorry Amelia, I really am. I don't know whatever for... I do wish you would tell me."

Before Amelia could reply, a door slammed somewhere in the back of the house. Heavy footsteps became louder, and then David lurched into the room. Robey, out of the corner of her eye, caught the look of a frightened mouse in Amelia's face. David's hair was uncombed. His face, once so smoothly handsome, was unshaven and his features bloated. The neck of a whiskey bottle protruded from the top of a brown paper sack dangling from his left hand. So this was why Amelia wanted her to leave. She struggled not to show her shock.

"Well hello David," Robey extended her hand in greeting, trying to sound cheerful. David took it only momentarily and turned to Amelia.

"Well my love. What did you do? Finally write to one of your old girlfriends for a shoulder to cry on?"

"No, David I didn't. Robey just came. Robey has some problems of her own she wanted to talk to me about."

"Liar! Don't tell me! A person doesn't come hundreds of miles to a place she's never been just to drop in for tea and a chat about her problems." He turned to Robey and she found herself frightened by the rage in his dark brown eyes.

"Well, what has she told you? That her husband is a drunk and lost his business and we're living—or existing—off my father's scraps of charity?"

"She hasn't said a thing David, you're mistaken." Robey protested. She had no stomach for other people's quarrels and felt an urgent need to leave as quickly as possible. She wondered if Amelia would be safe.

"Like hell she didn't tell you!" David yelled. "Well it's all true, but why don't you ask the damn little bitch the big why?"

Amelia nodded her head and tried to smile, and Robey sensed a silent plea that she still be her friend. There would be more time later to talk, she was sure. Saying goodbye, she let herself out the door. An urge to run down the path to the sun-drenched street was hard to control, but Robey deliberately walked slowly away. She was trembling, nerves shrieking. On the sidewalk, she forced herself to look at the other houses and concentrate on the architecture in order to gain emotional perspective. It would be afternoon before she trusted herself to think again about Amelia and David and her morning's experience.

Amelia pulled the heavy drapes aside and watched her friend as far down the path as she could see. She heard David move around the living room, but she stayed, intentionally, at the window keeping her back to him.

"Well, I really blew it didn't I?" David stated flatly, his rage spent. Amelia remained silent, tears filling her eyes, making the outdoor scene opaque.

"I'm sorry, Amy." He used the short of her name only when trying to get back into her good graces. He had once used it, she remembered, at times of endearment and passion. She was unmoved now, unable to respond as she had so many times in the past. A coldness stiffened her body, and for the first time in a long while she knew exactly what she must say and do.

"Sorry doesn't make it anymore, David," she turned and leaned against the wall. David sat with his head lowered, hands dangling between his knees.

"Whether or not you believe I wrote Robey matters not a whit to me. What does matter is that she is a fine sensitive person who was in the position of being hurt. She came to me for comfort. Roger and both babies, Sally and Bud, were all killed last summer in a senseless automobile accident." She used the words like daggers, enjoying seeing them hit their mark. "And you had to come in and hurt her more with your venomous drunken hate."

David's eyes widened as he realized the enormity of what he had done to Robey.

"I'm sorry Amy. I didn't know." His hand lifted in a futile gesture and dropped again to his knees.

"Sorry? I doubt it. I doubt that in your state it would have made any difference had you known." Disgust spewed from every word and Amelia was surprised at the strength she had to fight with David for Robey. Strength she had not found to defend herself. David looked at her, unable to understand the change in her attitude. She had never stood up to him like this before. He had once called her a 'stupid little doormat.'

Amelia stared back, for the first time standing her ground, thoroughly sickened by this weak shell she had once loved and married.

"Get out out of my sight." Her words were barely audible and then, when he didn't move, she screamed, "NOW!" David quickly stood, grabbed the brown bag containing his bottle, and rushed out the door, stumbling down the steps.

Amelia crumpled on the sofa, sobs shaking her slender body.

Before long she slept in exhausted slumber. Her dreams found her alone. David was in them no longer.

4

THE CORNER DRUGSTORE ACROSS FROM THE HOTEL was more pharmacy than lunch room, but since there were three round metal tables with menus propped up between salt and pepper shakers and wire ice cream parlor chairs by the window, Robey came in, sat down and waited for someone to take her order for a sandwich. Looking around, she noticed shelves stocked with a multitude of medical wares. The top shelves, however, seemed thick with dust. In the dim light Robey imagined herself in a past-century apothecary shop where cobwebs were used for packing open wounds, and turpentine and creosol were swabbed to battle infection. A stack of local newspapers on the end of the counter by the cash register caught her eye, so she purchased a "University Press" to read with her lunch.

A synopsis of national news was spread over the front page and photographs of the Garden Club's prize fern shared the Society page with two dowagers passing the gavel of authority in the Woman's Club. Two couples announced their engagement. One birth and one obituary were side by side. "Well, even-steven on that," Robey smiled. At least Knobbe Cove was holding its own.

Thumbing to the classified page Robey found very few ads in the help wanted section. Most jobs, she supposed, were filled by University students needing extra spending money. One position was available as a maid at the hotel for the coming summer, but Robey immediately dismissed this from her possibilities of employment. The thought occurred she might not be able to stay in Knobbe Cove after all. David and Amelia had their own problems and, evidently, she was unwelcome, at least by David. That eliminated her main reason for coming...or for staying. Now there seemed to be no work to keep her busy, so that took care of that! While she didn't need the money, she did need a reason to get up in the morning. Robey knew she couldn't hang around the hotel forever, living among strangers. She needed roots of some kind. Outside the window people stopped others on the street, greeting, laughing and going their way, their destinations predetermined. Robey felt a pang of loneliness and homesickness.

Sun blazed from a cloudless sky and magnified its heat through the unwashed panes, making a ray of dust motes across Robey's table. Her eyes dropped to the paper again and the church notices seemed to jump from the printed page. There were three churches in town with notices of Sunday services, but a sketch of the formidable brownstone Covenant Church drew her attention as she recalled her original intent to talk to Pastor Hill. She had found Amelia herself, but Robey still felt a need to talk to someone about her future, someone who would be objective and might be able to give her proper direction. Maybe Pastor Hill would be the very person.

Robey slowly ate her sandwich and sipped her Coke, trying to imagine what he could possibly be like.

The side street leading to Church Street was now familiar and Robey turned toward the brownstone building. From a block away she noticed a child leave the side door, skip down the path and through the iron gate. Relieved that someone must be inside, she hurried her step, smiling at the girl who, when she passed her by, was making a hopscotch game with chalk on the pavement.

This time, when Robey pushed the pearl button, a shuffle of feet beyond the arched portal responded. When the heavy door opened, a tall gray-haired man, leaning on metal crutches, waved her into the dimness of the vestibule. Inside, the air wasn't much warmer than the March chill outside. Robey gathered her coat tighter around her throat.

"Come in. Come in. I'm Graham Hill," he introduced himself and indicated the door to the church office. "What brings you back?"

"Back?" Robey was startled by what she assumed was his clairvoyance and said as much. He laughed and pointed out the window to the dark brick house.

"No, nothing mysterious. I don't read minds. That's where I live, and I was sitting by the window reading correspondence when you came past early this morning. You left before I had a chance to get over here. I'm not the fastest person on crutches, not the slowest, but not the fastest. I've never seen you around before. Do you have a brother or sister at the University?"

"No. No brother or sister." Robey smiled, not telling him any more, enjoying his apparent puzzlement just as he had seemed to enjoy hers a moment before. She felt comfortable in his presence, and his deep voice, very soft in spite of its low register, reminded her somewhat of Roger's.

Graham laboriously seated himself, leaning the crutches against a file cabinet behind his desk. Robey sat down on a brown leather armchair she found positioned in such a manner she could see out the side window without having to turn her head. She realized Pastor Hill would be able to see and study whoever was in this chair without them knowing it, especially if their eyes were distracted by the outdoors. She turned to face him squarely.

"Well, you're too young to have a son or daughter there, so I'll have to guess again and say you are a new teacher."

"Again. No." Robey answered, still not quite certain she wanted to explain everything to this man, but she knew he was really curious as to why he had found her at the door of his church and was due an explanation. "Why did I come?" she thought. The silence became awkward, so she took a deep breath and plunged in.

"My name is Layne...Roberta Layne. I'm an old friend of Amelia Wentworth, Pastor Hill." She was astonished to see the startled look spreading across his face. Pastor Hill was evidently one of those men who couldn't mask their emotions. 'Not too good for a minister who was supposed to be able to counsel without showing shock or too much sympathy,' Robey mused. She thought he was going to say something, but when he didn't, she continued.

"Yesterday I came into town to visit...and I did this morning ...but, well," she groped for further words that would not lead to telling all that had happened, not wanting to betray her friends situation or tell tales out of school.

"You found her a recluse. Is that it?" Pastor Hill turned in his swivel chair and faced the window. Robey found now she could study his face. His clean-shaven features under the shock of gray hair were handsome in a very rugged sense... A bit Lincolnian, she decided. His elbows rested on the arms of the chair; his fingers entwined beneath his chin.

"Do you know the Wentworth's well?" Robey asked.

"Yes, I did, that is. It has been several years since they've attended services. How much do you know about their present situation?"

"How do you mean?" Robey parried his question.

"Did you get to talk to her for long?"

"Yes, and no. If you mean did I learn much about how their lives are now, I guess I learned a bit more than I wanted."

"You saw David, then?"

"Yes, I know about his drinking and about his losing their bookstore. Amelia didn't tell me, but when David came home while I was visiting, he was very drunk, very belligerent, and quite frank about it."

Suddenly Pastor Hill swung around and faced Robey. His eyes seemed strangely angry.

"Believe me, Mrs. Layne, what has happened is none of your business and you'll do well to stay out of it!"

Robey was quite taken aback and put on defense by his attitude. "I never intended prying, if that's what you mean," she snapped.

"Then why did you come here today?"

"I really don't know," she said exasperated. "I really don't." She got up from the chair angry and hurt, unwelcome tears stinging her eyes. Why did she have to feel this way? She should not care what this man said. She had come to Knobbe Cove to seek some consolation...and perhaps some strength. She had found neither with Amelia and now felt more frustrated than ever. Drawing her coat about her, she started toward the door, not intending to even say goodbye.

"Mrs. Layne. Come back and sit down. I'm sorry." His voice sounded genuinely contrite. "I really don't know what made me be so...so...unthinking and inconsiderate. Of course, you don't know what to expect at the Wentworth's."

Robey stood with her back to him, her hand on the doorknob, trying to get herself under control. Disappointment had given way to anger, and it was this she fought before turning back to look at Graham Hill.

"Is there something more I can say?" He looked now like a schoolboy caught with a peashooter, wondering when the teacher was going to slap his knuckles. "Is there something I can do for you?"

"I did come here to ask your advice. Get some counsel," she faced him. "But I'm not sure at this point if you're the one I want to know my personal problems."

"Let's start over again, Mrs. Layne. For reasons I cannot tell you, you took me quite by surprise when you began talking about Amelia and David. An episode, let us say, I thought relegated to the past. Let us, for the moment, forget the Wentworths and consider what else you wished to tell me. Believe me, despite my recent rudeness, I can be a very good listener, at least so I've been told."

Robey looked deep into his face, trying to read behind his gray eyes. She found strength and confidence there. Suddenly Robey felt she could trust this man. She had never confided in a minister or, for that matter, anyone other than Amelia or Sarah, but she needed relief from the jangling nerves, the dead lump where her heart should be and, she admitted to herself, she needed help. Slowly she sat down again, clutching her purse on her lap.

"Alright. I came here, that is, to Amelia's, hoping she would help me over a really bad time. My home was up North—Chandor, Connecticut. The house is still there, but my home isn't. My husband," she choked on the words and it was a few moments before she continued, "my Roger... and my two children were killed in an automobile accident over a year and a half ago."

Robey watched Graham's face carefully as she said the words and noticed not a trace of pity. "I think I've gotten over the questions such as 'why wasn't I in the car with them?' or 'why them and not the murderers and rapists of the world who seem to come and go so freely to do their satanic work?' I think I've gone past questioning God or blaming him. I don't know."

"Why did you decide to leave the home you were so happy in? After all, it was a place where you lived with love, wasn't it?"

"Dreams... nightmares... I suppose. I was constantly reminded of them. Constantly."

"You should have been. I would hate to think someone I was married to would want to stop remembering me once I was gone."

Robey stared hard at Graham's face but saw no glimpse of cruelty there, and yet she felt he must have been purposely trying to be cruel.

"How can you say that? Of course, I'll remember them forever!"

"And as long as you remember them out of self-pity for losing them instead of remembering them out of love for having had them, you're going to have those nightmares."

"Are you always so stringent with your counsel?"

"When I deem it necessary. Mrs. Layne, you seem to be a vital young woman. I never had the pleasure of knowing your Roger, but I'm certain you were a strength to him and him to you. You coming all this distance to see Amelia denotes that strength. A weaker person would have remained in Connecticut and wallowed in self-pity and bitterness and perhaps be destroyed by them. Whether or not you know it, your leaving was an admission you had to go do something about your life. Right, or wrong?"

Robey got to her feet and strode to the window, her coat sliding off her slim shoulders. She stared out at the boxwoods trying to gather her thoughts. Graham Hill watched silently, giving her all the time she needed. At length she turned and leaned against the windowsill.

"Yes, I can't really complain. I'm physically well, and I think I have all my mental faculties. Sometimes I wonder about that.

Lawrence LaPorte said I was running away, and now I wonder if anyone could ever run away from, or toward, anything. Wherever I go, I'll take myself along, if that makes any sense. And I guess I'll have to rebuild my life on me." She hesitated, her mouth taking on a grim line. "No one is going to hand me a new shiny carefree existence, I..."

"Who's this Lawrence LaPorte?" Graham interrupted.

"My attorney. He's taking care of everything for me. There's a construction firm my husband owned and ran, and, of course, the house and estate...a lawsuit pending over the accident. I can hardly believe life could become so complicated in such a few minutes."

"Will you go back to Connecticut now?"

"No, I still think not. I'll start a new existence somewhere."

"You're a very strong person. Most would be frightened to live among strangers, having had such solid roots up until such a short time ago."

"I'm not as strong as you think. But I still prefer it this way. Maybe one day I'll go back and stay awhile. In the meantime, I need something to do. I don't need the money, only something to occupy my time. I guess I was depending on Amelia and the bookstore to supply my future. I never thought any further ahead."

Robey lapsed into silence and for a few minutes only the clock ticking loudly on the wall punctuated her thoughts.

"You can't stay at the hotel forever, Mrs. Layne." Graham broke the quiet. "I don't know whether we should call it a sign or not, but only yesterday I was thinking it would be much more efficient around here if I had an assistant in the office—a volunteer, mind you. The building is big, as you have probably noticed, but we have a fairly small congregation and there are no funds to pay a secretary or worker." He drummed his fingers on the desk, looking up at Robey. "If, as you say, money isn't your need, then perhaps you'd like to accept room and board at my home across the way as recompense for such work."

Robey shifted her eyes to the house. In daylight it seemed slightly rundown. She noticed a six-foot board fence she hadn't seen in the dark last night, which she assumed enclosed a backyard. The house reminded her of the old mansion she and Amelia, as children, used to believe was haunted. Even the porch swing was moving slightly from a strong breeze gusting around the corner. She and Amelia used to say the ghosts were sitting there, and they'd run past it each day on their way to and from school. Live there? She felt Graham's eyes on her back and she inwardly laughed at her fears. If she couldn't live in a house, haunted or otherwise, with the minister of the church, then she just better find a hole and crawl in!

"My sister, Iris, lives there, too, Mrs. Layne. If that is the reason for your hesitation."

Robey blushed red as she turned. "I really hadn't thought you weren't married with a big family. I just didn't think of that. Yes, I'll accept your offer, for the time being, at least. We can try it and see if it will work out. You have no idea how relieved I am. For a while, I had no idea what direction to take. All roads and doors seemed to be closing one by one." She grinned, her eyes sparkling. "Yes, yes, I'll do it."

"Good," Graham slapped his large hands down on the worn arms of the chair. "Glad to have that settled. Now how about you going down to the hotel and retrieving your things. While you're gone, I'll call Iris and tell her about our arrangement."

Back at the hotel room Robey hurriedly repacked and took the time to sit down at a small desk to write Sarah a letter on the hotel stationary.

Dear Sarah,

Just to let you know I arrived safely. Events moved swiftly—perhaps too swiftly. But nothing was as I had hoped it would be. Don't tell LaPorte, he'll only say I told you so.

I talked with Amelia and David very briefly this morning. Things are not well with them. David no longer has the bookstore. When he came in the house it was still mid-morning and he was already under the influence of too much liquor. Amelia was embarrassed, and I left as quickly as I could. My heart goes out to them both, I wish I could help.

Did you ever have a dream where you are falling, and you reach for a rope only to find that when you have grasped it, the other end isn't tethered to anything solid? That's the way I felt when I left Amelia and decided to visit the minister of a church here. It was a godsend that I did, for he, Pastor Hill, had all the solutions for me, at least for now. I am going to move into the manse and become a church secretary, a Girl Friday of sorts. I have no idea what I will be doing, but it is a new beginning. An identity, I guess you could say, besides being the widow Layne.

Hill is a bachelor, but his sister keeps house for him. He walks with crutches and, although I don't really know, I believe he has used them for a long time. I wonder what is wrong with his legs. I suppose if I stay here long enough, I'll find out.

I feel elated and excited about all of this. The last time I felt this way was when I was a little girl anticipating going to the circus for the first time. It was a whole new world for me.

You can write me in care of the Baptist manse. Wish me luck, and let's keep in touch. I'll write Lawrence tomorrow and let him know where to have the post office forward my mail.

All my love, Robey

Pastor Hill had settled back in his chair, and after watching Robey disappear down the street, he dialed the phone, drumming a yellow pencil on the desk while waiting for his sister to answer. He should have gone over to the house and spoken to her face to face, he supposed, but he admitted to himself he was a coward where Iris was concerned. The distance of the phone line would suit better for the news he would be giving her.

"Hill residence," Iris's crisp voice came over the wire.

"Me, Sis. Got some news for you."

"Oh?" Suspicion immediately crept into the crispness. Iris did not like surprises.

"I've a new assistant, a Mrs. Roberta Layne."

Silence at the other end of the line made Graham ask if she were still there.

"Yes, I'm here, Brother. Who on earth is Mrs. Layne, and how do you intend paying her? You know there's not an extra copper in the till for it, and I bet you didn't even consult the trustees."

Graham knew Iris would ask about pay first, had, in fact, counted on it to lead into the boarding arrangement. "Well, we can't pay, as you know. But she needs a place to stay, and I told her we would supply room and board in exchange."

A longer, deeper silence than the first one greeted this revelation and just about the time Graham was again going to inquire if she was still there, Iris asked, "Where does she come from? She obviously isn't from here, or she wouldn't need a place to live."

"Up North. Chandor, Connecticut."

"What brought her all the way down here?" Iris wasted no words getting to what she considered vital statistics.

"It's a long story, Iris, but she's newly widowed." He hesitated before uttering his next few words. "She came down here to find Amelia Wentworth."

"Amelia Wentworth!" The tone in Iris's voice made it obvious that she was really stunned by this turn of events. "Did she find her?"

"Yes, but you know what a hermit she's become. Mrs. Layne didn't feel welcome. David was there, so she just felt totally at sea and threw out a line for help. Then everything just seemed to fall into place."

"Why doesn't she go back to Connecticut if Amelia doesn't want her?"

"I don't know just how much I should tell you. We talked a bit today. She lost her husband and two children in a tragedy and she's fighting painful memories back home. I dare say another reversal might bring on illness. She seemed close to nervous prostration today." Graham had to admit to himself he didn't honestly believe this, but he felt he needed something to convince Iris and her maternal instincts she so amply applied to him. He hoped she would welcome Robey.

"I'll get the room ready, brother, but I hope it will only be temporary. You could have consulted me first before offering."

"Sorry, I should have, but done is done." Graham grinned, knowing he had deliberately not asked, since Iris liked the power of saying no to suggestions. An incurable optimist, Graham was sure things would work out satisfactorily, once Iris met Mrs. Layne. He would never be so wrong.

5

By the time Robey arrived at the manse, early evening shadows stretched long fingers across the streets. She parked in front of the old house and lugged her belongings down a brick walkway up onto the front porch, making three trips back to the car. Graham Hill, hearing the thump of the valises on the porch, came to the door and opened it wide.

"Didn't realize you would have so much to carry, Mrs. Layne, or I'd have asked our Sexton, Douglas, to help."

"It's alright. I may look small, but I'm capable of taking care of my bags." Robey tried to put him at ease with a broad smile.

Standing erect from placing the last bag inside the door, she faced a short stocky woman who bore only a slight facial resemblance to her younger brother. It was the grey eyes, Robey thought, and perhaps the nose, but in stature they were the exact opposite.

"This is my sister, Iris," Graham made the introductions. "Iris, meet Roberta Layne, the lady I spoke to you about this afternoon. Were you able to get the bedroom ready?"

"It's ready, Brother," Iris said coolly.

"Hello," Robey extended her hand but Iris, wiping her hands on her apron didn't reach out to shake hands, so Robey lowered hers, not certain Iris had seen her gesture.

"I do hope I'm not putting you to a lot of trouble. I'll do my own room, of course. It won't be necessary for you to clean up after me."

"The room is to the right at the top of the stairs. The door is open. I must get back to the kitchen and finish cleaning up after dinner," Iris spoke crisply, then abruptly turned, marching down the hall toward the rear of the house without looking back.

"I hope you had dinner before you came, Mrs. Layne," Graham whispered in the voice of a conspirator. "If not, there's plenty to snack on, and if you'll join me later, we'll indulge ourselves. Iris pretends to get furious with me when I raid the refrigerator, but I always seem to be hungry just before bedtime. I understand it's a terrible nutritional habit…eating just before going to sleep. At least, Iris tries to convince me it is."

"I'm not certain I'll join you tonight, Pastor Hill. I did have a salad and a bowl of soup at the hotel."

"Well, I must get back to some phoning before it's too late in the evening to bother people." He glanced once more at the stack of luggage. "Are you sure you won't need help to get those upstairs? You could leave them there until morning and get Douglas to help."

"No, no, I'll manage. Thanks anyway."

Robey was aware that Graham Hill wouldn't be able to handle any heavy load and watched as he disappeared behind huge doors that slid out of the wall. Before they closed, she had a glimpse of his study and was impressed by the shelves of books that evidently made up one full wall of the room. Then she began to trek up the steps with her possessions.

"Wish LaPorte were here," she mumbled to herself on the third trip up the steep stairs, "he'd have made it all in one climb." She had never lived in a world without a man to do the hard jobs, and she found even little things, like carrying luggage, very tiring.

Roger had always washed the outside windows, set out the loaded trash cans on the curb, pushed the lawnmower, and packed boxes into the attic. Well, it would be different now, she realized, for Graham Hill was the only man in this household and it was certain his affliction, whatever it was, kept him from performing any kind of difficult physical task. Iris, on the other hand, even as short as she was, looked like she could move mountains all by herself.

Robey plopped down on a straight-backed chair to catch her breath and looked around the large, high-ceilinged room. A dark mahogany wardrobe leaned against one wall and looked as though it would be more than adequate for her clothes. It would have to do, Robey realized, since no other closet was evident. The bed boasted an ornately carved headboard reaching halfway to the ceiling. Next to it was a small marble- top washstand. Across the room stood a bulky chiffonier with brass handles, a companion piece to the wardrobe. "Probably all from the Federal period," Robey surprised herself by remembering what she had once been taught in a retailing class in high school. Several small hooked rugs covered bare spots in a faded and well-worn oriental carpet. The only illumination came from the opaque glass bowl affixed to the ceiling covering a lone light bulb and a floor lamp with an equally opaque silk shade that stood by the chair on which she sat. Rising, Robey looked behind the washstand for an electrical outlet where she could plug in a bed lamp or her radio but saw none.

Unpacking, she placed lingerie, sweaters, and neatly folded blouses in the ample drawers. She hung the rest in the wardrobe and placed empty luggage and shoe boxes on the floor of the massive piece of furniture.

She noticed that the door to the hallway had a bolt as well as a keyhole, so the room could be locked from within. She felt more secure seeing the bolt there but laughed at herself for needing that kind of security. However, all the while she was working, she had a feeling there was something unusual about the room, something she couldn't quite put her finger on. Then, before going back downstairs as she gave a final inspection of her new accommodations, she grasped the cause of her concern.

Robey had never thought of herself as having claustrophobia, but each of the three tall windows in the room were heavily draped, giving the room an aura of there being no outside, no continuance of life beyond the four walls. For a short moment she felt stifled and rushed to the window beside the bed, pulling on the braided cords hanging there. The olive-green brocade opened reluctantly, as if they shielded something Robey should not see. Strangely, no light, not even from the streetlamp she knew wasn't far behind, entered the room, and Robey stepped from the side of the window to face it directly. Black shutters pressed themselves against the outside of the single-pane windows and for an instant the feeling of entrapment, which had almost faded away, again surged through her. She tried opening the window but found it nailed shut. Almost frantically she hurried to the remaining windows, pulling the drapes open, alarm growing with the blackness facing her at each one.

"Come on, old girl," she spoke aloud, "Miss Hill had very little time to prepare for me and tomorrow's another day."

Exasperated at herself for letting every little thing shake her, she realized she was, indeed, physically trembling. "Perhaps a warm glass of milk and a light snack might be just what I need," Robey said aloud. Dispelling the dark silence, she stepped out into the upper hall and heard Pastor Hill going to the back of the house downstairs, his crutches softly thudding the stairs in the otherwise quiet house. Robey leaned over the balustrade and softly called to him, "Hold up there, I think I'll take you up on your invitation after all."

He looked up, leaning on his crutches and smiling. "Come on. We'll get to know a bit more about each other over a sandwich." Robey felt the warmth of his smile and saw the twinkle of a little boy going to raid the cookie jar in his eye.

"Are you sure it's alright?" She asked when she caught up to him. "I think your sister overheard your invitation. Is that her room across from mine?"

"Yes, she won't join us. She's an early to bed and early to rise person."

Entering the kitchen which was, Robey surmised, as big as her own living and dining room combined back in Chandor, she saw an old wood stove squatting next to a modern electric range. Heat still radiated from the top of the old stove, giving evidence that Iris used it to cook on during the winter and early spring months. Although Robey had often seen pictures in early American magazines depicting such kitchens, she had never really been in one furnished as was this one. There was a large oak safe where pies and cakes were kept fresh and deep metal-lined drawers for bread and flour. The rose-patterned linoleum was clean but worn almost through in front of the white enameled sink. A wood box, filled for the morning, occupied a small space between the two stoves. Shiny pots and pans hung from black wrought iron hooks above the butcher-block table in the center of the room. The wonder reflected in Robey's face wasn't lost on Graham.

"A minister doesn't make enough for all the up-to-date equipment and jimcracks, Mrs. Layne, and I'm not sure Iris would use them if I did. She still opens cans with one of those small hand-held openers that leaves jagged edges."

"I was just thinking how different it all is, Pastor Hill. I love it. It has such charm, although I'm sure it must be a lot of work for your sister to keep it so clean."

"Iris doesn't have anything else to do. What I mean is, she could have learned to type or teach...or nurse—she'd have made a great nurse. But she likes to keep house, and she's good at it. Sit down," he waved her to a chair at the table. Robey watched as he expertly leaned on one crutch, reached into the refrigerator and set out the makings of sandwiches on the oil cloth table.

Robey made sandwiches of thin sliced beef, lettuce, tomato and cheese as Graham continued talking.

"I might as well warn you, though, Iris doesn't like too many people, and she won't take an immediate shine to you, I'm afraid. There's not much use in trying too hard to get next to her. I think she gets suspicious of people who try. When she's ready she'll come round," he said. "You see, she is one of those self-inflicted martyrs. Know what I mean?"

"Yes, I think I do. But don't people like that usually have, or think they have, a reason?"

"She does, she does." Graham took a big bite out of his sandwich. Robey waited while he swallowed. "You see, our brother, Ward, who is between Iris and me in age—I'm the youngest—is mentally ill and in an institution somewhere. There are eighteen years difference in our ages, Iris' and mine, I mean. And there was only sixteen months between Iris and Ward."

"How long has he been there...in the institution?"

"Twenty-seven years. I barely remember him. Iris and Ward grew up together, and when I was five—in fact, it was the day after my birthday, Ward was committed by the court at the petition of my uncle Rem. Our parents had both died. Mother when I was born and father in a coal mine accident when I was four."

"Your uncle and aunt raised you? After your father died, I mean."

"No, Iris raised me. She was of age by that time and really my next of kin. A year later, when I was five, Ward became too much for her, but she wouldn't give him up. He was twenty-one by then. Anyway, our Uncle Rem stepped in and...well...I've been told Ward was pretty much uncontrollable at times and the families in town were afraid for their children when he got into a temper. Iris took it very hard and never forgave Uncle Rem. He's never been back to this house and to this day Iris refuses to speak of him. Any mention of his name sends her into a bad snit. I said 'never has been' as if he were still alive. Uncle Rem died about twelve years ago. Iris wouldn't even go to the funeral."

"That's terribly sad, Pastor Hill. What a burden for a young woman to lose both parents and a brother, too, under such tragic circumstances."

"Well, she decided to forgo any life of her own to raise me, and I guess I should say that I am grateful to her; she has been a grim guardian, intolerant of any interference. That's why I've never married, I guess. I wouldn't want to leave her alone. Where would she go? What could she do? She wouldn't stay here with another woman in charge, and I certainly wouldn't want a wife of mine to have to constantly cope with Iris' foibles."

"Now who's being a martyr?" Robey said half-jokingly. Graham smiled, nodding his head in agreement.

"I suppose so. Only there's so much more to it than that."

"Does anyone visit Ward?"

"No. Iris said the last time she did—about seven years ago—the doctors asked her not to come back. He evidently became quite violent and hard to handle whenever she left. He doesn't, according to what Iris tells me, have any understanding of what goes on around him."

"You've never seen him since he left?"

"No. Iris wouldn't take me with her when I was little and after

I was grown and able to understand, well it just didn't seem right; like I was going out of curiosity rather than a loss of a close relationship, which we never had. Iris assures me he's well taken care of, and I believe her. She wouldn't ever allow him to be mistreated in any way. Besides, he wouldn't know who I was at all. To him, I guess, I'm still that five-year-old."

Robey sat picking at a few crumbs on her plate, in deep thought. "Does she have friends here she visits?"

"She used to go see an old girlfriend of hers on weekends, but it has been quite some time since she's done that."

Robey was surprised at herself, delving as she seemed to be doing into a stranger's business, but Graham didn't seem to mind in the least. 'I guess,' she thought to herself, 'since I was so open with him today, he feels he can be equally open with me.'

"Well, it seems to me she could have had some other life than what she has... friends, I mean. And you—you're really cheating yourself by doing just as she has done by not marrying. As I said, making a martyr of yourself, Mr. Hill."

Graham laughed in agreement, a wholly pleasant sound from deep within the man. "Please, if we're going to analyze each other so thoroughly, we should at least be on a first name basis."

Robey grinned, raising her glass of milk in a toast. "Alright, to us ... call me Robey... and please pass the bread, and I'll make a couple more sandwiches. I didn't know how empty my stomach was. That salad I ate for dinner at the hotel wasn't very filling."

In clearing up the crumbs and putting things away after they had satiated their hunger, Robey looked out the window into the night and remembered the shuttered windows in her room

"Oh, by the way, who can I get to help me unnail the windows and open those shutters upstairs? I'm a fresh-air fiend. I like open windows at night." Robey was loathe to admit to the uneasiness she had felt, so childish.

"I'll send Douglas over tomorrow. It's a shame he wasn't around to help with your bags this evening. He does most of the odd jobs here and at the church. Can you start work tomorrow or do you want to familiarize yourself with the town a bit more?"

"I'll start work. Probably get to know people better if I have a purpose in meeting them. You know, I'm really looking forward to my first day as a part of the labor force."

"Volunteer force, you mean, don't you? Remember, there's no money to be had, although I have an inkling you will probably more than have earned it if there were." Graham snapped the light switch off, throwing the kitchen into darkness and he and Robey started down the hallway. Between the study in the kitchen she noticed another door and, trying to put the house in proper perspective in her mind, asked if it was the dining room.

"No, that was Ward's room. Iris keeps it locked. If I've ever been in it, it was before I was five years old. I used to ask about it. With a kid's curiosity I wanted to explore, but she'd never open it. Said it was piled up with Ward's stuff. The room above is locked, too. We used to put guests in there. I was a bit surprised Iris gave you the room she did, since the other overlooks the flower garden. I think she's using that for storage, too."

"Where is the dining room, then?" Robey pursued her query.

"Off to the left from the kitchen." Graham pointed in the direction. "We seldom use it. The living room is just to your left at the bottom of the stairs, behind the sliding doors. Except for an occasional tea, we don't use it, either. For their meetings, the ladies of the church prefer our upholstered chairs to the bare wood ones in the Sunday School rooms for their monthly meeting. My study gets the most use here after the church office is closed for the day. Iris practically lives in the kitchen. She's a great cook. Smelling what she bakes is almost as good as eating it."

Robey started up the steps and Graham laboriously came behind. "Goodnight, Robey," he whispered.

"Goodnight, Graham," Robey responded in an equally low voice. After she shut her door and turned on the light, the question came to her. Why didn't Graham use his brothers' downstairs room instead of having to pull himself up that long flight of stairs on crutches? It certainly must be inconvenient for him, but then, perhaps he was using the room he had had since a boy and didn't want to change. Robey knew it was none of her concern, but the thought nagged at her even after she had snuggled down between the sheets. Iris, she decided, was going to be quite a challenge. She had retired while Robey was still unpacking and had given her no indication that she intended to be cordial. Robey's mind ran over the day's events, and she was astonished at what the day had brought.

Iris Hill stared at the ceiling of her darkened bedroom and tried to put the confusion in her mind in proper place. This morning had been so orderly—the routine of years. And now this woman had foisted herself into her life. She remembered back to other times when outsiders had succeeded in upsetting routine, including Graham's fifth birthday party. Uncle Rem and Aunt Edwina had not been invited. They had barged in. Iris let her memory carry her back.

Colorful balloons dipped and bobbed from the ceiling and orange streamers twisted in the breeze whenever a door opened or shut. The children and their parents had all arrived and presents were stacked on a table in the corner by the parlor door. Childish squeals pierced the air. Graham was blindfolded and trying to pin the tail on the donkey. At this point, Iris recalled, Uncle Rem and Aunt Edwina came up the front steps and entered the house without knocking. A sour taste came up into Iris' throat at the memory.

"Why didn't you tell us you were having a party for Graham?" She heard Aunt Edwina whine. "We'd have been glad to help."

'Glad to take over, you mean,' Iris thought. They had never believed she could take care of Graham but, because Iris was of age, they had no alternative but to let her.

Children were laughing and clapping their hands to Farmer in the Dell, oblivious to the tensions sparking between the three adults facing each other in the hallway.

At that moment, Ward came lumbering out of his room. He had overalls on over a plaid flannel shirt, but his feet were bare. His hair was uncombed in his face and he had gone unshaven since Iris did this for him. She had been totally involved in the party all day and had, for once, neglected this duty.

Iris tried to turn him around back to his room to lock him in, but her effort was in vain. He was physically strong and had seen the children and the birthday cake. In his child's mind he had but one purpose—to join the party. Ward grabbed the first gift he saw and ripped off the wrapping. If only Uncle Rem had left him alone, Iris cringed, but he didn't! He tried to take the present away, and it became a wrestling match. He pushed Ward to the wall and now, understanding only that he was threatened, Ward took hold of a small vase stand by the leg and hit his assailant sharply on the head. Uncle Rem crumpled to the floor, and Ward looked at Iris pitifully, knowing he had done something wrong—very wrong. Iris could hear screams coming from Aunt Edwina. Parents stood in the doorway in stunned disbelief.

Iris now lead the docile Ward to his room, and locked the door. When she returned to the front hall, she found Uncle Rem sitting on the floor, where Aunt Edwina applied to his head wound a cold wet dishtowel snatched from the kitchen. The last of the children were being ushered out the door, and Graham was standing in the archway, tears wetting his cheeks. His party was over, and his five-year-old mind couldn't understand.

The next morning, assured by Uncle Rem, the judge signed the papers for a lunacy commission, and they met in the afternoon in the parlor, a padded wagon waiting outside the house. After Ward was committed, Iris would never forget his face as he was led away by strangers...looking back...pleading...not comprehending. After he left, she vaguely heard the Sheriff telling her how much better things would be.

Third-people intruders—Uncle Rem, Aunt Edwina, the Judge, the Sheriff, had always been bad news. Amelia Wentworth had been bad news. And now this Mrs. Roberta Layne.

"Well, Mrs. Roberta Layne," Iris said to herself in a whisper, "you just better not interfere with me." She turned over on her side and pulled the cover over her shoulder. "Please, Lord, make her leave us alone, please," she pleaded silently.

It would be a long time before sleep finally overtook her thoughts.

Graham, in his own bed, rehashed the events of the day. Robey was a very attractive woman, he decided, but not one to devote her life to a career. Where, he wondered, would she fit in this quest of hers to make a new life? She didn't seem hard and ambitious like so many women who could barge ahead and be content climbing a corporate ladder. Of this he was certain. He could picture her waiting at the doorway for her husband and two children to come home to her; cooking fine meals, keeping a clean and cheerful house, doing all those things a man likes for her to do for him. Yes, he decided, that had been and should be again her lot in life.

Graham chided himself for trying to plan Robey's future. Yes, *I'd better practice what I preach and let the good Lord take charge.* A grim memory of the last time he had truly tried to help someone straighten out her life invaded his reverie. Amelia had come to work at the church in desperation, hoping to earn enough money to keep from having to beg David's father to bail them out of their sinking financial ship.

The Wentworths had come to church regularly for a short while after David brought his bride to Knobbe Cove. It wasn't long, however, before Amelia came alone and then she, too, had ceased to appear at Sunday services. He was surprised to find her one day standing in his office in answer to a classified ad for a church secretary, asking for both advice and a job.

"Honestly, Pastor Hill," Amelia sounded exasperated, "I don't know what to do. David just will not take charge of the bookstore to make it profitable, and he won't even let me in to help. He's going to lose it if he doesn't do something soon."

"Do you know why he won't let you help?" Graham was afraid, perhaps, she wasn't a good worker and David just didn't want her to mess up his book cataloging system, which is essential for all good libraries and booksellers. He could certainly understand that.

"Yes, I think I know why. I've heard gossip, rumors about his drinking during the day. I've heard he sometimes closes early when he's had too much."

Graham had looked deep into Amelia's eyes and found nothing there to disprove her words. She seemed remarkably cold and collected about it, but he realized she had faced the problem squarely and was determined to do something positive about her circumstances.

"I'm sorry, Amelia, I really am. Do you want me to talk to David?"

"No, no, please don't. It probably would only worsen the situation. I don't ever want him to know he's been discussed. He would be furious, I know."

"What will he say about you working here?"

"He won't mind, I don't think. I told him I wanted to work at least until we started a family. We've only been married a little over two years, and I'm not really ready yet. Perhaps soon...if David..." She seemed to be searching for words.

"If he changes for the better, you mean?"

"Oh, I sound so terrible, don't I? I love David, I truly do. And I will —no matter what—but I guess the rosy existence I thought was ahead of us when we married just wasn't meant to be. Reality set in and the reality is that David's father has spoiled him and given him everything he ever wanted. David doesn't know how to take responsibility for his life. So, I'll have to."

"Well, the job here is yours and maybe, the Lord willing, I may be able to help both you and David. I'll try to find a way."

"Famous last words," Graham muttered to himself. What a tragic mess that had turned out to be! Five years had gone by, and he still had no way to carry out his intentions for Amelia and David. Perhaps, he mused optimistically, this attempt at helping another distressed damsel will end up better or at least, hopefully, not quite as disastrously.

6

A SHARP RAP AT THE DOOR ROUSED ROBEY, BUT QUICK footsteps retreated down the stairs before she could answer. She stretched, cat-like, putting first one leg outside the bed, testing the room temperature before pushing the quilt off her body. Since no sun filtered through the offensive black shutters, she wondered if it was morning. She felt as though she had just dropped off to sleep, a sleep that had been dreamless and deep from which she had awakened more refreshed than she had been for a long time. Her travel clock on the washstand indicated 7:30 AM. Wrapping her quilted robe around her shoulders and shoving her feet into white satin slippers, she picked up the towel and washcloth Iris had left folded on the marble top of the stand and slipped out the door heading for the bath.

In its extreme spaciousness, the bathroom resembled all the other rooms in the house that she had seen. A freestanding shower inhabited one corner with a round white enameled base and a singular white duck cloth curtain hanging from a large circular pipe. The large iron bathtub with eagle claw legs dominated one side of the room, and an ancient toilet, graced by a plain wood seat, was made functional by a chain dangling from the water closet affixed halfway up the wall. Astonished, Robey was greatly amused. Was she still in this decade? Or had she, during the night, somehow been traversed back a century through time?

Sounds of talking rose from the kitchen downstairs which Robey realized was directly beneath her, so she hastened her bath. No need to have Iris upset by being late for breakfast her first morning.

In her room, she wondered what time Graham would go to the church and how long they would stay there each day. "I'll soon find out," she said aloud to herself, pulling a bright orange sweater over her head. She patted her dark auburn hair into place and appraised the results in the mirror. Roger had always liked the orange sweater with the brown houndstooth suit, and she had to admit, with her coloring, oranges and rusts were her best colors. She rapidly made the bed and put things in order, and with a last glance at the shuttered windows, Robey picked up her purse and jacket and descended to the kitchen.

"Good morning, Miss Hill," she greeted the aproned woman placing a plate of ham and eggs in front of her brother. Iris barely looked at her. "Good morning, Graham," she was determined to remain cheerful and not let Iris set the mood for the day, but her smile quickly faded when Iris glared at her in open hostility at what Robey presumed was her using Pastor Hill's first name. Iris's expression was not lost on Graham who, after greeting Robey and motioning her to sit down, turned to his sister.

"Iris, I have a feeling our association with Mrs. Layne—Robey—will be long and enjoyable. As for me, I feel she's, well, I won't say God sent," he chuckled, "but even that remains to be seen."

Iris placed Robey's plate on the table in front of her and sat down at her own place before making a comment. She creamed and sugared her coffee and stirred it slowly. When she raised her eyes her hostility was shielded, as though she had decided not to wage war...yet.

"My brother tells me you came to visit Amelia Wentworth, Mrs. Layne," emphasizing the Mrs. and leaving no doubt as to her displeasure.

"Yes, but I'm afraid my welcome was less than I expected. I should have written first that I was coming. So, I suppose it is pretty much my fault. I shouldn't have presumed Amelia would be receptive to a surprise visit."

"One *does* usually write before coming such a long distance," Iris stated flatly. Robey shivered under her coldness. "Mrs. Wentworth used to do the things in the church my brother will be expecting you to do. Did he tell you that?"

Robey couldn't conceal her surprise. "No, no, I don't believe you mentioned that, did you, Graham?"

Graham's face clouded, visibly disturbed with his sister.

"Iris," he wiped his mouth on the linen napkin and stood up, reaching for the crutches. "I haven't had time to go into every detail of Knobbe Cove with Robey in the short couple of hours we've had to converse. You sound as though I were trying to hide the fact." He faced Robey, "Excuse me a minute, I forgot a phone call I promised to make first thing this morning." He made his way down the hall to his office leaving the two women alone at the breakfast table.

Iris's face had colored deeply at Grahams words, making her light grey eyes seem even paler. Her lips tightened into a thin line with anger at her brother's rebuke, and the meal was finished in silence. She almost grabbed the dishes from the table as Robey walked down the hall to join Graham and leave the house.

A brisk wind during the night had cleared the last of the storm clouds from the sky. Only white wispy broom-swept fluffs lingered in the robin egg blue of the early spring heavens. A few brown pin-oak leaves broke loose and scampered down the street, and here and there a crocus pushed its green cap above the ground. 'At least,' Robey thought, 'spring is welcome in Knobbe Cove.' Except for Graham, Robey certainly felt like an unwanted alien. Indecision wormed its way back into her emotions. 'Why should I stay here when it seems I shouldn't have come in the first place? First Amelia and David and now Iris. Maybe I'll go back home. That would please Lawrence and Sarah.' Her chin went up and her shoulders visibly straightened. 'But it wouldn't please me,' she stubbornly insisted to herself.

The sight of the church put other thoughts in Robey's mind and she was soon in the office, hanging her coat on the rack stand behind the door and placing her handbag in a desk drawer which had, evidently, once been Amelia's when she was employed as church secretary.

Graham greeted her from the doorway. "Come with me to the storeroom, and I'll show you where everything is kept." She followed him across the hall where shelves held a variety of bulletin covers, mimeograph paper, stencils and Sunday School books and tracts.

"Copier's pretty old—still have to hand tone it and it doesn't collate—but it gets the job done. I'll show you tomorrow how to use it when we update the bulletins for Sunday."

"How many folks are there in your congregation?"

"Not more than a hundred most Sundays. Easter and Christmas are different, of course, but not a whole lot. Teachers and students leave for their homes during these holidays, but they're replaced by those who are holiday regulars. Twice a year Christians, I call them. The biggest crowd is at graduation time when folks come to collect their students."

The telephone jangled in the office and Graham quickly swung on his crutches and crossed the hall. Robey was amazed at how dexterous he could be. She followed him and sat down quietly, wondering what had happened to him to make him so handicapped. Was it an accident, childhood disease, or was he born that way? His brother, Ward, had a mental problem...perhaps...

The question nagged to be answered, but Robey knew it was too soon to ask. If Graham had wanted her to know he would probably have told her last night in the kitchen. Heaven knows, she thought, we talked about enough personal things. Only Sarah knows as much about me. Robey hoped there would be many evenings in the kitchen—without Iris. She realized she was being unfair, as unfair, in fact, as Iris had been to her, and that certainly wasn't a charitable or Christian way to be, but, well, she didn't care. Iris presented a threat to her peace of mind. Exasperation at her own attitude assailed her and she decided, despite Graham's assurance that Iris would never get to be a good friend to her, to make a very special effort to know her better and, if possible, like her. After all, she reasoned, if they were to share the same house, they had better not get on one another's nerves.

"That was Webster—Webb—Brown, chairman of our trustees," Graham explained as he re cradled the phone receiver. "He's coming over to discuss the program for the Easter service. Why don't you bone up on your typing? You do type, don't you? I forgot to ask!"

"Yes—very slowly—but accurately. I used to do a lot of my husband's rough drafts at home on our word processor. He said he could think better when he could bounce his ideas off me."

"Our computer is as old as the copier, but you'll get to love it... It'll grow on you, as they say. I don't have anything for you to do just yet, but you'll find work around here simply grows like topsy. One thing will lead to another and pretty soon you'll be wishing you had said no to me." His smile showed slight creases in his cheeks that were almost dimples, and his face beamed youthfulness despite the shock of gray hair. Robey, trying to figure his age from what he had told her about Ward and Iris last night, came up with thirty-two. Her thoughts were interrupted by a tall man with a small black mustache who stopped momentarily at the office door, waved at Graham and went on without introduction. Graham followed him down the hall through arched doors to the church sanctuary.

Robey sat down at the old computer and turned it on. After a short wait she clicked on word processor. She was not sure she was ready to telephone Lawrence. Things should be going more smoothly than they were. Yet, she remembered she had promised to let him know her situation, so perhaps, she thought, she'd drop him a short note. Glancing out the window, she saw a small black man leave the manse and head toward the church. In a short few seconds he made his entrance into the office.

"Hello," Robey was certain this was the sexton Graham had told her about. "Are you Douglas Washington?"

"Yes, ma'am. You must be Mizz Layne."

"That's me. Were you able to open those shutters in my room?"

"All done. I'll be over later this afternoon to wash the windows, there's all kinds of spider webs in them. Always happens when windows get shut up like that for long."

"Thank you so very much. I surely do appreciate it. That room needs plenty of sunlight."

"Sure does," Douglas agreed. "Where's the pastor?"

"He's in the sanctuary with Webster Brown."

Douglass turned and strode away, leaving Robey to wonder just how old he was. His hair was steel gray, but his step was young and agile. Slight and wiry, he appeared to have more energy than many people with less years. Douglas reappeared shortly with both Webb and Graham in tow. Graham entered the office and scrabbled through some papers in the middle drawer of his desk. The other two men stood outside in the hallway, talking.

"I'm going down to the bank with Webb. Douglas tells me John King, the loan officer there, has returned and we're trying to negotiate some funds to fix up a few things around here. Might as well get him fresh from his Bahamas vacation. Maybe he'll have a little pity on we stay-at-homes. When you leave, lock the door from the inside—just push the button beside the knob. I'll try to remember to get you a key made downtown today. We had an extra, but I don't know where it went."

Graham and Webb left, and Douglas came back into the office and sat down in the leather chair beside Graham's desk, which Robey had occupied the day before. He watched her carefully as she explored the drawers of her new work site, as though trying to make up his mind whether or not to like her. Robey, determined to have one ally besides Graham, gave him a broad smile.

"Tell me, Mr. Washington, how long have you worked for Pastor Hill?"

"For him and his family—most of my life, Mizz Layne."

"Was Pastor Hill's father a minister...of course not," she quickly corrected herself, "he told me he was a coal miner...but how did Mrs. Hill's brother and sister come to live in the manse when he..." Robey realized she was completely puzzled and not making much sense. She also wasn't sure she should be asking such a question of a complete stranger—a stranger to her, anyway. How nosey she must seem to him—but the question was out, and she couldn't retract it. "I'm sorry, Mr. Washington, I have no business asking things like that about Pastor Hill."

Douglas laughed. Somehow, he really liked this pretty woman who, he understood from Graham, would be working here from now on. "Ask away. I see why you're confused. The house isn't really the manse. Not owned by the church, you see. It belonged to the pastor's grandmother—on his mother side. When she married the pastor's father he moved in with her family. It was done a lot in those days. Typhoid took her Ma and Pa. Since she was an only child, the house was hers. She was expecting her second baby at the time. Mizz Iris was her first. It was a miracle both of them didn't die, too. People said the reason the baby, Ward, was the way he was had something to do with typhoid. I don't know."

"You must know everyone in Knobbe Cove, Mr. Washington. I want to do an effective job here, so can I ask you to sometime show me the whole town and tell me who's who?"

"Of course. First off, please call me Douglas. As for the town, there's not much, but it's a good town. We're in three sections here, I guess." Douglas settled back and lit a corncob pipe. The first puff of smoke enveloped his head in a blue haze. "There's the town folk, like the pastor and the rest who live right around the Cove. And there's the backwoods folk—that's me and my people—mostly black but a few whites who like to live up against the foothills. We mostly farm and do summer work in the Cove."

"You said three, Douglas. Who are the others?"

"They are the mountain folk. An odd bunch. Some are meaner than snakes and others just don't want to do anything much. Don't do nothing for anybody. Some of them steal from tourists to get by in the winter."

"You have much trouble with them?"

"No, not really. If any of them gets too bad, we take care of them. You see, they don't even stick up for each other. My folk kind of work as one mind and body when we get mad..." Douglas shook his fist and flexed his small but obviously hard muscle to emphasize his words. "We don't have to do much of anything anymore, just let the word get out that we're after someone and that takes care of that. He usually disappears on his own for a while. If he don't—then often as not he finds himself miles from home on a dark night wearing nothing but a couple of extra bumps and maybe a black eye. We never get real violent, but if they throw the first blow we serve up the second."

"I see," Robey grinned. "Backwoods justice?"

"Yep, that's what it is." Douglas stretched his spindly legs. "Well, better get back to work." He rose and was gone in what seemed to Robey one swift movement. She looked out the office door and saw no sign of life.

Robey spent a few minutes getting familiar with the computer and then typed a couple of lines to the attorney and Sarah. In the middle of Sarah's letter, Robey abruptly stopped. "I'll finish this by hand later," she said aloud, printing out what she had written. She shut down the computer, locked the church door behind her, and went back to the house. If this was to be her home, she would have to have an understanding with Iris.

7

ROBEY ENTERED THE HOUSE, STOPPING TO LISTEN TO see if she could tell where Iris was working. Not hearing anything, she went in search of her in the kitchen and, not finding her there, mounted the stairs on her way to her own room. There, in the upstairs hall, she found Iris placing clean linen in a huge walk-in closet next to Robey's room.

"Good morning, Miss Hill," she tried to sound as cheerful as possible. Iris turned to face her but remained silent.

Robey took a deep breath. "I know you disapprove of me being here, Miss Hill, but...well...I really don't understand why, unless I'll be too much bother. I'll try not."

"There's no bother, Mrs. Layne. Whatever my brother wishes is no bother to me."

"Then what is it? If we are to live together under the same roof we should be on the best of terms and somehow, I feel I've—we've—gotten off to a very bad beginning."

Iris was not used to such outspoken honesty from strangers. She closed the closet door, locked it, and turned again to face Robey.

"Most people seem afraid to speak their minds in front of me. You're different, aren't you? Let's go down and have a cup of coffee together. There are a few things I expect you should know to be forearmed, if you are determined to work with my brother."

Robey felt a wash of relief that she had been taken up on her attempt at an open relationship, but a bit alarmed at the tone of foreboding in what Iris seemed intent on telling her. Forearmed? She followed Iris down the steps and through the hallway to the kitchen. This wasn't going to be as hard as she thought it might and she was certain Graham would both approve and feel relief. Still, instinctively, Robey knew she had better only listen and ask few questions. Iris lifted the huge gray enamel coffee pot from the wood stove and poured two cups of the dark steaming liquid. That done, she sat opposite Robey at the table and told her a story she found difficult to believe.

"As I said before, Amelia Wentworth once had the job you have undertaken. It was about six years ago when she came to the church looking for part-time work. Her husband's book-store was doing poorly, and they needed the extra money." She paused, remembering Robey was getting no salary and hastened to explain. "At the time the church was paying a small stipend. The congregation was large…then…and could afford a paid sec-retary. Mrs. Wentworth's hours were supposed to be from 9:00 in the morning until 2:00 in the afternoon, but soon she was ar-riving earlier and staying later. Brother insisted it was the volume of work, but I know it wasn't so." Iris's voice was almost a whis-per. "She was throwing herself at him shamelessly. He wasn't al-ways a cripple on crutches. He was tall and handsome then…and looked like one of the university football team members. But for all that he was naive. He never dated many girls for some reason and those he did he never took seriously. Brother has never been suspicious-minded. He's too trusting and too willing to see the good in everybody. I sometimes think he'd see good in the devil! He fell into Amelia Wentworth's trap."

Robey let out a gasp of protest as Iris plunged on.

"Oh, yes. He's too stubborn to ever admit that's what happened. He'd never betray her, but everyone else knew what was going on inside that church office day after day. I walked in on them one day," Iris's eyes dropped to her hands dramatically, "He was there with his arms around her, and she had her head buried in his shoulder. Talk was already going around Knobbe Cove like wildfire. About five months after she started working, she told Brother she was expecting a child. David, poor boy, had started drinking because of the gossip and Amelia did nothing to help put the rumors to rest."

"This doesn't sound like the Amelia I know." Robey felt defensive.

"What could she say?" Iris continued, ignoring the remark. "Of course, David could never be quite sure who the father of the child was. From what I understand he begged her to stop working at the church and she refused. Things kept getting worse. I tried to reason with Brother, told him to get rid of her, but he wouldn't. I knew it would all end in tragedy. It couldn't help but do that. And it did."

Iris stood and walked over to the window, her back to Robey.

"Our congregation became smaller as respectable people refused to attend and listen to what they considered hypocritical sermons. Brother never publicly said anything, but privately to me he defended her. Said he felt sorry for her, that her husband didn't understand his responsibilities and was gambling and drinking all their money away. Of course he was! The shame and disgrace of a wife carrying on with the pastor would drive any man to such ends."

Robey noticed the bitterness that dominated each word Iris uttered...or was it bitterness? As she listened further to the story, she realized it was a deep hatred of Amelia and could very well be a destructive fury if Iris wanted to act on it. I suppose, she thought, it would make any person furious not to be able to stop a beloved brother from making a fool of himself. Still, Robey felt wary, amazed Iris would tell her all this. Had she no loyalty to Graham? He certainly wasn't put in a very good light by her revelations.

"One day Amelia and my brother started out together to Lighthouse Island. You'll go there, too, in a few weeks. There's a family there who keep orphaned and unwanted children. There aren't many in these parts, but we have no place for them to go except send them away to a State institution. The Willises have tremendously big hearts and just can't seem to turn away any child. The State helps pay for their upkeep. Brother wants to start a regular orphanage here—it's a dream of his—but there's no money. The Willises earn a good living cabinetmaking. Sell their work all over the East Coast. Brother goes out several times a year for communion and ministering. Anyway, you'll go when he goes." Iris fell silent, seemingly searching for the lost thread of her tirade against Amelia. She looked around at Robey. "Where was I?"

"You were telling me about Graham and Amelia going to Lighthouse Island...the Willises," Robey prodded the older woman back onto the original track of conversation.

Iris looked a bit startled. "Oh, yes, I was telling you about that, wasn't I? It's not hard to get off an unpleasant subject, is it?"

'Why tell me at all,' Robey thought. But then she remembered Iris saying she wanted her to be forearmed. Perhaps she did mean well at that.

"Well," Iris continued, her voice quiet but clipped, "they were on their way in my brother's little outboard and had just gone past the part of the Cove that juts out onto the water when a large boat came around the Knobbe and ran them down. There was no way my brother could get away from it, from what he told me, and the boat—my brother's boat—was literally cut in half. It was horrible, horrible. I'll never forget when they came for me and gave me the news."

Robey realized Iris always referred to Graham as her brother or the Reverend. And she said it's so possessively! Robey listened in a state of mental confusion, not wanting to believe everything Iris said, and yet not wanting to be a dupe and discount it all. Perhaps she might be able to verify the facts by a talk with Amelia and then again, she remembered, Amelia might not talk to her at all.

"What happened then?" She urged Iris to complete the narrative.

"My brother was injured terribly. That's why he walks on crutches today. I guess he's lucky to be alive at all. He spent months in physical therapy and even with that he can barely stand alone. He has feeling in his legs but they just won't support him. Amelia lost the baby and by the time my brother got out of the hospital some of the congregation was gone and there was no job for her."

"Who was responsible for the accident?"

"They never really found out. The rock formation—the Knobbe—makes a blind spot. Boats are supposed to sound their horns or clang bells and slow down as they come around, but there was no warning according to the Reverend. The big boat was empty when the police boarded, and no one could prove who was piloting, but then no one really tried. You see, the big boat belonged to David Wentworth."

Robey's hand flew to her throat. "You mean David purposely tried to kill them?"

"He said he wasn't in the boat, but he was drunk as usual when they found him. His clothes were dry. They would have been wet, I suppose, if he had jumped from the boat where they found it out in the water."

Then, she negated the logic of the alibi. "He probably had time to change clothes. Who else could it have been?"

Iris looked up at the clock and rose to begin preparations for the noon meal. When she said no more, Robey realized she had been dismissed. She slowly pushed up from the table and walked to the front door, staring across the street at the church, trying to absorb the narrative she had just been told. Amelia and Graham? What could have happened to her to make her change so? She and David had been so in love.

As she looked out over the porch, Graham and Webb Brown stepped up on the curb in front of the building, said a few words to each other and parted. Graham caught sight of Robey in the doorway and came across the street. As he came up the sidewalk, she tried to place him in the role of homewrecker, the other man, and couldn't. But then, she remembered, he wasn't on those crutches five years ago. A picture of him standing erect without them escaped her, try as she could to materialize one. She would, she resolved, be a bit more careful of her confidences with him until she really got to know the whole truth of his relationship with Amelia.

Robey recalled that Amelia had stopped writing to her five years ago—and the accident, she figured, had been about that time. So, perhaps Iris's story did have some whole cloth to it. Graham crossed the porch and Robey opened the door for him.

"Well, waiting for me? Thank you." He smiled broadly.

"No, not really," Robey answered cooley. "I was just standing here idly thinking when you came up."

If Graham noticed the chill of her tone, he decided not to question it. "I hear Iris in the kitchen. Lunch about ready?" he called out as he clumped down the hallway. "I'm ravenous. We had a real favorable session at the bank, and I feel like celebrating." He faced Robey, who had been right behind him, "The only way to celebrate in this town is to get drunk or eat a hearty meal. Considering what we're celebrating, I better settle for being a glutton."

"Come on, Robey," Iris invited, "sit here and I'll dish it out."

Robey looked up at Iris and searched her face to see if she could tell what had prompted her to use her first name. In fact, the way she had said it denoted conspiracy, as if she were trying to tell her they had secrets together. Did Iris really expect for the two of them to become allies against the Wentworths and, for that matter, Graham as well? Robey, instead of being able to relax, now found herself becoming more and more apprehensive at the awkward situation Iris had put her in.

8

*T*HREE WEEKS PASSED QUICKLY WITH QUARTERLY reports, ordering supplies, answering letters and getting used to Graham's file system. Robey began to feel comfortable and at home in the big house and went out of her way to be helpful to Iris.

A letter came from Lawrence describing a small settlement out of court on the accident. Oddly, had Roger lived and been incapacitated she could have received a settlement in the upper six figures. As it was, the judgment was small, and Lawrence said that since the car had been stolen, he doubted he could squeeze any real money from anyone. Robey dismissed the case from her mind. Only Lawrence's urging had made her sue to begin with. Now, it was over at last.

Lawrence also indicated in his note that he had been able to store all her possessions at the old warehouse on the back lot of the company, and he was in the process of repainting the house in order to rent it to what he termed fairly well-to-do prospects.

The letter seemed impersonal, with no hint of a repeat of the declaration he had made the day she left Chandor. Robey assumed she had been able to impress him with how she felt. It would be a relief not to have to pussyfoot around words, keeping him from being encouraged whenever she wrote to him, and not having to read his letters looking for subtle meanings between the lines.

She reread the letter and put her mind at rest. He had evidently decided not to pursue the issue. Robey filed the letter away in a small briefcase she had brought along, holding what she had considered important papers.

Sitting at the lunch table, Graham pulled a letter from his coat pocket. "I have a job for you this evening, if you're not doing anything else."

Robey assured him she was free, and he explained.

"There's and old couple here whose only son is in France. He went there during the Second World War, and just never came back—found himself a wife and now has a large family. He's not too well off, so I guess his money has gone for living and not traveling, but he does send his folks a bit of money every month. Neither of the old folks read. One never learned, and the other is almost blind. The mail comes to me, and I put the money in the bank for them and see that someone reads the letters to them. Douglas does it once in a while. I do it sometimes, and guess what? Now I have you to do it!"

"Do they come over to the church, or do I go to them?"

"Ordinarily they come to the church during the day, but last month just before you came, Grandpa Kaslav fell and broke his leg. He's home, but Mama Kaslav doesn't want to leave him alone. They're up in their eighties, real nice people. You'll like them."

"Where do they live?"

"They're three blocks behind the church. I took the liberty of sending word by Douglas that you'd probably be there this evening. Do you mind?"

"I'll be glad to go," Robey agreed, taking the letter from Graham, thankful it was typewritten so it would be easy to read.

For a short few minutes they all concentrated on the food set before them. Then Robey broke the silence.

"Iris tells me you are interested in a home for orphans, Graham."

He grinned at the mention of his pet dream.

"Yes, I hope it's more than a pipe dream. The Willises keep about fifteen kids out on the island," Graham hesitated. Robey could hear a sharp intake of breath, then he looked at Iris with questions in his eyes. Robey realized he had become aware his sister had probably told her about the accident, since she knew about the Willis children.

When will I ever learn to keep my mouth shut, she admonished herself silently, and glanced at Iris. She was sitting, solemn and unsmiling, studiously picking at the remnants of food on her plate. Robey wanted to reach out and touch her and tell her how sorry she was she had betrayed her confidence. Iris hadn't told her not to say anything, but there were just certain things one didn't casually refer to and a tragic accident was one of them. Now, she knew, she would have to start all over again trying to win Iris as a friend. She doubted she would ever be her confidant.

During the remainder of the meal, Robey felt Iris's accusing eyes on her and she determinedly changed the subject and talked to Graham about what the improvements and repairs were to be at the church.

"How soon will you get the money for the church?" She changed the direction of conversation.

"Oh, that's a long way off, couple of months or so, I'd guess. The loan committee at the bank only meets every two weeks. Things move slowly here. We should get a commitment at the next meeting. They'll investigate the solvency of the church finances and the cash prospects. They'll also need an itemized list of what we intend using the money for."

"Do you think there will be any difficulty?"

"No, no, we don't owe anyone now. The mortgage was burned

years ago. It's just that needed repairs will cost far above what we can get in a lump sum through Sunday donations. Don't worry, it looks like a sure thing."

Robey wanted to assure him she would be glad to supply the needed funds, but caution made her hesitate. Better, she thought, to wait and see if it was really needed.

Iris had not contributed to the latter part of the lunch conversation, evidently still in deep resentful thought, and Robey was grateful when the meal came to an end and she and Graham again made the short trip to the church for an afternoon of work.

Time flew by. When Robey next looked out the window it was early dusk and almost six o'clock.

"Do you think Iris would mind stashing my dinner in the fridge? I'll eat when I get home, but I'd like to go to the Kaslav's first."

"Sure. No trouble," Graham replied, not looking up from the draft of his next Sunday's sermon.

The air now had a cool spring softness drifting in gentle gusts meeting from around street corners between the houses. The Kaslav house wasn't hard to find, a small stone building right on the sidewalk, lacking both a porch and yard. Robey thought perhaps it had once been a gatehouse to the three-story mansion dominating the entire block several hundred feet behind. The larger house boasted a widow's walk, two-story white columns and porches on each floor. A semicircular driveway bowed from each end of the street, with the Kaslav house guarding one entrance and a tall iron gate blocking the other. The big house looked vacant and the stables, visible through the newly budding trees, seemed ramshackle. Robey filed the picture in her mind as another question to ask Douglas or Graham. She knocked at the front door of the gatehouse. No one opened the door, but a cheerful "come in" could be heard from somewhere within.

Robey slowly turned the porcelain knob and pushed the door open, stepping through to face a couple seated at their dinner table beside a window, their only illumination the waning daylight. Mr. Kaslav's head was ringed with cotton white hair, but a shiny baldness slid from front to back of his head. His shoulders were broad and heavy, and his leg, in a cast, was propped up on a quilted cushion overflowing a small footstool.

Mrs. Kaslav was willowy and frail, yellowed gray hair framed her face and was loosely twisted into a bun at the top of her head. Her fingers smoothed a bright gingham bib apron as she stood in greeting.

"I'm Robey Layne," Robey extended her hand and it was taken into a surprisingly strong one. "Pastor Hill sent word that I'd come with your son's letter."

"Yes, yes," the old lady flustered, "can I get you some coffee?" Not waiting for an answer, she put cup in saucer and reached for the pot. Robey smiled at her eagerness to please and sat down in a chair next to the table. A warm friendliness permeated the room and it reminded Robey of Sarah's kitchen back home.

"May I turn this on?" Robey reached for a lamp switch.

"Of course," Mrs. Kaslav beamed. "We just never do unless we have something to look at that's interesting. We like sitting in the dark."

Robey read the letter to them and repeated parts they wanted to hear again. She found them easy to talk to and could tell they were lonely and in need of attention. Time passed without notice until she glanced out the window and saw the streetlights come on.

"I'll come back, if you want me too, even if there's no letter,"

Robey offered. "But I must go now." She rose and walked towards the door, Mrs. Kaslav followed, thanking her profusely, and asked her by all means to come as often as she liked.

Dank darkness closed in around Robey as the door shut behind her. A ground fog from the Cove roiled around her feet. She pulled her coat collar around her throat and looked up at the purple sky as a rising moon appeared . . . and then disappeared, playing hide and go seek with low, heavy threatening storm clouds. Robey walked down First Avenue, noticing streetlights, yellow and soft, in cahoots with the wind, working together to make a ballet on the pavement of swaying shadows of tree limbs.

For a short time Robey enjoyed nature's play, but suddenly, out of the corner of her eye she saw another shadow that seemed to be darting between parked cars across the street. She involuntarily quickened her step and glanced over her shoulder. This time she saw no movement other than the tree ballet, and she tried to convince herself she was unduly alarmed, but as she continued down the street, the anxiety returned and could not be dispelled.

At the next intersection, University Lane and First Avenue, Robey stopped and realized she had to walk past the cemetery in the next block. A tangle of apprehension enveloped her, and she fought off unreasoning fear.

"I'm an adult, not a child afraid of the dark," she admonished herself. Stiffening her shoulders, she decided to face her unknown dread and turned around completely, looking back up on the street she had just traversed. With relief she saw no person or unusual shadow, neither darting, swaying, nor still, within the scope of her vision.

"Really, old girl," she spoke aloud. "Let's stop this foolishness. This is the safest place on earth." She tried to add some bravado to her mood. "Remember, they're all afraid of the backwoods folk."

She started walking again and set out across the intersection with a determinedly slower stride. Halfway down the block, just as she reached the streetlight, she heard a quick shuffle of feet behind her and before she could look around, she was grabbed and roughly thrown to the ground.

Robey flung her arm up to protect her face, knocking her assailant's cap from his head. He momentarily stared at her, and a chill shuddered down Robey's spine. His face had a deathly pallor and his wispy hair and beard were pure white. She tried to scream but found she couldn't get a sound beyond her lips. In the light she could see his eyes were light, but the pupil seemed to be black holes beside his bulbous nose. It seemed an eternity of time as they looked at each other, before he hit her once in the face. Not a hard hit, but almost a hesitant slap, as though he didn't really want to hurt her. Just as Robey was certain he was going to hit her again he stood erect, snatched his cap from the ground and swung away from her, taking several strides toward the cemetery. She was about to get up and run when he turned again towards her, reached down, picked up her purse which had been flung aside in the attack, and then darted through the gravestones, the darkness swallowing him. Robey watched until he was entirely out of sight.

The moon, which had perversely hidden behind clouds during the assault, came out again and illuminated the stones marking the graves of ghosts who had witnessed the scene but could never tell. Robey looked around to see if anyone was coming to her aid, but the street was deserted. She rose to her feet, still badly shaken and frightened. Her heart thumped in her chest and her stomach churned. Brushing dirt from her skirt and the elbows of her jacket, she checked her hose for rips, but there were none.

He won't be back, she told herself. He has what he wanted. Must be one of those mountain men Douglas mentioned. Well, you can be sure I'll tell him about this. Her eyes scanned the grave-yard, hoping against hope she wouldn't see the man's figure coming for her again. She caught sight of an object on top of one of the flat stones. Her eyes strained to make out the form and yes, it was, she was sure of it, her purse! Now why would someone steal a purse and then carefully lay it where she would be able to recover it? There had not been time for him to examine the contents or steal anything. Confusion dulled her mind and for a brief second she considered entering the grounds and retrieving her property, but when the clouds again covered the moon, shrouding the street in darkness, she dismissed the idea. A screech owl's wail shattered the silence and the hair rose on the back of her neck. Her skin popped great goosebumps. Robey almost ran the rest of the short distance to home. She was breathless when she arrived.

When she entered the house, Graham was seated at his desk and he could see, through the door, she was upset. He called for her to come in and sit down. Iris, standing in the kitchen door, holding her apron in her hand, turned sharply away back into the kitchen. Robey wondered that she wasn't curious about her excitement which must have been as apparent to her as it had been to Graham.

Telling Graham about the adventure helped settle her nerves. She included her questions as to why the man had attacked her under a streetlight, where she could see him clearly and why he had so neatly laid the purse, apparently unopened, on top of a marble marker.

"He wanted the handbag. It was obviously the reason for pushing me down, because he came back for it when he started to leave."

As she unfolded the story, she became aware someone—it had to be Iris—was listening outside the door. Turning her head, she saw Iris's image reflected in the mirror atop the hall coat rack. Why wouldn't she just come in? She decided to invite her in, but before she could put thought into action her attention was drawn back to Graham, who was offering to go to the cemetery to retrieve the purse.

"I'll go with you," Robey agreed, still uneasy. "It's a good suede bag, and if it should rain tonight it would be ruined."

When they stepped out of the office Iris was halfway up the stairs, still wiping her hands on her apron as though she had just come from the kitchen sink.

"Your dinner is set out, Robey. I'd eat it before it gets cold, if I were you."

"Thank you, I'll eat and then we'll go," she turned to Graham.

"I'll have something to drink with you. You've been through a shattering ordeal, but I think you'll sleep better if we get that purse tonight."

Iris came back down the stairs, saying she thought she'd like more tea. She then sat down with them, and Robey repeated the story as though she never knew Iris had been eavesdropping. Iris seemed totally absorbed in every word, clucking and tisking.

"Are you going to report this to the police?" Iris asked

"No, I think not. I wasn't hurt and, if I'm right, nothing is missing. I'll just tell Douglas. Maybe it was one of those shiftless mountain people he told me about."

"At least you weren't hurt, Robey. That's what counts." Iris said, rising from her chair.

Robey could see that Iris was genuinely relieved.

The handbag was still there on the gravestone when Graham and Robey entered the cemetery, and after they got back under the streetlight, Robey verified nothing valuable had been removed, only a compact that Roger had given her years ago, and it had been decorated with rhinestones, not real gems.

She and Graham slowly walked home. Robey was surprised at how much she enjoyed being with him and how safe she felt in his presence only an hour after her harrowing experience on the same street. But when she looked back from the sanctuary of their porch, she again shuddered, and swiftly entered the house, bidding Graham goodnight as she went up to her room.

Sleep didn't come easily after she stretched out between her sheets, so she sat up and wrote a letter to Lawrence, thanking him for his letter and describing the evening's events. She tried to sound lighthearted about it—not that she felt that way or wanted to spare him concern—but because she realized she didn't want to admit to him he might have been right about her leaving Chandor and coming to Knobbe Cove.

9

WHEN ROBEY DESCENDED THE STAIRCASE FOR breakfast, she found Graham waiting at the bottom to greet her.

"How are you feeling this morning? Get over your shakiness?"

"Yes, I'm fine now," Robey tried to put him at ease, "after I finally got to sleep, I must have dropped off the edge of creation."

"I could tell you were pretty exhausted by your ordeal, but I believe the Lord has a special sleep to help cure shock." Graham indicated Lawrence's letter in Robey's hand. "Is that a letter you want mailed?"

"Yes. I'll put it in the mailbox on the corner."

"Just put it on the table there by the door." He nodded his head toward a small walnut stand. "Iris has several letters to mail for me at the post office. I ran out of stamps."

Robey laid the envelope on the top of the others and walked back to the kitchen where the smell of bacon and coffee permeated the hallway. Iris put pancakes on plates from the warming oven, placed them on the table and reached for a pitcher of orange juice.

"Good morning, Iris," Robey smiled. "Graham said you had some letters to mail for him. Would you mind mailing one for me, too?"

"Glad to, Robey," Iris agreed, placing more butter on an almost empty butter plate.

"It's to Lawrence LaPorte, my husband's...my attorney. He's been a staunch ally, didn't want me to leave Chandor. Went so far as to say I was running away. When I couldn't quickly get to sleep last night, I wrote him about what had happened. He'll say," she paused to take a sip of the tangy juice, "I told you so. I can hear him right now. He might be right."

"Do you like him?" Iris asked to Robey's surprise.

"Yes, as an associate. I suppose he's nice enough, and he's sufficient in his job." She hesitated a bit before adding, "I know he'd like to be more...he told me so...but I just can't see him that way."

"Perhaps later, when you've had time to forget and adjust. You will, you know. You'll see everything in a brighter light as time slips past."

Iris sat down beside them with the coffee. Graham look quizzically at his sister, trying to fathom her unusual interest in Robey. He hoped she was genuinely concerned, but somehow, he felt Iris's motives had more than compassion in them.

"What's on the agenda for today, Graham?" Robey quickly switched the subject from her attorney. The scene of her last day in Chandor still rankled whenever she thought of Lawrence approaching her romantically. She hoped Iris didn't think her rude, but she didn't wish to pursue the present train of conversation.

"We'll have to make a list of needed repairs this morning for the bank, and I have to meet this afternoon with the loan committee again. Your time should be free after lunch."

Breakfast over, Graham and Robey left the house as Graham called back over his shoulder to Iris that they would be in for lunch about 12:30. The porch steps were wet with early morning dew and crisp air filled their lungs as they stood momentarily looking up and down the street, breathing deeply. Robey loved this little ritual they seem to have fallen into, understanding a need to rejuvenate their bodies with the clean fresh outdoors. They seldom talked, just enjoyed their own company and shared the world with the chirping birds high in the leafy trees lining the streets. After a few minutes, they moved off the porch and made their way across the narrow street to the brownstone church, unaware that Iris had been, for days, watching them from the living room window, a mixture of sad consternation and anger on her face.

As they entered the office deep in their individual thought, Graham broke the silence. "Sit down, I want to talk to you a bit about Iris."

Robey settled in the chair opposite the desk and, remembering her talk with Iris, wondered what Graham's story was going to be.

"Years ago, I don't know how many," Graham began," I discovered Iris was, as they say, telling tales out of school. She really didn't mean to disclose confidences, but her life with me is pretty mundane and lonely." Graham paused, but when Robey said nothing, continued. "I realized then, if I were to be effective in a counseling role, I could have no one at the house for Iris to overhear."

"She was listening last night, Graham. I saw her reflected in the mirror in the hall."

"I know. I followed your eyes and saw her, too, but, well, to return to what I was saying, when I discovered what was going on I'm afraid I was quite brutal in my censure, not understanding at all. Iris was crushed. She had given me all her life, and I had turned on her, she said. I know I could have approached the situation differently. I should have simply told my appointments to come here to the office instead of the house office. That would have removed temptation from earshot."

"I'm sure you didn't intend being cruel, Graham."

"That's the worst part, I did. I was self-righteous and holier than thou, and that's not a good position for a minister of the good book to find himself in. Anyway, the result was, as you saw last night, that she steals little bits of excitement, I guess, to spice up an otherwise dull existence. Now, she would never ask me about anything, never in a million years."

"Well, I intend to fill her in on everything I can," Robey declared and, seeing Graham's eyebrows rise, hastened to add, "of course, only pertaining to me and no one else. Why doesn't she belong to a club or do charity work or something? She might even find a real nice guy!"

Graham threw back his head and laughed. "Iris? Oh, yes, how simple it would be if she did that." He was suddenly serious. "But she won't. She can't."

"Can't? Why?" Robey felt his pronouncement unjustifiable and final.

"'Cause of Ward."

"What does Ward have to do with it? He's in an institution. She doesn't have to look after him anymore. I'm sure you'd get along with almost any man she should choose, and it would probably be good for you both to have someone else in the house."

"Sounds like you've got it all figured out but, as I said, it just isn't that simple. True, Ward isn't a problem anymore, but Iris believes insanity—or mental illness as we call it today—runs in the family genes. We had a great uncle who lived out his days in a sanitarium. I was never certain what kind, could have been for tuberculosis back in those days, but Iris insists it was the state home for the insane. She won't let herself get involved with people and, I guess that's one of the real reasons I'll never marry. I'm not sure, either. That, and my present condition."

"Neither condition should keep you from having a happy normal family life, Graham. I wouldn't give two cents for a woman who would turn down the man she loves because he has to rely on crutches to walk. And as for the mental illness thing, you should get a professional opinion before accepting out of hand to remain a bachelor."

"Who's counseling whom?" Graham grinned.

Robey couldn't help but notice how young and boyish he looked when he smiled—a rugged and craggy smile, but, yes, she could see where Amelia might have been attracted to him.

Amelia! Robey thought perhaps she would try to see her again in the afternoon when work was done. It was difficult for her to realize over a month had passed since she had visited, her second day in Knobbe Cove. Her life had been so full. She hoped things were better for Amelia and David, too.

"Let's get this correspondence cleared away, and I'll dictate a few notes for Sunday sermon. Then we'll check on the repairs needed."

Graham tackled the morning's mail enthusiastically, gave the dictation and, while Robey typed, made a few phone calls. As the last letter was stuffed into its envelope, he swiveled to face Robey. "Come on and bring a pad and pencil. We'll make a list as we go along."

The warmth of the office faded into the coolness of the hallway leading to the sunday school rooms and the sanctuary. They wandered from room to room searching out flaws, listing chipped paint, water stains under a window, leaky radiators, and shabby draperies needing replacing. In the short time Robey had been here she hadn't taken the opportunity to explore the back corridors. In fact, she had never, that she could recall, been behind the altar or in the innermost rooms of any church. These hallways remind- ed her of corridors pictured in travel brochures about the great cathedrals of Europe in the early centuries. Tall dark-beamed ceilings arched over parquet floors, and she knew the church must have been very elegant when the doors were first opened to worshippers. Now it needed much care and polish to restore that grandeur.

Graham swung along, dictating, oblivious to the musky aroma from a few seldom used and rarely aired storage areas.

"Need to reinforce those steps to the choir stall." Graham pronounced and then repeated the repair as he became aware that Robey was not writing, but had stopped, overcome momentarily by the startling lights emitting from the huge round stained glass window above the balcony at the front of the sanctuary.

"Do you feel it, Robey? I always do. It never fails to overwhelm me when I'm alone in here. It's seldom so bright on Sunday mornings. It's only the afternoons when the sun is just right in the Heavens." Graham stood close behind Robey and his words were spoken softly into her ear. "It's almost as if the window were alive, an entity to itself. If I had never felt the presence of God in this building before, I certainly couldn't deny it now. It's so beautiful."

The hues of the window vibrated and danced in the rays of the outside sun. Some changing depth of tone each time a cloud was windblown across the sky. Blues, reds, and golds spread across the pews in the sanctuary and at one point, a small chip from the cross in the center let in a brilliant sharp ray of sunlight.

"Yes," Robey agreed, "it has a soul of its own."

"Do you know? I could never quite put my finger on it, but I believe you just did. I like to stand here, behind the pulpit, looking down on the room where my people congregate, when it's quiet and the solitude almost echoes. Then that window has a special glory for me."

They shared that glory for a few more moments, and then Graham broke the spell. "Got to get to work. I have an appointment to take this list to the bank. Did you get that last repair about the choir stall steps? They're pretty creaky."

"No," Robey admitted that she hadn't listed them. "I'll put it down right now."

After checking on the choir robes, which needed replacing but didn't go on the list because an ice cream social was planned for that purpose, Graham indicated that the last place to examine was the organ loft in the belfry.

"The bell needs a new rope, I know."

"You mean someone still has to pull a rope to ring the bell on Sunday morning?"

"You city bred people just don't appreciate tradition!" Graham said jokingly, "we would never get one of those electric bell ringers! Each Sunday we appoint one of our little folk to pull the bellcord. I think they begin dreaming about getting chosen while they're still on the cradle roll. We've never lacked a bell ringer."

The steps to the organ loft were very narrow, and even from where they stood Robey could see they would need something to shore them up.

"I'm afraid you will have to go up just ahead of me and give me a hand," Graham complained, "the steps are too steep for me to use my crutches without someone giving me balance." He left one crutch leaning against the wall and took Robey's hand, half hopping, half leaning on her. At the top he swung around to sit on the organ bench and looked around in the dimness for evidence of repair need.

"Yes, the bellcord is in for replacing and the rug at the top here is dangerously frayed." He pointed to the offending rip. "Someone could trip on it and have a bad fall."

Robey felt for and found a light switch on the crook neck lamp sitting on the organ and turned it on. Instead of illuminating the cubicle, it brightly lit the hymnal standing open above the organ stops, throwing the rest of the area into unfathomable darkness.

"Now you've done it," Graham chuckled and turned off the lamp quickly. "Sit down here beside me for a couple of minutes until your eyes get used to the dark again. Don't move around, you might bump into something and hurt yourself."

Robey sat down and found herself close to Graham, so close she could feel the heat of his arm beneath the sleeve of his turtle-neck sweater. Her heart leapt and a familiar thrill pulsed enticingly through her. Her first impulse was to move away, but she didn't want Graham to know she was disturbed by the contact, so she remained there, half guilty by being so aroused by him. She was alarmed and impatient with herself since she had decided months before to never feel anything for any man ever again. She and Roger had been faithful in all things to each other. It had been a wonderful marriage and she felt luckier than most. She saw no reason to not remain faithful now, so she felt disgusted that she would react so sensually to the first new man she had met and been alone with.

"I'm fine now," Robey stood up and walked a few steps to a door and looked at the ornate gothic carvings. "When they built this church they didn't skimp on the furnishings, did they? Just how many people would ever see this doorway up here?"

"Very few, I suppose. However, years and years ago there used to be tours conducted for every new member. Then things started getting run down and the interest lagged. I'd like to start the tours up again once we're fixed up. Might generate some money out of a few pious pockets. Guaranteed, this loft will have to have major work done, it's downright dangerous. Wonder why Clive never mentioned it to me?"

"I've only met him a couple of times," Robey referred to the organist and choir director, "but he seems to be all music and oblivious to practical things. I've known quite a few people like that. They are geniuses but don't know one end of a screwdriver from the other."

"Never really thought about Clive that way, but I do believe you're right. Still, he should have seen such blatant disrepair, especially since it could cause physical harm."

"Yes, I noticed the railing was pretty rickety as we came up." Robey tried to be all business, but she was finding it difficult to dismiss her unwelcome feelings for Graham. Her mind went back unwillingly to Iris telling her she should be forearmed. From advances from Graham? Well, she said to herself, from now on I intend to keep a little more distance between us. I was practically on his lap.

Graham scooched around on the organ stool. "We're getting very little work done sitting here, and the day's going fast. I hate to be the heavy, but we'll have to get that list typed up and get to lunch.

Robey was glad the tour was over. She needed to escape somehow. Graham put his arm around her shoulders and heaved himself erect, then Robey slowly preceded him down the unstable stairs so he could use her and the bannister as a crutch. She was keenly aware of the physical contact of his hand on her shoulder and hoped Graham didn't notice. The bannister wavered with each awkward step.

"You're right, the bannister should be foremost on our list." Graham, standing in the hall now on both of his crutches, shook it sharply, and it responded, swaying from the bottom step to the very top.

All work finished, Robey donned her cardigan again as Graham slipped into his dark blue blazer. Outside, the spring air greeted them with warmth and the late morning sun pierced the budding tree branches, coaxing new foliage from red and green knobs on the scraggly limbs. Tulips and snow bells poked from the freshly warmed earth.

Iris had lunch ready, and Graham sat down while Robey helped her with the last of the table setting.

"Your letter is mailed," Iris said as she sat down.

"Thank you. I know already what his reply will be. Come back, little Robey, the world is too scary for you out there. You'll never make it."

"Oh, come on now," Graham grinned. "He can't think you're that incapable of taking care of yourself, can he?"

"Maybe he'd like her to be that scared and dependent," Iris said without stopping her halving ham sandwiches.

"Iris! What a thing to say!" Graham sounded shocked.

"Just saying what I think," Iris retorted.

Suddenly, Graham realized he knew very little about what Iris thought. They had almost stopped having real conversations. He looked at his sister and absently wondered who she talked to. Perhaps she talked only to herself. For a moment he felt her loneliness, and guilt for his neglect stung his conscience.

"We went all over the church building today listing necessary repairs, Iris." He picked up half his sandwich as he spoke. "There's so much to be done, especially that bannister to the organ loft."

"The bannister? What's the matter with it?" Iris stood between them ladling out hot tomato soup.

"It's ready to fall down. I won't go back up again, I assure you, until its fixed."

"What about Clive?" Iris's voice showed her concern.

"He hasn't said anything. Probably doesn't lean on the bannister to go up."

"I see," Iris said and seemed to dismiss the problem from her mind. She finished her lunch silently, lost in her own thoughts. Robey studied her whenever she thought she wouldn't be caught looking. Funny, Robey mused, that Iris wouldn't be more interested in Graham's work at the church. Just as she was about to continue telling her about the rest of the needed repairs, Iris finished her lunch, abruptly stood and, leaving the dishes where they were, headed upstairs to her room. Both Graham and Robey let their eyes follow her out the kitchen door to the hallway, perplexed at her unusual behavior.

10

Back in the church office, searching the large ever-cluttered desk for the loan papers she had just filled out that morning, Robey picked up the check for Douglas's monthly wages.

"Graham, I meant to ask you about Douglas."

"Douglas? What about him?"

"He's delightful to talk too. Much more…" She hunted for the right word, "outgoing and well-spoken than fits the worn overalls he always wears."

Graham laughed. "I know what you mean. Well, he is well-educated, at least by standards for most of our backwoods people. Used to teach some before they started requiring college degrees for the job. Never made enough to not need to work at other jobs, so he always helped my family and worked here at the church as Sexton. Does odd jobs all over the Cove. He'll be seventy-two on his next birthday, if my memory serves correctly."

"Does he have any family? He's never said."

"Oh, yes. His wife, Leola, is still living and he has seven children and twenty-three grandchildren at last count."

"I had to ask!" Robey smiled. "Where are his children now?"

"Two sons are here in Knobbe Cove. One lives with them and the other has his own family. Neither had much gumption. They

earn a living cooking and waiting tables in the restaurant downtown. The other five have scattered all over a wide area. One's in
the army; one's a nurse; there are two teachers, and one girl married
a lawyer in Whitney."

At the moment he was being discussed in the church, Douglas
was sitting in his kitchen, his feet propped up on the table with the
ladder back chair in which he sat tilted precariously on the slick linoleum floor. Smoke wreathed his head and his wife, Leola, waved
it away as it drifted her direction.

"Was a terrible thing that happened to the new lady," she
amented, wiping the freshly-washed lunch dishes and placing them
neatly on a shelf over the sink.

"Yes, it was." Douglas said softly and banged his pipe on the
side of a brass ashtray, dislodging the small plug which had gone
out. Reaching into his pocket, he extracted a package of Grainger
Roughcut and, using his forefinger, tamped a new supply into the
corncob bowl.

"Are you going to hunt for him?" Leola persisted in her line of
thought, hanging the towel to dry and leaning on the back of the
chair opposite his. It seemed to her he was reticent to talk about
the attack and that was unlike him.

"Several of us are going to patrol the streets for a few nights.
Maybe he'll show himself."

"I hope so. Seems such a shame for that nice lady to have
to walk around looking over her shoulder to see if it's going to
happen again. That's what I'd be doing if'n happened to me!"

Douglas stood up, came around table and took Leola in his
arms, giving her a big squeeze. "Don't have to worry none about
that, Hon," he said teasingly. "Any man pick you up under a lamp
post will drop you at the next."

Leola grabbed the wet rag from the sink and threw it at him

as he scampered out the door, missing him and hitting the wall. A pleased grin lit up her face as she watched him cut across the yard towards his Jeepster. "That man," she said aloud, "be the death of me yet."

When Graham left the church, Robey went back to the house to rid herself of the heavy coat she had worn earlier. She needed some cosmetics from the pharmacy and thought, perhaps, she would visit Amelia again. She wanted to clear up the doubts she had about Iris's story and hoped that Amelia would be very frank and honest with her. On her way back down the stairs from her room, she glimpsed Iris sitting at the kitchen table writing on a stationary tablet. As she neared the door, Iris looked up, saw her, and turned the pad over so Robey couldn't see what was written there. Robey flushed at this obvious rebuke of her presence.

"I'm going to the pharmacy, Iris. Is there anything I could bring you?"

"No, no," Iris was quite emphatic. "Nothing." She sat there, her arm lying across her letter, protecting it. Robey felt like telling her she had no intention prying into her business, but pity for the strange woman held her tongue.

Robey smiled stiffly, turned and left the house, aware Iris's eyes followed her every step down the hallway, through the door, and onto the porch.

The stroll downtown was pleasant, broken several times by people nodding to her. Each day, she thought, there are fewer strangers. At the pharmacy she purchased a new powder compact, replacing the stolen one, some nail polish and a new lipstick. Stepping back into the brilliant afternoon sun, she shielded her eyes momentarily and then set her foot toward Railroad Street, small trepidations nagging at her mind.

Graham had slowly made his way in the opposite direction from

Robey. On his walk to the bank, he thought only of her. He, too, was feeling impatient at himself for the emotions that had washed over him like a fever when Robey sat so close, touching his arm. He had to admit to himself under other circumstances he would have been tempted to put his arms around her and pull her into an embrace. His imagination carried him further to the invitation of her full pink lips which he knew would be sweet and soft if he kissed them. It had been many years since he had kissed a woman—not since the accident. He shook his head visibly to scatter these thoughts and pull himself back to reality. The reality was that he would have to be very careful not to think of Robey's warm lips or her sparkling blue eyes in this way again. It would lead to an impasse he didn't want, one he was certain she also wouldn't welcome. But, still, he had to admit, with Robey today in the loft, he had felt more a man than he had in the past five years. In fact, he also had to face the truth that he even felt a pang of jealously at the mention of Lawrence LaPorte—someone he had never met—and someone Robey evidently was not interested in romantically. He had no right, he told himself, when he wasn't going to do anything about his budding feelings anyway.

Robey approached the house on the corner of Railroad Street with some apprehension, hoping her welcome wouldn't be as short lived as her first visit. When she raised the brass knocker this time, the curtains moved aside, and Amelia flung the door wide and they embraced warmly. Amelia's countenance shone, showing her pleasure, and she seemed so much more like her old self. Robey sighed with relief, and all doubt about the visit fled.

"I've already heard about your job at the church," Amelia opened the conversation in a rush. Robey's eyebrows raised in surprise. "News," Amelia explained, "travels fast in Knobbe Cove—good or bad. I still have a few friends beyond these four walls."

Slipping off her shoes, Robey sat down on the sofa and tucked her feet up under her. She looked out the living room door to the hallway and, Amelia, following her eyes, read her thoughts.

"David is away this week at his father's place. Asking for a handout, I suppose." She spoke bitterly.

"Heard the whole story, at least what I was told was the whole story, from Iris Hill."

"Glad you seem to have an open mind," Amelia hesitated a bit. "You do, don't you?"

"Of course. You know me, I need to hear at least both sides to a story before I make up my mind. And it is, simply that you and Graham were—to quote her—carrying on and David ran you both down in his boat one day.

"That's putting it on the line, for sure!" Amelia was caught off guard by Robey's frankness. "However, there's a lot you don't know."

"Fill me in."

Before answering, she went to the kitchen and returned with two tall glasses of tea. Offering one to Robey, she slipped out of her own shoes and snuggled down in the big overstuffed platform rocker. For a few moments she gazed deeply into the amber liquid as she turned the glass slowly with her long tapering fingers. When her eyes again met Robey's, they brimmed with tears.

"He had started drinking soon after we arrived here seven years ago. I hadn't realized that he had a severe problem with alcohol before we married. His father once sent him to a place to dry out. For a short while he was alright; during that time I met and married him. Then, as soon as the responsibility of earning a living was put on his shoulders and something went wrong, he turned back to the bottle. He soon ruined the bookstore, closing it for no other reason than he wanted to go out on the boat and drink.

He spent more than the profits, and there was nothing we could do but sell."

"Didn't you help him in the store? Couldn't you see what was happening?"

Amelia stretched her legs and took some newspapers to stuff under the fireplace logs. "It's a bit chilly in here, don't you think?"

"Yes," Robey had to agree, but she wondered if it weren't more inner than outer discomfort. The fire leapt to life and Amelia sat on a pillow by the hearth staring into the flames. She shook her head, bringing herself back to the story.

"When we first got here this house was a monster," her hand swept in gesture. "David's father gave it to us as a wedding present, but it needed so much work. You know me, I love to redecorate, and by the time I had sanded, painted, papered, and bought lots of new things, with money I found later we did not have, it was already too late at the bookstore. When I asked David if I could come down to the shop to work, he wouldn't let me. He said he wanted me to be at home for him. He even insisted I call before I visited the place, to be sure he was there, he said. I know now he was too ashamed for me to see him drunk, and he was afraid I would find the liquor supply he kept hidden in the back room."

"How did you find out?" Robey asked softly.

"I went down one day without calling first. I had gone for a doctor's appointment, regular checkup, in the morning and thought maybe it would be nice if we could eat lunch together. He was there, drunk, and arguing with a customer. He practically shoved him out the door and locked it behind him.

"Faced with the fact I now knew his secret, he accused me of spying, treating him like a child, taking away his manhood. He was very sarcastic and really made little sense. Then he walked out and went to the boat, leaving me standing there. I can tell you, Robey, it was one of the darkest hours of my life."

"How terrible for you," Robey rose and put her cup on the coffee table. "What did you do?"

"What could I do? I had a talk with his father and learned a lot more about his background. David found out we had gotten our heads together and there was another awful scene. I pleaded with him to stop his drinking and get us back on an even keel. That's when I learned there was no even keel. We were broke, stone broke, and the shop was about to go under. Believe me, Robey, I was devastated. Even the events that followed weren't quite as bad as that first knowing."

Amelia fetched a handkerchief from her pocket and dabbed at her eyes and blew her nose. "Sorry."

"It'll do you good to get it all out."

"I couldn't just sit around wringing my hands, so I went to work for Graham Hill. David protested, but we needed the money, and I let him know I didn't care what he thought at that point. The money wasn't much, and I guess the work did more for my self-esteem than it did for the bank account. Besides, Graham helped me get some perspective. He's very good at counseling."

"Yes, I know. He's helped me considerably since I've gotten here." Robey wondered if she should ask the next question but decided to dive in feet first. "Is that how you fell in love with him?"

Amelia gasped and shook her head in disbelief. Her shoulders sagged, and then she pulled herself erect. "I never fell in love with Graham, Robey. David is the only man I'll ever love. The time might come when I can't live with him, I don't know, but I think I'll always love him. As for Graham, that's a vicious lie Iris started, I'm sure of it. Oh, I don't have proof she did, but she hates me, that I've always known. She hovered over Graham every instant she could while I was around. Then one night she had to face the fact she had told around town what should have been confidential communique with one of the church members. He was furious with her. I was in the storeroom and couldn't help overhearing it all. I was astounded at the tongue-lashing he gave her. I could hardly believe it was gentle, reticent Graham talking. As Iris left in tears, our eyes met and oh, Robey, I have never seen such naked hate, such, such..." Amelia groped for words and couldn't find them.

"Graham told me of his tirade with Iris after I caught her eavesdropping on one of my conversations with him in the office at the house, but that's another story. Let's get back to you right now. What about the accident?"

"Well. That's ahead of events...I'll get there. About the time of Graham's fight with Iris I found out I was pregnant. I was torn between happiness and fear. I'd love to have a baby, but I knew David didn't need any more pressure, and unless he straightened himself out, I didn't want to bring a child into the world. When I told David, he took it as though I had handed him a poisoned apple. He went on a weeklong binge. So, I went to Graham for help, in tears. He put his arms around me trying to help stop the sobs which just didn't seem to want to stop. I lost control of myself, Robey, I really did. "

"I should think you were entitled after all you had been through."

"I guess, but the timing was lousy. Iris walked in on us and accused him of being involved with me. I believe she had also overheard the cause of my distress and, you don't need to ask, it was David's baby, not Graham's as rumors proclaimed."

"I wasn't going to ask, Amelia. I think I know you well enough to be sure in my heart you're still a moral person. Really, that's why I came today. I just couldn't believe, wouldn't believe, Iris's tales."

"Thanks. Helps a lot to know. Well, rumors really swept this little town and everywhere I could hear Iris's voice in them.

Graham and I talked and decided it best I quit working for him. At that time, I decided...you won't believe this, Robey, but I had decided to leave David and come back to Chandor and visit you. I had visions of David regaining his senses and coming after me on a white horse or something. I wrote you a letter, but never mailed it."

"How come?"

"What was to be my last duty on the job was almost the last thing I ever did in my life. We were to see the Willises on the island. It was a beautiful day, and I tried to savor every minute of it. Our spirits were high and, I think, by silent mutual agreement, we didn't speak of my leaving. Then we started across the Cove, nearing the huge jut of rock to the left."

"I've seen the Cove, Amelia. It's pretty quiet now but Graham says soon it will be the busiest section of town."

"Yes, and it was fairly busy that day. Just as we got to the point, a boat...David's boat," Amelia hesitated, almost visibly tearing open old wounds, "bore down on us full speed. We heard shouts from the shore and Graham tried desperately to maneuver out of its way but couldn't. That's all I remember about the accident itself, but afterward," her voice faded at the remembrance of pain, "they told me I had lost the baby."

Robey stood up and walked over to the window, noticing the closed shutters, but her mind was on Amelia's words. "Could you see who was piloting the boat?"

"I looked up just as we collided, but the face at the wheel was a blur —a split-second blur—but I'm certain the face was pale, and David was deeply tanned from being out on the boat so much.

"Of course, if it had been David, no, it wasn't..." She shook her head, unable to put that kind of accusation into words. "I told the police about the man I saw—at least glimpsed."

"There was an investigation, wasn't there? What became of that?"

"David said he was alone in the bookstore, drunk. He had the only keys to the boat, but he had been known to lend them freely to others who used the boat for fishing parties. They could have had duplicates made."

"Wasn't anyone charged with the accident?"

"No. All of us concerned let the furor die down. The police kept looking for the pilot but never found anyone. All their leads led to dead ends. David swore to me he wasn't in that boat, and I believe him. In the semi-conscious days that followed, David was very attentive and concerned for me, but I could feel he was relieved about the baby," she said. "Graham lost the use of his legs and, so now Iris has more reason than ever to hate me and smother him with care."

"How did David's father take it all?"

"He's been an angel to me. He paid all the hospital bills, above insurance, including Graham's. You see, he believes David was at the wheel of the boat. It weighs heavily on his mind."

"That's sad," Robey said quietly, returning to the sofa.

"He gives me money to run the house, knowing any money he'd give David would go for booze. I've turned away from David. I become physically ill every time I see him drunk. Funny, when I lost the baby, I remember each wracking pain, but I can't remember the joy David and I had seven years ago. The good Lord knows I wish we could be as we used to be without his problem, but it can't be. I need someone to lean on, and I can't lean on him. I grieved for the lost child and cursed David and his negligence. I've wallowed in self-pity and can't seem to reach God. My rose-covered cottage is a thorn-crusted prison. I don't go outside any more than I need. A call on the phone brings me food from the grocer and medicine. The cleaners still pick up and deliver around here. I send the bills to his father. All this," her arm swept in a wide circle, "will be mine, I am informed, if I stick it out with David until, I guess, he drinks himself to death." Bitterness spewed with her words. And then she said, almost in a whisper, "but I'm not staying for the house. I'm staying because I promised to, for better or worse. I know David's sick."

Silence cloaked the room shared by the two women who sat staring deep into the embers of the fireplace.

"I'm sorry, Amelia, I really am." Robey was the first to speak. "Is there anything at all I can do to help?" She got up from the sofa, put her arms around Amelia's shoulders and pulled her close.

"No. Let's keep in touch. You'll never know how much your visit has meant. Here's my cell number." She went over to a small desk and swiftly jotted the number on a slip of paper. "Call me, and if I hang up, you'll know David's here and you should try again later. I'll call you at the church when I think you'll be there." Her face brightened at a thought she put into words. "How about lunch tomorrow? David usually doesn't get back until Friday when he goes to his dad's. It isn't far away...but...well, it's away from me."

"I'll try. It will depend on what Graham has for me to do. We've been busy with arranging repairs to the building, and then it's about time for another letter for the Kaslavs." At the mention of the old couple Robey remembered her first visit to them.

"Oh, yes, I had almost forgotten, although I don't know why. It was an unforgettable experience. A couple of weeks ago I got mugged beside the cemetery!"

"I heard something about that," Amelia was intrigued. "Tell me about it."

Robey related her adventure and when she finished Amelia looked puzzled.

"You say the man had a very white face?"

"Yes, why?"

"It's probably just coincidence, but remember? I told you the man in the boat had a very pale face, at least as far as I can recall."

"That was five years ago, Amelia!" Robey tried to impress upon her the unlikelihood of them being the same person. "Have you heard of any such man since?"

"No, but I haven't been out walking Knobbe Cove streets, either." Amelia ran her fingers through her long hair, stood up and paced around the room. "You're right. It's ridiculous to try to read into events what isn't there. I'll put it out of my mind if I can."

"I've made you dredge up some unpleasant memories, haven't I?" Robey stood and put her sweater around her shoulders, ready to leave. "I'm truly sorry, but I'm glad to know for sure Graham is an honorable man. I couldn't stay if he weren't."

"He's honorable, Robey, but I warn you, don't turn your back on Iris. Be careful. And don't do anything she can interpret in the wrong way. She'll spread it all over town."

"I've been trying to make friends with her. I told Graham I would include her in my business as much as I could, not shut her out. Do you think that's a mistake?"

"I don't know. I really don't. Things happened so fast for me I never thought whether she spread talk out of loneliness and rejection or just plain vindictiveness."

"Well great, I'll be careful" Robey grinned, "I'll try not to become the second red lady of Knobbe Cove."

"Laugh if you will," Amelia smiled warmly, "but do watch your step. She won't need much to go on."

Robey said goodbye and strolled down the path to the street. Although she was reassured regarding Graham, she had a nagging doubt somewhere in her mind, and it disturbed her. She passed the graveyard and stopped for a minute by the streetlight where she had been accosted. How innocent and serene the cemetery looked in the daylight! Small evergreen bushes stood guard over sleeping bones interred for many, many years. Here and there new green shoots pushed their way out of the stems of last year's now dead brush.

"Roger, oh, Roger. What have I gotten myself into?" She asked the empty air. "I should have stayed where I belonged."

Upon returning home Robey found a letter from Sarah waiting for her on the hall table. She took it upstairs, curled up on the bed and read it.

Dear Robey,

Everyone here is fine, Jack, me and the boys. We sure do miss you and are planning a trip this summer. We'd like to swing down south to see you for a day or two if it's convenient. Write us where we might get sleeping quarters.

I haven't seen LaPorte since you left. Once, his car was parked outside your house but by the time I got my boots and jacket on he was gone. I've seen the painters there with all their paraphernalia, but I didn't go over. I didn't think it was my business to be nosey.

A small article in the newspaper tells of the nice settlement LaPorte got for you on the accident. Congratulations! However, I don't want to disturb you, but rumor has it he has lost quite a few clients lately. That new law firm, the one that opened in the shopping mall, remember? Well, from what I can find out they charge far less for the same services LaPorte gives, and they advertise. I know you feel beholden to him for handling Roger's business, but it appears he has been charging exorbitant

*fees all along. I clipped out an item from the newspaper about
it the other day. Seems he is not alone in his high fees. He and
his associates were brought before an Ethics Committee of some
sort for trying to fix prices. They went to the new firm and
tried to convince them to comply with their rates schedule and
the new firm complained. I've enclosed the clipping. Sorry not
to send one about your settlement, but Jack used the paper to
light a fire before I could stop him.*

The letter went on with trivial bits of information about
Chandor, and Robey could imagine the same people practicing for
the bowling tournament and softball teams.

After finishing, she turned her attention to the news clipping.
It was decided, the article announced, there had been nothing
illegal about the fees Lawrence and his firm were charging if people
wanted to pay. They got a slap on the wrist for approaching the
new firm to raise their fees. Robey was certain all the publicity
caused by the complaint had worked to his detriment, but if what
was reported was true, she had a difficult time feeling sorry for
him.

Back in Chandor, LaPorte was looking again at his books and
cursing his present position. The stupidity of his move rankled.
He should have known better, but the deed was done and now
he had to think of ways to recoup the losses that were becoming
more and more evident every day. Brown, LaPorte and Simpson
no longer had a monopoly in the upper-class legal department
of Chandor. They could, like their competition, advertise, he
supposed, but being of the old school he thought anything like that
would cheapen, not enhance, his practice.

Laporte's only big accounts now were a few Estates from old
timers, several tort cases for which he would achieve a third of

the settlement if he won in court, and the Layne account. New cases were evidently being entrusted to the new untested law firm. Of course, Brown and Simpson had their own cases—the only shared aspect in the partnership was the overhead. Except for that it was every man for himself.

In his hand was a letter he received just a few days ago that might open a door for him. Perhaps he could still marry a fortune. It was that or admit defeat and lower all his fees to what he thought would be a ridiculous figure, certainly an income that wouldn't keep him in silk shirts and designer suits.

He opened the letter and read it again, then sat back, swiveled his chair to face the window, put his feet up on the radiator and let his thoughts wander several hundred miles south.

During dinner Robey shared the contents of her letter from Sarah with Graham and Iris.

"Will you be going back to Chandor soon?" Iris asked, looking at the clipping, as if it had already been determined that Robey would return to look after her interests.

Robey looked at her, realizing the thought had never occurred to her. "No," she answered quickly, "I have no plans to go back. It would take quite a bit to get me back there, especially after beginning to feel so much at home here. Lawrence was wrong when he wanted me to stay and face it out. There's just so much I could take. I needed to get away from it. And now that I have, I feel freer than I have in a long time, and," she added, "happier."

"I thought, perhaps, now that you had that big settlement maybe you'd want to travel. Especially now that the weather is getting so nice." Iris continued, obviously hoping Robey would get wanderlust and leave.

Iris didn't fool Robey one bit. She read her loud and clear, and she didn't intend for her to drive her out of her new life. As for the settlement and Sarah's remark about it being large, she had dismissed it from mind. Sarah and Jack had worked hard all their lives for a pitifully small amount of income. Anything over five thousand dollars was a fortune to Sarah and Robey knew it.

"No, I will not go back. Just where I'll end up, I still don't know. As for traveling, I'm just not ready."

"Well, you're welcome here as long as you can stay—forever, if need be." Graham reached over and patted Robey's hand. The clipping fell from Iris' fingers and floated unnoticed to the floor.

11

CLOUDS DRIFTED IN A DELFT BLUE SKY AND A COOL breeze caressed Robey's face when she exited the church in late afternoon. Having finished clearing her desk, she stood momentarily wondering what she needed to do to keep herself busy and, thinking of nothing urgent, she began walking toward the corner.

Across the street in the house next door to the Hill home, two people sat on the porch swing. Robey had yet to meet the Lodge couple and thought, perhaps, this might be a good time. Crossing Church Street, she pushed the white picket gate open and walked between low rows of daffodil fronds left over from the spring bloom. The swing slowed and Arthur Lodge rose to greet her as his wife put down the newspaper she had been reading.

"Hello, you're Mrs. Layne, aren't you?" His almost bald head bobbed when he spoke.

"Yes, and I felt it was time we met. I've admired your flower garden for quite a while now."

"Come up and sit a spell, and I'll get us a glass of iced tea," Charlotte Lodge didn't wait for Robey to say whether she wanted some or not and disappeared behind the screen door.

"We've seen you coming and going and should have called you before, but you looked so very busy. Mr. Lodge again sat down and crossed his legs.

"Yes, I've managed to have a lot to do. It's been wonderful meeting new people and doing new things. Pastor Hill says I need to keep busy, it's good therapy."

"Oh, we heard all about you. You don't need to explain. A small town like this couldn't keep a secret if it tried. Iris visits frequently, and Charlotte goes down to the beauty parlor, and I often go down to the hotel barber shop," he chuckled to himself. "More to catch up on what goes on than to get a haircut." He ran his hand over his almost entirely bald head.

"Sounds like any small town," Robey laughed.

"What you really mean is that we're nosy, don't you?" Mrs. Lodge smiled, pushing her way out of the door with a tray filled with tall glasses of tea, a sugar bowl and a dish of lemon wedges.

"Curiosity is a very natural thing, Mrs. Lodge," Robey stirred her tea slowly, "and I wouldn't give two hoots for someone without a healthy portion of it."

"Well, I'm glad to hear that someone doesn't mind knowing they're being talked about. You might be a rare one at that."

"I hardly expect to come from out of seemingly nowhere, start working in a church, live with the pastor and his sister and have everyone just accept it without question. No, I've known all along that I've probably set some folks on their ears."

"I understand how you feel. When we came here as young marrieds right after World War II, it was the same thing. We're English," Arthur explained. "I came to America to go to the University here when a buddy of mine, an American, made it all sound so wonderful. I couldn't resist. We were roommates for four years, and then I went back to see to a small inheritance when my father died. Mom had been gone for quite a while. I met Charlotte on that trip, and we decided we'd marry and come back to America."

"What a romantic story!" Robey put her glass down on the tray. "Have you ever gone back?"

"No." It was Mrs. Lodge who answered. "Never did and never regretted it a moment. We became citizens as soon as we could, so we're really Americans now."

"How come you settled here in Knobbe Cove?" Robey sipped on her tea.

"I came back to teach in the University where I had been awarded my degrees. Retired about ten years ago. I have a stupid heart condition that doesn't take too well to stress. Used to play soccer and golf—all those physical things. I can't do them now. So here I am puttering around in the garden, taking a few trips now and then. It's a good lazy life, can't complain."

Robey watched the shadows lengthen and stood up, placing her empty glass on the tray. "I must go now. It won't be long before dinner, and I like to at least help Iris set the table. So far, she's refused any help with preparing meals, but I understand. I never liked anyone in my kitchen, either. Although I do manage to help with the dishes."

"Yes, she's told us that you help her out on occasion. She can be an odd one. It took us a long time before we really felt we were friends with her. She comes over often to chat. Come to think of it, I guess we're about her closest friends. She attends church and shops downtown, but I don't think she has anyone else in town she visits. She's always been a loner since we've been here."

Robey found she did not want to discuss Iris and sidled towards the steps. "Thanks for the tea. I really must be on my way."

"Glad to have met you," Mrs. Lodge waved from the swing. "Come again."

The Lodges sat silently for several minutes until Robey was out of sight. Neither picked up the newspaper again or even sipped on the tea remaining in their glasses.

"It's a shame. She's so nice." Arthur said without turning his eyes from the path Robey had taken.

"Yes, she is," Charlotte degreed. "But it's inevitable. Iris will find a way to get rid of her. She'll have her way. I just hope no one gets hurt . . . really hurt . . . this time."

Two more weeks passed, and June was nudging the calendar into a summer already promising to be hot and humid. Gardens broke out in riots of color as pink and white dogwoods, magnolias, huge hydrangeas, almost as tall as trees, burst into bloom. Lilac and butterfly bushes, like perfume atomizers, spread their heady aromas throughout neighborhoods.

"I feel I'm in the garden of Eden," Robey told Graham one day standing in the churchyard. She stretched her arms wide and made a quick spin.

"You're just full of it, aren't you?" He laughed, watching her, quietly envying her mobility. He suddenly turned serious and stared over the boxwoods. "I used to feel the same way you do now, glad to be alive every minute, but, well, somewhere I lost it and began to simply exist." He hesitated a moment. "But do you know? I do believe," he shrugged his shoulders, "I do believe just watching you has made me aware again of what fun it can be to just be alive. I feel really good, too."

"That's a nice compliment, Graham. Thank you." Robey was genuinely pleased. "Kind of makes things complete. Knobbe Cove seems to have accepted me . . . lots of folks stop and chat with me on the street. Had a visit with the Lodges a couple of weeks ago and they informed me I've been the talk of the town for weeks."

"You don't mind?"

"Of course not. It would be unrealistic of me to think no one around here would be curious. I'd be, in their place."

"Well I can assure you it is all good. Your ears haven't been burning, have they?"

Robey's letters to Sarah and Lawrence LaPorte reflected her contentment, and she wrote of her new acquaintances and friends. She was just about convinced that any fears for the future she had once nurtured were completely unfounded. Even Iris had become more friendly—not talkative or warm—but at least the open animosity was gone or well hidden.

She left the church and strolled over to the house, picking up the mail from the black box hanging beside the front door and began separating it as she stepped inside. There was a letter for the Kaslavs and a letter for Iris, and as Robey placed it on the hall stand, she hesitated and slowly raised it to her eyes again, turning it over. There was no return address, but the handwriting was familiar. But whose? The answer suddenly crowded her mind. Of course, she mused, it's Lawrence's! But why should Lawrence LaPorte be writing Iris? The question was doomed to remain unanswered for, just as she was attempting to look at the postmark, Iris came barreling down the hallway and snatched the envelope from Robey's hand.

"That's from an old friend of mine in Wisconsin." Iris flared without hardly looking at the letter or Robey. She rushed up the staircase and disappeared behind her door, leaving a very bewildered Robey staring after her.

"Don't be foolish, girl," Robey spoke sharply to herself. "Many people have similar handwriting." She still couldn't help wishing she had had time to see the postmark. Amelia's warning about Iris's treachery came to mind. Could she have written to Lawrence? Telling lies about her? If she had, Robey wondered, how could she find out what they were? She admonished herself for being so suspicious and the problem was temporarily pushed into the recesses of her mind as Graham came in, obviously elated.

"I had almost forgotten to tell you, but there's going to be a celebration at the docks soon. Each year just about this time, when the University students are ready to go home, we have an art, crafts and just about everything else fair. There are street dances, all kinds of booths—a real blow out."

Graham's excitement was contagious, and Robey urged him to tell her more about it.

"Sort of starts out the summer season in style. The weather should be pretty hot from now on. Barring hurricanes, we usually have good weather. And, this year the fair coincides with the arrival of our one and only annual carnival."

"Wonderful," Robey laughed. "It's about time something went on in Knobbe Cove. I've been here almost four months and, except for getting attacked on the street, it's been quiet as a tomb."

"Want me to arrange a few more muggings?" Graham teased, "just to pep things up?"

"No, no thanks. Once was quite sufficient."

"Really, Robey, are you feeling more at home?" Graham took her hand in his. A warm tingle shut up her arm and swept through her whole being at his touch. She had noticed it often lately even when he was just handing her a stack of papers to file and their fingers met. She no longer felt alarmed at it since she had almost hypnotized herself to not fall in love with any man; but she did like the closeness her relationship with Graham had become. Always and forever just good friends, she decided.

"Yes, I am feeling more at home. I think things will work out. Even Iris seems to have accepted me now, or is resigned, I don't know which."

"Speaking of Iris, where is she?" Graham looked over his shoulder into the kitchen, expecting to find her listening. "I want to ask her about plans for the fair. She usually knows all the details."

"She received a letter from a friend in Wisconsin and went up to her room to read it in private."

"From Wisconsin?" Graham was genuinely surprised. "As far as I know, she's not acquainted with anyone from Wisconsin." He looked thoughtful for a moment. "Could be someone who moved away from here, though."

"Oh, well, come on." Robey handed him the money from the Kaslav envelope and put the letter in her purse.

"Let's both go over with the letter this evening. Douglas says Mr. Kaslav is still pretty shaky on that leg, even though the cast is off. And they want to take communion, too. I have your small bag ready."

"My, you sound like you are really beginning to take charge around here." Graham pushed the door open, and Robey stepped back out into the sunshine. Her shiny auburn hair glistened, and she swung her arms in rhythm with her stride. Graham watched her with great pleasure and Robey was aware of his eyes on her. Memories of how Roger used to look at her flooded back. Embarrassment and guilt blended into a blush.

The Kaslavs were effusive in their welcome and lit candles for the communion. First, Graham read the letter from their son who had a gift of putting words on paper in such a way you felt him in the room with you just having a conversation. Robey listened spellbound to Graham's voice, dramatically emphasizing even the most mundane phrases, making them come alive and interesting. She was so engrossed that she was startled when he came to the end of the letter and turned to her for his valise with the holy elements.

Handing the wafers and wine to him she settled back to lose herself in the meaning of the offering of the blood and body of Jesus. She had, of course, heard Graham before in the church, but here…with so few…it was more personal and she partook with them, eager to feel the deep emotions of the sacrament. When she looked up from prayer their eyes met, and her stomach tightened and made her tremble. Yes, she thought, I could easily adore this man and trust him with my life, was this God's will? She quickly glanced away, not wanting him to see or sense her feelings.

Standing in the kitchen after breakfast the next morning, Robey's attention was drawn beyond the screen door leading to the backyard. Wisps of smoke were swirling in the air by the tall board fence.

"Something's burning!" She cried in startled alarm as she swiftly pushed the door open and stepped out onto the back porch.

Graham laughed. "That's Douglas out there, smoking bumble bees out of the holes they bore in the wood fence. They build their nests in there and become a nuisance for him when he mows. They hate the sound of the mower—or maybe it's the vibration—but whatever it is, they'll come at him with blood in their eyes every so often. He tries to discourage them from building in the fence."

"One day," Iris grumped, "he's going to burn the fence down."

"I've seldom gone out in the backyard. Seems all my outdoor sitting has been done on the front porch." Robey started down the wide wooden steps. "It looks so beautiful…and serene."

Graham had come up behind her. "Go back and get our coffee cups and let's go on out and watch the action. Be ready to run if a bee comes after you."

"Be careful, Brother," Iris warned, "you can't get out of the way very fast."

"I'll be okay. Don't worry. Douglas will blow smoke my way every so often. He used to do that when I was a kid. Never did get stung."

Robey's eyes swept around the large yard; it wrapped its way around almost three sides of the house. The fence totally enclosed the area and had a gate in the back which led to an alley where trash and delivery trucks served the houses on two streets. In front, a gate with rusty hinges stood agape behind the huge hydrangea dominating the left side of the front porch. On the side next to the large house, three boards were missing.

A white wrought-iron bench, picnic table and several molded cement birdbaths furnished the yard. Red rambling roses clamored over a fan trellis and tea roses of several hues, mostly in bud, stood guard over sunny pansy faces huddled in the darkly mulched beds.

"This is just delightful," Robey exclaimed, as she sat at the picnic table and put down the coffee cups. She looked over her shoulder just in time to see Douglas sprinting around the corner, a large black bumblebee in hot pursuit. Seeing them sitting there, he turned and thrust a smoking newspaper torch at the angry insect, discouraging its flight.

"She doesn't have a nest to go back to. Maybe she'll try the Lodge side of the fence." Douglas panted.

"Get some coffee from Iris, and join us," Graham invited.

"No. Thanks anyway." Douglas stamped out the few embers still glowing on the paper. "The graveyard needs a weeding. Want to get there while the ground's soft, so's they'll pull better. I'm basically lazy, you know. Rather do it the easy way."

"Never thought of it that way before, Douglas, but I just realized how lazy you are. You work so hard and get things done quickly just so you can goof off."

"That's it, Pastor," he grinned. He waved a grimy hand and disappeared through the front gate, pulling it shut behind him.

Robey was still chuckling when she rose from her side of the picnic table and began exploring. A small rock garden nestled in the corner with deep purple Johnny jump ups, white periwinkle, and pink creeping phlox invading the short-clipped grass. Several azaleas clumped against the fence and enveloped the trunk of a tulip poplar which stood at the further corner of the yard. Blossoms of all manner and hue hummed with honeybees that Douglas had no urge to banish.

"I know where I'll come to read from now on. This is a bit of paradise."

"Spent much of my childhood here. Used to help Douglas some, and he'd bring his boys over to play. Lot of wonderful memories here. Even kissed my first girl under that very tree where you're standing." He moved over beside Robey and looked up into the branches and, leaning his crutches against the tree, supported himself by hanging his arms over a low limb. "Used to climb this old maple clear to the top, too."

"Which was the most memorable? The kiss or the climb?" Robey teased.

He reached over and tweaked her nose, leaving his hand cupping the side of her face. "I'll never tell, although she did, and boy, did I get in Dutch with Iris."

They were almost face to face and he looked deep into Robey's eyes. She returned his gaze, unable to look away, and his hand slid from the side of her face to the back of her head, drawing her lips close to his. The long lingering kiss, soft and gentle, surprised them both with the depth of its emotion. The tree limb was between them, or they would have found themselves drawn into a fevered embrace.

Opening her eyes, Robey stepped backwards, not believing what had occurred. She had promised herself to guard against this happening and yet it had and the turmoil within was overwhelming. She snatched up the coffee cups and swiftly headed toward the house.

"Sorry, Robey," Graham called out after her. "I had no right. I just couldn't seem to help myself." He reached for his crutches, balanced his body momentarily against the tree and hurried after her, but by the time he reached the screen door, it had slammed behind Robey and she was heading up the stairs to her room.

Once her door was closed and the inner latch locked, secure from interruption, Robey fell across the bed looking up at the ceiling, deep in thought.

"What do you do now, old girl?" She asked herself. "Run away again or face up to the fact that you've fallen in love?" No answer came but, mulling it over in her mind, Robey decided she'd have to talk with Graham. It was too soon, much too soon for her to enter into a romance, and if he couldn't promise this wouldn't happen again, she'd have to move out and only see him at the church office. She wasn't going to leave Knobbe Cove, not while Amelia needed her, and she still enjoyed her work. "But I must be honest. I am falling in love, and a future with Graham Hill wouldn't be the worst of fates."

At the remembrance of the kiss, somehow, she knew the memory of Roger was being relegated to the past where it belonged. And she did not feel a bit guilty.

12

WHEN ROBEY ANSWERED THE PHONE AT THE OFFICE, she was surprised but pleased to hear Amelia's voice coming over the line.

"How about you and me go shopping tomorrow in Savannah? I know plenty of nice places where you don't have to spend too much, and we can still have a good time."

"Sounds marvelous," Robey readily agreed, "and let's have lunch in some real posh restaurant. My treat. Do you know, except for eating on the road when I came down here a few months ago, I haven't been out to dinner but once and that was a church potluck dinner at Ebenezer Temple."

"So, it's about time for both of us. I hate to tell you, we'll have to use your wheels. I don't have a decent car of my own, and it has been years since I've driven anywhere in traffic."

"No problem. I'll pick you up about 8:30 in the morning, maybe we'll even take in an afternoon movie."

After putting the receiver back into its cradle, Robey sat looking out the window but not seeing beyond it. Amelia sounded more like her old self, so perhaps things were better at their house. Robey hoped so. She still wished for the relationship she thought she would have when she first came to Knobbe Cove—the three of them good friends—maybe like the three musketeers.

Early morning found the two women rolling along the main highway to Savannah, car windows open and hair blowing freely behind them. The day promised to be hot, but they intended to spend most of it inside air-conditioned department stores at the mall.

"I've been saving up a little nest egg for some new clothes for what seems years. A bit here and there has added up. Should have gotten something new before, but I don't like to shop alone, much more fun to have someone along."

"Remember how we'd spend so much time after school window shopping?" Robey reminisced. "We seldom bought, but we sure did look—a lot."

Amelia laughed. "Oh, what a long time ago that was. What were we, all of fifteen...sixteen years old? Yep," she said now with a bitter tone, "we had the whole world at our beck and call. How I wish things could have been different."

"How are things?" Robey glanced sideways at her friend as she drove. "We haven't talked for a while."

"David's gone. A couple of weeks ago he hit me in drunken anger." She heard Robey gasp and hastened to assure her; "I wasn't physically hurt, although I did have a bruised cheek for a few days. He apologized, of course, said he didn't mean to and would never do it again, but I made him leave." She drew in a deep breath.

"I'm sorry. So sorry, Amelia."

"Don't be. Was the best thing that could have happened. I had a good excuse to get him out of the house and believe me, Robey, when I tell you, it has been a long time since I've had such peace of mind."

"Do you know where he is?"

"I think he's at his father's house. As disgusted as his dad gets with David, he'd never turn him out."

They rode in silence for a short while, and the traffic began to pick up congestion near the city, so Robey found her attention drawn to her driving in unfamiliar territory. Soon they pulled into a parking space in the mall, got out, locked the doors and headed for the salesrooms. Before long all thoughts of the morning's conversation were gone from mind as they tried on suits, dresses, sweaters, and shoes. Three times they made excited trips back to the car to load their booty in the trunk and then they found a restaurant high over the city at the top of a hotel.

Robey decided one glass of white wine wouldn't hurt her driving, especially since they were going to eat Italian pasta, so they ordered and sat remembering classmates, teachers, and even the haunted houses they used to run past as little girls. They giggled so much they were certain other people were noticing, but they couldn't seem to contain their delight, especially when they recalled pranks perpetrated on parents and neighbors. Time quickly passed, and they soon realized there would be no movie, or they would be caught in the rush hour traffic going back home.

"Eat dinner at my place," Amelia invited. "We'll spend a bit more time looking over our purchases and seeing if we want to take anything back next week."

"No reason not to. I'll call Iris as soon as we get back and let her know not to expect me. I feel like a girl again...we've had so much fun."

The rest of the evening went as fast as the day with neither of them talking anymore about their personal troubles. In fact, Robey did not tell Amelia about the kiss, not yet, she had decided. When Robey pulled away from the house about 9:00 o'clock, she was happier than she had been for many months.

As Robey turned out the light, she heard the patter of rain on the roof. The sky had threatened rain earlier while she and Amelia were coming home from their day's excursion in Savannah, and around the time dinner had been served, a solid cloud cover darkened Knobbe Cove. Amelia remarked hurricanes had been known to sometimes strike this early in the year, but the clouds didn't show the usual yellow sulphur tinge associated with them. Now, burrowing under the covers and turning on her side, Robey mumbled to herself, "Go ahead and rain...at least we had a beautiful day." She stretched, realizing she was bone weary after all the hours of shopping, walking, and driving, and closed her eyes tightly in hopes of immediate sleep.

The light had not been off long when sounds of furtive whispers came to her through the door. It was too late for either Iris or Graham to be up and about...unless something were wrong, she thought. She sat up on the side of the bed, shoved her feet into large fluffy slippers, and reached for the robe draped over the bed post. Closer to the door she was able to discern Iris's voice, but the man whispering was not Graham. In the dark she kicked the desk leg, bumping the piece of furniture against the wall. The noise resounded throughout the room. Rubbing her toe, she opened the door, but the hall was empty. Blackness was pierced by a slim sliver of light beaming through the keyhole of the locked room. Iris's door was slightly ajar, and Robey could feel her eyes upon her. She didn't want Iris to know she was aware someone was in the room across the hall, so she quickly glanced right and left and shrugged her shoulders, then retreated behind her own door.

Once again in bed she looked up at the ceiling where she could, in the dim light from the window, make out the rococo plaster decorations around the base of the small ceiling globe.

"I wonder who the man in the locked room is," she mused to herself. "A secret love for Iris?" The thought sent her mind reeling into imaginary courting scenes of Iris and the faceless, nameless suitor, until she dropped off to sleep.

She had been asleep only a couple of hours when she was awakened by a sense of alarm. At first Robey thought it might have been the increasing rain, for the sky now spat hailstones and wind whistled through the shutters, but she became aware of a strange odor in the room, a damp smell, a musty, mildew stench that filled her nostrils in assailed her senses. She stayed under the covers trying to control the chill that crept up her spine.

"What a weird feeling," she voiced aloud, and when she spoke, she heard a shuffling noise over the corner near the wardrobe. Terror gripped her and she lay still, almost not breathing. "Who's there?" She barely whispered. No answer came.

Time passed. A half hour? An hour? Robey could not be sure, but the odor was no longer in the room. Had it been real, or imagined? Had she really been asleep and dreamed at all? If real, it could have been, Robey tried to rationalize, an old house, already damp, responding to more moisture from without, especially when there must have been a big change in air temperature to bring on hailstones.

The idea also occurred that a mouse might have been scampering under the wardrobe. Yes, that was it, of course. "This is an old house and old houses usually have mice around somewhere." Robey talked softly but rapidly to herself, building her courage. She was wide awake now and knew it would be difficult to fall asleep but she didn't intend to lie awake all night. Doctor Fairhope, in Chandor, had given her some sleeping pills after Roger's death, and she had brought the last of the prescription along with her. They were now in box on the floor of the wardrobe. Bolstered by the quietness of the room, Robey got out of bed and tiptoed to the door where she turned on the switch, bathing each corner of the room in welcome light. The bolt on the door was still tightly closed so no one could have gotten into the room, but for a short moment she considered looking under the bed.

She walked quietly over to the wardrobe, not wanting to wake anyone else, and opened the left door. In order to see the boxes were which were neatly stacked on the floor in the back, she had to stoop down and in doing so, she reached out her left hand and touched the rug to balance herself. A shudder shot through her, and her hand involuntarily jerked back at the feel of wetness on the carpet. Beside the wardrobe was a large damp spot.

"Big enough to be made by someone standing there dripping wet," Robey said aloud, but that's impossible, the door was bolted!

The rain increased in intensity and Robey's eyes were drawn to the window where a rivulet of water rand down inside one pane. The wood in the old frame was warped. Of course, there must be a leak on the roof. She looked up and could not see where it could have come from, but the explanation was such a logically satisfactory one she embraced it thankfully without further question.

The prescription box was the second one down and she extracted one pill, being careful to replace the rest back in their proper place on the bottom of the wardrobe. She took the tablet with water she always brought to the side of her bed at night, and crawled back under the covers, resolving to tell Graham about the leak in the morning, and wondering if the sedative would really help. She dreaded sleepless nights...she had experienced too many.

Brilliance streamed through the window and Robey opened one eye reluctantly and looked at the alarm clock, which had failed to go off. She dimly remembered a knock on her door earlier, but a sleeping potion always lasted much too long with her, and it kept nudging her back to slumber. Even now her eyes felt heavy. She knew she was late for breakfast and Iris would complain...not that she would really say anything, but her attitude would leave no mistaking her annoyance.

While dressing, Robey's thoughts went back to the previous night's events. But in the bright sunlight her fears vanished. The damp spot on the rug was gone and she wondered if, perhaps, she had imagined it, the door was still bolted, and she knew no one could have entered the room.

On the way downstairs she glanced at the usually locked room across the hall and wondered if she would meet Iris's overnight guest this morning. Iris was at the sink finishing dishes and Graham was drinking a second cup of coffee. There was no one else to be seen.

"Well, sleepyhead, it's about time you emerged from your cocoon on such a pretty day.

"I'm sorry I'm late, I just didn't get awake. My alarm clock didn't go off. I must not have set it." Robey looked at Iris, but if the older woman intended explaining last night's whispering, she gave no indication. Perhaps, she thought to herself, he is her secret boyfriend. I'll just keep my suspicions to myself. It's none of my business, anyway. Picking up her coffee cup she went over to the stove and filled it. Turning away from the stove she came face to face with Iris. For a moment they stood staring deeply into each other's eyes, both seemingly attempting to fathom what the other knew.

"Sit down, Robey. I'll fix you some scrambled eggs. The sausage is gone . . . it gets hard in the pan if you try to keep it too long." Disapproval filled each word.

"That's fine, Iris," Robey tried to ignore the chastisement in Iris's voice. "I could make the eggs myself. And I'm truly sorry I overslept."

"Makes no difference," Graham held up his cup for a refill,

"does us all good once in a while to sleep in. Besides, I ate your sausage so it wouldn't go to waste."

"Good. That makes me feel better. By the way, there was a damp spot on my rug near the wardrobe last night. Do you suppose there might be a leak in the roof somewhere?"

"Could be, we've had roof trouble before. It really needs replacing. I'll have Douglas look at it."

"What plans does the church make for the celebration you were telling me about? Anything special?" Robey sat down and stirred cream into her coffee, her mind still half on Iris and last night's whispering.

"I'll announce it Sunday. The merchants and townspeople make most of the necessary arrangements. Sales, favors, prizes. We serve a dinner in the activities room. It's an old-fashioned Baptist potluck dinner groaning board."

"I don't want to change the subject, but I wrote Sarah the other day..."

"She was your neighbor in Chandor, wasn't she?" Iris interrupted.

"Yes. I told her to plan to come down for a visit this summer. She asked in her last letter if she might. I know she'll enjoy Knobbe Cove. She and Jack and the boys would, of course, stay at the hotel. Or is there a cabin somewhere they could rent?"

"At the hotel! A cabin! Of course not," Graham emphasized his words with a jab of his spoon. "They'll stay here in our vacant rooms, which haven't been used for...let's see... I believe it has been almost seven years since we've had guests. Iris," he turned towards his sister, "when Robey lets us know when Sarah and her family will arrive, ask Douglas to help you clean out the rooms. They must be filled with cobwebs by this time."

Robey looked at Iris and noticed her face was ashen... Then

it turned so red Robey thought she might be in danger of a seizure. Their eyes met momentarily, and Robey's suspicions that Iris had a secret male friend were confirmed. She promised herself to say nothing about it or, for that matter, anything more to Sarah about a visit...at least for a while. She wondered, though, how often the man came, or had she just happened to discover her tryst on his only nocturnal visit?

13

DOUGLAS, ONE FOOT PROPPED UP ON THE SEAT OF A hardback chair, stared out the front window of his house in deep thought. He had been there almost a quarter hour without speaking to his wife, Leola, who was mending, slowly moving back and forth in her bentwood rocker.

"Leola..." He hesitated a bit, "I've got a problem," he finally spit out the words.

"Yes, you sure do if you don't get that dirty boot off that chair seat."

Douglas looked down, removed his foot, dusted some dried mud from the chair and plopped himself were his foot had just been.

"Come on, Hon, I need your help," he reached over and patted her hand, making her stick her finger with the needle.

"Ouch!" Leola stuck her injured finger in her mouth and sucked on it.

"Sorry, I didn't mean to do that," Douglas picked up her hand when she laid it back in her lap and kissed it." I'm just extra clumsy today, I guess. Lot on my mind."

"Figured you had some woes when you didn't light that pipe of yours," Leola reached into her apron pocket and handed him a pack of matches.

Douglas struck a match on the sole of his boot, lit his pipe, and moved forward on the seat, resting his elbows on his knees, cradling the pipe in his palms.

"Well," Leola prompted when he again lapsed into silence, "what's this big problem?"

Douglas cleared his throat. "I've been keeping a secret for seven years and right now I don't know whether I should keep it any longer."

"Secret? From me?" Leola's fingers stopped sewing and rested on the arm of the chair." I can't believe it. I thought we never had secrets!"

"There's one. Just one. Seven years ago, I promised Iris Hill I'd never tell, but somehow I'm afraid maybe somebody else is going to be hurt by this secret."

"Sounds terrible, Father. I think you better tell me. You know I won't say anything outside these walls, 'less you say I can."

Douglas smiled at his wife. In all their years together, he had never known her to be a gossip. "Do you remember Ward... The Hill boy who was sent away to the State Institution?"

"Yes. Well... I don't actually remember *him*. Don't think I ever saw him... but I recall what happened back then."

"About seven years ago Ward escaped from State. He found his way home, and I found him one day in the Hill's cellar. I was working in the yard and went to get a rake I kept there. I didn't know who he was, hadn't seen him for years. Mizz Iris came down when she heard me yell at him to leave."

"She threw her arms around him and calmed him down. He was pretty upset, I guess, at someone trying to oust him from his own home. I know he didn't recognize me, it had been a long time. Well, the upshot of it was, Mizz Iris wouldn't send him back to the institution and made me promise to keep quiet about him being there. He was so scared and meek, I never thought he'd be a problem. Mizz Hill just pleaded and begged and cried…so, I promised."

"I understand," Leola sympathized, "I heard she really loved him. It would be awful hard to send him back." A deep silence built between them as Leola thought over the situation and Douglas waited. "Where was the pastor?" Leola finally spoke.

"Luckily, over at the church. The phone rang before I left, it was the authorities at State telling Mizz Hill of his escape. Guess they hunted a couple of days hoping they'd find him before they notified anyone he was missing. Anyway, she told them to keep looking, and she'd let them know if he came home."

"You say she had to calm him. Was he ready to fight you?"

"No, he cringed from me. It was pitiful. He seemed harmless, childlike."

"What did the pastor do when he found out?"

"Mizz Iris decided not to tell him, either. Afraid he'd send him back. I told her it would be awful hard hiding a grown man in her house, but she was bound to try."

"She fixed up a place in the cellar. I'm the only one who ever went there. And she locked him in. He seemed satisfied with that, guess he was used to locked doors at State. She'd let him out in the garden every time she could. With the pastor spending most of his time across the street, it was pretty easy. She'd take him his meals in his old room on the first floor."

"Seven years he stayed there, and no one's found out? It's hard to believe. I couldn't keep an extra cat but what you'd find out in five minutes."

"Of course, for a few months after the accident, while the pastor was in the hospital, Ward had the run of the house, but when Pastor came home with those crutches to recuperate, Mizz Iris had to do something."

"What was that?" Leola bit through a thread when she finished a sock hole she had resumed darning.

"She enlisted the help of the Lodges next door. They agreed to take him in for a few weeks. Guess she told them the whole story, I don't know. But I took a couple boards out of the fence so Ward could go through without being seen from the street."

"Iris Hill seems to be pretty devious, Douglas. Isn't it a bit hard being loyal to her?" Leola looked up from her task and met her husband's eyes.

"That's just it... why I find myself in this dilemma. Remember me telling you a few weeks ago about Mizz Layne being attacked on the street by the graveyard?"

"Sure do," Leola stopped short. "You don't mean it was this crazy guy... Iris Hill's brother?"

Douglas hung his head and reached down to pick some mud from his boot heel. "Yes, I think so. Now I don't *know* so for sure, but the description fits."

"What are you going to do about it?"

"I already talked to Mizz Iris. She said Ward was staying at the Lodge's now because Mizz Layne is boarding at her place. She said she was certain he wasn't the one. I don't know what to think... or do."

Leola rocked in the chair, her lips a tight line across her face, her mind trying to absorb all Douglas had told her.

"She's an evil woman, Father. No, don't protest," she put out her hand to stop the words he had on his lips. "She is. She's telling all kinds of things around town about Robey Layne. I heard them from the help at the hotel and even, I'm sorry to say, from our Ladies Aid at our church. Most of them work in the houses in town, you know. They don't miss much."

"She's not evil, Hon, just lonesome. She loves both her broth-

ers, and I guess she's doing what she thinks best. As for talk, I've
not heard anything."

"You callin' me a liar?" Leola's eyebrows shot up her forehead
in indignation.

"No, no, you say so then it's God's truth... But I was just saying *I* hadn't heard."

"Well, can't say is there's anything to be done... not right now.
Mrs. Layne is alright, and you can't prove anything... and after all
this time... seven years, it would do no good. Probably only make
a terrible mess. Guess we might as well keep *our* secret a while
longer."

Douglas grinned. "I knew you'd know what to do. I sure do
feel better now."

"Sure *you* do, but now I'll be looking at every new face in town
and wondering if it's Ward Hill. What does he look like?"

"He's not too tall, his skin is real white from staying cooped
up, I guess. And his hair is white. Has a white beard, too. Funny
thing, he looks like a man much older than he is and acts like a
child. He'll do anything his sister tells him."

"How does he spend his time?" Leola put the tea kettle on the
fire and went to the cupboard to get down cups and saucers.

"Plays solitaire, reads, or I should say looks at the pictures in
magazines. She feeds him and talks to him as much as she can."

"Wouldn't he be better off in a place where they have programs
and exercises?"

"Probably so... but he's real good with his hands. She keeps
him supplied with craft stuff and then takes what he makes over
to the hospital for the gift shop to sell. Just donates it, they think
she does it all."

"So, he's not so dumb, after all. What a tragedy! Sounds like
he could be educated," Leola said, pouring hot water over coffee
grounds in the dripolator.

"We'll just have to push this into the back of our minds for now," Douglas stood behind Leola and put his arms around her shoulders. "Thanks for listening…and all the advice and understanding. I knew I could count on you."

Leola turned in his embrace and rested her head on his shoulder. "No more secrets to confess?" she asked, tilting her head back.

"No, no more. You know, Mrs. Washington, I love you." He reached past her and turned out the flame under the coffee. "We don't need that right now, do we?" He asked, guiding her toward the bedroom door.

Two days passed before Robey had any reason to question her decision to come to Knobbe Cove. Graham and Webb had gone into town for the final signing of the loan papers for the improvements. She hadn't realized getting a loan could be such a complicated business. After the list had been made, the loan committee had sent an inspector to the church to verify if the needs were accurate and if there was anything structurally unsound about the building.

"They are extra cautious," Graham had explained at breakfast, "because churches are dependent upon their congregations to supply funds. Congregations can be very fickle in their giving at times, and it will be several years before we will be able to pay back every dime. Besides, foreclosing on a church would be a black eye on their image."

"But they verified the list last month. What is holding it up?" Robey complained, anxious to get done with the paperwork and see some results.

"Impatient youth, all in due time," Graham had mocked her jokingly as he left with Webb.

She smiled to herself at the memory. Turning to go up to her room she encountered Iris on the bottom step. There was something very odd, almost ominous, about her countenance and Robey couldn't place it. Was it her eyes? No, perhaps her stance. No, not that, either, but whatever it was, Robey was more than slightly startled to see her, for she hadn't heard her descend the steps and had not, in fact, realized that she had been upstairs. The last time she had seen her was in the kitchen only a few minutes before. She didn't think she could have passed her in the hallway without her being aware of the movement.

Iris held out a white envelope. "Brother wants you to give this to the organist this morning. If he doesn't come into the office, put it on the organ where he'll see it."

"What is it?"

"I don't know, I'm sure it's none of our business or my brother would have told me." Her rebuke was bare and cutting. There was unmasked distaste in the tone of her voice, a tone that had returned the night Robey had mentioned Sarah's future visit and Graham had offered Ward's room as accommodations. Robey felt tears sting her eyes. She had tried so hard to like Iris and make Iris like her. What she had done, she could not imagine. She took the envelope in trembling hands and went out into the cool morning air. Frustration bogged her mind, notions and ideas tumbled around needing to be sorted out, put in perspective. On top of it all was an itch to run. She had not been asked to come; she had pushed herself into Iris's life. She had had no right to interfere in and upset what had probably been a most comfortable household. She had been so happy for such a short while in Knobbe Cove, and she was alarmed at how quickly Iris could dispel that happiness.

At the church she found herself alone. How quiet and mystical a church could be. Each footfall on the carpets was so silent.

She busied herself with letters and bulletins and kept a watch out for Clive to give him his sealed envelope. She picked it up, turned it over a couple of times in her hand, not understanding why Graham hadn't given it to her himself. Straightening Graham's desk and putting the finished correspondence where he would see it as soon as he sat down, she glanced at the calendar pad next to the phone. There, in Grahams hand, was a notation Clive was out of town and choir practice had been cancelled for this week. Beside the pad was a note from Clive explaining a family emergency and assuring Graham the choir knew their anthem and not to worry.

Perhaps, Clive wasn't going to be here at all. Maybe Graham had let it slip his mind. Robey thought she had better give the note back to him. On second thought, she remembered Iris's instructions to put the note on the organ. Evidently Graham didn't want to take a chance on missing Clive on his return, and the organ was surely the best place to assure he'd see the note.

Robey walked through the sanctuary slowly, looking long at each stained-glass window as though she were in an art gallery. Each changing color made the pictures alive and throbbing. How ironic, she thought, that the windows, like so many lives, were subtly affected by something so unreachable, so wispy, so intangible as a cloud or a sunbeam, or someone else's attitude. Here and there Robey reached down to put a hymn book back into the bracket behind a pew or gathered a bulletin or scrap of paper left from last night's prayer meeting.

Behind the altar a small door led to the corridor below the organ loft and Robey let herself through it. There was an odd aura in the hallway...as though just prior there had been sound, and the echo was still there waiting for silence to begin again. Could someone be in one of the rooms? Maybe just inside the door? She thought of the night of the storm when she was so certain for a while that someone was in her room. Robey didn't believe in haunting spirits as such, but if asked, she would have had to say she could feel vibrations. And she felt them now.

Standing silently apprehensive, she peered down the long hall and could see light coming through the back door of the church— the door leading to the cemetery. Her first urge was to walk the length of the dingy hall to see if anyone was there, but she couldn't summon the courage.

If someone had been there, they would now be gone or have made themselves known, she reasoned. She was furious with herself for her cowardice. It was difficult to not turn back into the sanctuary and run out the other door into the safe sunshine of the street.

Momentarily, she forgot her mission and when she looked down and saw the white envelope in her hand she was jarred back to reality. "For Pete's sake, this is stupid," she said aloud, setting her body into motion toward the door to the organ loft. She pulled the door open none too gently and was halfway up the stairs before she remembered how shaky and unstable the bannister was. More cautiously, she finished ascending into the gloomy niche. Turning on the light to see where to place the note had again the effect of making the dark recesses of the small loft pitch black. She placed the envelope on the music rack and reached up to turn off the bulb, hoping her eyes would adjust quickly to the dimness. Before she had time to touch the switch, a noise startled her and she stood erect, wary, alert, and very alarmed.

"Who's there?" There was no answer, but she could hear short breaths coming from the corner near the ornate doors to the pipes. "Who's there? Is that you, Clive? Did you get back early?" She knew deep within it wasn't Clive, but she had to keep talking, trying to edge herself away from the organ and toward the steps.

She stared intently into the darkness, unaware of a stealthy move behind the organ until the light clicked off, plunging the entire room into unfathomable darkness.

Robey screamed involuntarily and ran toward the steps, where a dim light from the hall downstairs outlined the stairwell. All thought of danger, other than the one pursuing her, fled from her mind. Her heel caught in the ragged hole of the rug, and she was propelled toward the bannister. Robey grasped it desperately to save herself from falling. She hung over the steep stairs for a brief moment, unable to right herself, as a rasping sound grew from a soft grind to a shattering break. Again, she screamed, looking down at the floor below, just moments before plummeting the distance amid splinters of railing and metal brackets.

How long she lay there, Robey didn't know. When she began to regain consciousness her ankle throbbed, her head hurt and her side ached. She heard a door slam in the distance and the familiar clump of Graham's crutch coming closer and his voice, talking to Webb Brown, calling her name.

And then he was there, horrified, concerned, calling to Webb to hurry and phone Doctor Kent and bring cold, wet towels.

Graham sat down beside her on the floor, took off his jacket and folded it under her head. "Robey, whatever happened? What happened?"

Robey's eyes cleared and she tried to get up, but Graham gently restrained her, pushing her shoulder down, making her lie still. "Don't move until the doctor sees you." His eyes looked up at the place where the bannister had been. "A fall like that could have broken some bones."

"Graham, there was someone there, in the organ loft." Robey whispered.

"Someone there? Who?"

"I don't know. I didn't see his face." She shuddered involuntarily. "I didn't see him. I just know he was there."

Graham scooted over to the bottom of the stairs and peered up into the blackness and yelled for whoever was there to come out. There was no answer, or other sound.

"There was someone, Graham. There was."

"If there was, we'll find out, Robey. But whoever was there must be gone. Why *did* you go up there? You knew that bannister was fragile."

"I was taking the envelope up for Clive."

"Envelope? What envelope?"

"Iris gave it to me this morning, said you told her to tell me to give it to Clive when he came in...or put it on the organ music rack if I didn't see him."

"Clive is out of town; his mother is worse, and they are moving her to a nursing home."

"Yes, I know that now. I saw his note and your marked calendar, so that's why I went up there. I thought it important that he get it as soon as he got back."

"I gave that envelope to Iris last Monday before Clive left. Remember the day I had to leave before daylight to get to Savannah? I wonder why she took so long giving it to you. "

Robey had, despite Graham's wishes, moved around enough to realize nothing was broken and she sat up, holding her head in her hands. A big knot had risen on her forehead and her arms were scraped and brushed-burned in several places from the carpet. Graham put his arm around her, rested her head on his shoulder, kissed her forehead and gently rubbed the muscles in her neck. The knot on her head continued to increase in size.

"What a terrible, terrible thing to have happened. If I had had any idea you would have gotten hurt by that shaky bannister, I would have paid out of my own pocket to have it fixed before this. I never dreamed... Oh, Robey, I am so sorry."

"It's alright, Graham. You couldn't have known I..." She was going to say had been so clumsy when the events leading up to her fall rushed back to mind. "Graham, there was someone up there. He didn't push me or anything, but he scared the wits out of me, and I just didn't think of anything but getting out of there."

Robey told Graham everything she could remember... but as she told it, the narrative took on the tone of a hysterical woman, frightened of her own shadow. It was so unreal, so mystery-bookish. Robey wouldn't blame Graham if he didn't believe a single word she said.

Doctor Kent swept through the door carrying his medical bag. He extracted the stethoscope and small flashlight to check Robey's pulse and reflexes and, after feeling arms and legs and getting her to turn and twist, he pronounced her sound.

"Well, young lady, it looks like you are pretty lucky. The worst that has happened seems to be a broken heel... genus shoe, he dangled Robey's heelless brown pump. "You've got a few bad scrapes and bumps and if I were you, I'd get to bed, drink some hot soup and tea, and rest the balance of the day. You're going to be pretty sore for a couple of days, so I'll give you a prescription for pain if you wish. If any of those bumps begin swelling any further, especially that ankle, put some ice on it and call me. With an educated guess, I'd say you'll be fine within the week."

"Thank you, doctor. I think I'll take your advice. Bed for me. I've had enough excitement for one day." She turned to Graham. "Everything in the office is done."

"Wouldn't make any difference if it weren't, you're not going near that office for a few days."

Webb helped both Robey and Graham to their feet. It took Robey a couple of steps to get her equilibrium. She went stocking-footed, carrying her shoes and the broken heel. The group walked out into the yard, each going their separate ways except for Graham and Robey who made their way slowly across the street and up the front steps of the house. Iris met them at the door wringing her hands in her apron.

"What happened? Mrs. Lodge just called to say she saw Doctor Kent go into the church with Webb Brown meeting him. I was just on my way over."

"The bannister to the organ loft broke when Robey grabbed it. Her heel had caught in the rug at the top of the stairs and she fell."

"Is that what happened, Robey I mean…"

Robey smiled. "That's what happened, Iris. Just like Graham said." Now why, she mused, would Iris disbelieve her brother? Iris was obviously overwrought, and Robey wondered if it really was all concern for her welfare. Of course, she reasoned, she might be feeling guilty, because she knew I'd not have gone up there in the first place, if it hadn't been for her.

"Can you make some hot soup and tea, Iris?" Graham asked his sister, "it's what the doctor wants her to have. You can serve it to her upstairs." He turned to Robey; "can you make it upstairs by yourself? Iris could help you, sorry I can't."

"I'll get there myself, Graham, and Iris, you don't need to bring the soup up, I'll come down and eat it in the kitchen. I'm really not hurt that badly."

"You go on up, Robey. I'll be glad to serve you upstairs. You should get off your feet and in a warm comfortable position. I'll bring the ice bag, too, for your ankle. It looks awfully swollen. Sure you don't need me to help you up the stairs?"

"Alright. I give in." Robey conceded. Her head was aching, and she found that the more she stood the stiffer she became.

"If you need anything, I'll be in the study," Graham called up the steps after them, before he turned and shut the library door behind him.

Iris quickly returned downstairs and disappeared into the kitchen.

Robey changed into a nightgown and was sitting up in bed when Iris knocked at the door and then pushed it open with her hip. She placed a bed tray across Robey's lap from which a bowl of hot chicken noodle soup and a pot of steaming tea emitted aromas intertwined with the smell of a fresh hot cross bun. "I thought maybe you'd like something sweet. Made them this morning. Here's the ice pack also."

"Thank you, Iris. That was thoughtful of you, and I do appreciate it. I'm sorry to be so much of a bother to you."

"Now rest. It must have been a horrible experience. I feel it's all my fault. If it hadn't been for Clive's letter..." Her voice trailed off.

"Now stop thinking that way," Robey felt sorry for her. "It wasn't your fault. I just got scared and..."

"I'd better go now," Iris interrupted, "you can tell me all about it later. Brother would be upset if I kept you from resting. We'll talk later, maybe tomorrow."

The hot soup and tea made Robey sleepy and she lay back on the pillows thinking of the moments before the fall. A warning signal from somewhere within cautioned her not to tell Iris of her suspicions that someone was in the loft, although she knew that Graham would probably do so. Still, it had happened that way, she knew it had. Yet, there had been nothing to see...nothing to touch. Just like the wet spot on the rug, the smell in the room that night, and the terror that had gripped her heart like a vise both times. Was she losing her mind? Had Lawrence been right? Should she, even now, pack up and go home?

She took a couple of aspirin from the drawer beside her bed, swallowed them, and then carefully lifted the tray onto the armchair beside the window. Snuggling beneath the covers, trying to blank out all thoughts, she slept fitfully, several times being aware of aches and hurts when she turned in bed to find a more comfortable spot.

It was dinnertime when she awoke, and she could hear Graham and Iris arguing downstairs. She strained her ears to hear and only wisps of the conversation managed to invade the room, but there was enough to surmise that Graham was upset with Iris. 'It was bad enough,' he said, 'that you had neglected to deliver the message in time for Clive to get it Monday, but to ask Robey to take it to the loft where Clive would see it thinking that it had been delivered on time...and to tell Robey that I had instructed her to put it there...' The voices droned on, Iris weeping, Graham's anger now receding.

So that's what happened! Poor Iris, Robey thought, trying to cover up her own negligence with a little white lie. Such a small matter. Such a big fuss for a small human error. Robey hung her legs over the edge of the bed and her bruises cried out in pain and stiffness, but she was determined to go down to dinner and not have Iris carry for her. Out in the hall, with the tray she was going to return, she realized she would have to hold onto the balustrade as she descended to be certain her sore ankle would hold her. She left the tray on the landing floor. Downstairs, Iris rose quickly from the table when she saw Robey enter the hallway. Dabbing her eyes on the edge of her apron, she hurried forward to put her arm around Robey's waist, giving her extra support.

"Here, sit down. You didn't need to come down. I'd have brought your dinner up."

"I had to come down. I don't like to interfere, Graham, but I couldn't help overhearing your discussion with Iris. It just isn't anything to get so riled up about. Life's too short, and it's over and done with."

"That's just it, Robey. It *could* have been your life."

"But it wasn't, and it isn't likely to ever happen again. So, let's just forget it. Please?"

"You're right, of course," Graham conceded. "I've acted inexcusably towards you, Iris. I'm sorry. Why I keep forgetting the gentle and forgiving ways of our Lord Christ Jesus and react the way I do sometimes, I'll never know."

"You were right, Brother and I was wrong," Iris turned her head and gently blew her nose into her handkerchief.

"Let's talk about the celebration," Robey abruptly changed the subject and Iris listened gratefully while Graham started telling them about the schedule of events he had heard about in town earlier in the day.

14

ROBEY STAYED IN BED THE NEXT MORNING, STILL bone-weary and sore, more bruised than she had realized at first, and she didn't come downstairs until lunch. Iris had served breakfast in her room with hardly a word, slipping in silently to get the empty tray after Robey had again dozed off.

The weather was warm but windy and the dogwood and lilacs laced the outdoors with color. Graham stood on the sidewalk on his way back to the church after lunch, looking up at Robey seated on the top step.

"You'd better go back to bed and rest."

"I'm going to rest in the garden, do some reading and maybe write a couple of letters."

"Wish I could join you. Maybe this evening." Graham swiveled on his crutches, looking beyond the house toward the fence.

"Maybe I'll get over to the office later," Robey tried to stretch her aching arms.

"If you must, but don't hurry. I'm going over the primary department lesson books with Mary Stevens first thing."

Graham swung across the street, and Robey turned back into the yard. She was always pleased to find the garden so well-tended. Her own, in Chandor, had often gone unweeded and unclipped, playing second fiddle to Roger's work and her busy schedule.

Snapdragons and daisies, showing pink, salmon, and white under the trees, were just beginning their summer blooming. The forsythia Robey had admired so from her window was barren now of yellow bugles, only graceful sweeping green branches formed a cathedral in the corner of the yard at the back fence.

Under the huge maple, the iron seats were freshly painted. Robey gingerly touched a seat and finding it dry, sat down, looking up into the tree where a nest could be seen securely propped in a forked branch. She wondered what bird had built it and if there were eggs or baby birds in residence. As if in answer, a mother blue jay swooped down and made a pass at her head, making her raise her arms to fend her off. She stood up and backed away from the tree and turned swiftly, right into the arms of Douglas, who was as startled as she.

"Oh!" She pushed herself away, "I didn't hear you come up!"

Douglas had pruning shears in one hand and a bag of rose food in the other.

"You be careful around jays, Mizz Layne. They'll peck your head real good for getting anyways near their young."

Robey was just about to reply when she noticed an odor coming from Douglas's sweaty work clothes. It was a familiar smell, but she couldn't at that moment place it. Now, where? Of course! The bedroom that night! The knowledge assailed her mind, spinning her thoughts.

"Something wrong, Mizz Layne? Did the jay get you?" Douglas's voice seemed to come from somewhere in a deep abyss, pulling Robey back from her thoughts.

"No. No, Douglas. Everything is alright. I was just surprised seeing you here, running into you, literally. I thought I was alone in the garden."

Robey slowly walked across the grass and pretended to be looking at the shrubs and new leaf buds on the crape myrtle, but her mind was bombarded by questions. Could Douglas have been in her room that night? Of course not. No one could. The door was bolted. She could feel Douglas's eyes on her, and she couldn't help thinking she accused him without reason.

The warm sun helped dispel the uneasiness she experienced as it intensified in the early noon position directly above her. Strolling around the back of the house she entered the rose garden, where buds poked their way through glossy leaves and full blooms topped long thorny stems. Douglas had retreated to the front of the house and over the fence Robey could see him on his knees, digging out broadleaf bordering the concrete walkway.

Robey turned and faced the back of the house. Looking up, she saw what she figured to be the windows to Iris's room and the two locked rooms, one upstairs and one down, both tightly shuttered except for a missing slat in the upstairs window. Iris's window was above the study window and the two shuttered windows topped a slanting cellar door with a coal chute beside it. As she turned away a glint light caught her eye, drawing her gaze back to the shuttered upstairs window. She was sure it came from the room across the hall from her bedroom. Was Iris's visitor back? She slowly edged toward the house, straining her neck, looking upward, but the light disappeared, and Robey rationalized it could possibly be the sun reflected in the pane. She stepped backwards and almost screamed when she stepped on Douglas's foot.

"I'm sorry, I just seem to keep bumping into you." She laughed in relief. "Douglas," she intoned solemnly, "this yard just isn't big enough for the two of us!"

Douglas laughed heartily, a delightful contagious sound, and Robey found herself joining in as they walked over to the wrought-iron seats.

"I didn't mean to scare you, Mizz Layne. I was just going to open the cellar and put these tools away."

Robey knew Douglas always seemed to have time to talk to her and decided to try some investigation into what, she told herself, was really none of her business, but curiosity overcame discretion.

"Douglas, have you ever done and work in those two rooms Iris keeps locked?"

Douglas didn't seem to think the question was out of line for he answered quickly. "Not lately, Mizz Layne. There's a small bath in the downstairs room, and I fixed a broken faucet once. Don't know how it got broken, but that's not my business. I just repair things others break."

"Graham told me Ward lived in that room."

"Yes, he did. Old Mr. Hill had the bath put in so Ward wouldn't have to go into the main house unless they wanted him there."

"You mean he was a discipline problem?"

"You have to understand, Mizz Robey. His body was large as a man, but his mind was like a child. Mentally challenged is what they call it today. Most times he was alright, but once in a while he'd want his own way and throw a tantrum just like any little kid."

"It must have been terribly difficult for Iris to take care of a little boy like Graham and a man like Ward. Graham told me he was sent away around Graham's fifth birthday, how old was Ward?"

"Early twenties, I think. Far as I know those rooms haven't been used for years." There was a hesitation in Douglas's voice that made Robey wonder if perhaps he knew about Iris's visitor and didn't want to lie about whether the rooms were occasionally in use. Probably should tell me to mind my own affairs, she thought to herself. She looked at her watch.

"Well, I better get over to the church. Graham told me to stay home, but it's time to do the bulletins, and he doesn't type very fast. He gets frustrated when he makes a mistake. So, I better do them."

Douglas reached out and put his hand on her arm, lightly restraining her from leaving. "I heard about that accident yesterday, Mizz Layne, and I'm terribly sorry. I could have fixed that rug, and the bannister, if I had ever thought such a thing would happen, but...well...with the loan money coming through, I thought it could wait until it was replaced proper."

"That's alright, it certainly wasn't your fault." She started away again and then stopped and looked back. "Douglas, have you ever seen anyone around the church who shouldn't be there? Like a prowler, I mean?"

"No, nobody Mizz Robey. All the doors are kept locked. Shame we have to, nothing really valuable there, but I've read of vandalism in churches in other towns north of here. We're just being cautious. So far, we haven't ever had trouble with anyone breaking in. Why do you ask?"

"Nothing, really. I guess I was just letting my imagination get away with me yesterday. I was all alone in the back rooms for the first time and was probably hearing the walls talk to me." Robey stepped through the gate to the front yard, and Douglas called after her.

"Tell the Reverend I'll be over as soon as I set in these bulbs. Yell if you need me before."

"Alright," she called back over her shoulder, but there were several questions she wished she had had the brass to ask Douglas. Like why Graham had to climb stairs when a comfortable room with bath was downstairs, and who Iris's visitor was. She suspected that Douglas knew.

She resolved to ask Graham about moving into the room at dinner, although she knew she should leave well enough alone, but perhaps Graham just needed someone on his side.

"Just whose side am I on?" She said aloud, "last night I was furious with Graham for treating Iris the way he did, and now I'm upset with Iris for treating Graham as a second-rate boarder in his own home." Her protection all these years of Ward's room, and probably his belongs, was evidence of an unreal tie to the past.

Robey's mind went back to the scene at the church and the tender kisses Graham kept giving her on the forehead, as if she were a little child hurt in play. A smile crossed her lips as she entered the office door. Graham, I haven't made up my mind yet, she mused to herself, but I don't think little placating pecks on the forehead are what the good Lord has in mind for us. It's certainly not what I've got in mind!

"Looks like you swallowed the canary!" Graham smiled at her. "What's up?"

"Nothing…not a thing." But even Robey was surprised at her thoughts.

Robey typed the bulletin master and turned to find Graham standing behind her without his crutches, bracing himself on the desk edge. He laboriously took a couple of steps toward her, grinning broadly.

"Hey," Robey cheered, "you're getting pretty good at supporting yourself alone."

"One day I'm not going to need those crutches. I've been exercising up in my room, you know, isometric kind of thing, and I can feel my legs, or rather, my rump muscles are a lot stronger."

"How wonderful. Does Iris know? It would make her so happy to know you might get back the use of your legs without needing props."

"No, I don't want her to know just yet. She was so frightened when the doctor advised the exercises—afraid that I might fall and do more damage. An optimist she is not. But I find I fall like a stuntman; I've never hurt myself." With that he slipped to the floor and Robey, concerned, dropped down beside him, wincing as she came to rest on her sore ankle.

"See, you ought to take lessons." He rubbed her ankle and then let his hand come up her leg to massage the calf muscle. "Feel better?"

"Lots. Thanks," she stretched her legs out in front of her.

"We've got to stop meeting on the floor like this," Graham's face was slightly flushed. Robey turned and put her hand on the side of his face and drew closer, looking deep into his startled eyes. Her hand cupped his chin and she kissed him softly and quickly, drawing her face away only momentarily and then kissing him again more eagerly.

"Robey," he muttered and drew his hand through her hair, his other arm circling her waist and pulling her into a close and passionate embrace. Then he thrust her from him and looked out the window.

"Let's get up. This is silly, sitting on the floor and..."

"And what, Graham? Just because you don't think you should get involved, married, which I don't agree with, why should you be celibate the rest of your life?"

Graham's eyebrows lifted as he stared at Robey. He couldn't believe she was suggesting...and yet she was...wasn't she?

Robey read his expression clearly. "Oh Graham. I didn't mean we had to have an affair, not at all. What I mean is, well, if you won't say it, I will. I think I've fallen in love with you, and I'm not about to wait around forever for you to stop being so noble and self-sacrificing."

Graham continued to gape at her in astonishment.

"I want to find out if, maybe, our relationship might, in spite of you, be something more than friendship. That is," she took a deep breath, "I want to marry you, unless you don't feel the same way toward me. In that case, just say so, and I'll never bother you again."

A long silence sat heavy between them while Graham seemed to be absorbing what Robey had just dropped like a bomb upon him.

"You really mean you'd consider being married to a man who may never walk without crutches the rest of his life?

"Yes, if I loved him."

"No dancing? No climbing mountains? Not even long walks in the moonlight?"

"Graham, if it were me, would it make any difference to you?"

"You know the answer to that without asking, Robey. But what about children? You know what I've told you about me. I don't think we could safely have any."

"We could adopt."

Graham threw back his head and laughed until tears of relief squished from the corners of his eyes. "Oh, Robey, Robey. How many dreams I've had about you. Somehow, I always knew you'd feel the way you do, but I didn't dare risk trying to tell you how I felt. It just didn't seem fair. I love you so much."

Robey rested her head on his shoulder, feeling as if she had always belonged there. "I'm not ready to say we'll marry soon, Graham. I still have lots of questions to resolve in my life—threads from the past that I must put knots in and pack away...but I do know right now that my day doesn't begin until I've seen you."

15

"LET'S STOP WORKING AND GO DOWN TO THE drugstore and get a banana split!"

"A banana split. Are you serious?" Robey laughed.

They had both been working silently for some time; he in the storeroom hunting old books, and she typing address labels—getting prepared for the annual membership canvas. Neither, if they were honest about it, had their minds on the tasks at hand.

"I feel like a kid in the throes of his first puppy love, never did have that feeling before. All the college boys take their girls down for a soda... so I can, too."

"Okay. I'd love to go sip a soda with you, Mr. Hill."

"Can you walk okay on that ankle?"

"No problem. My ankle's fine for at least a couple of blocks."

Graham was now in a talkative mood as they walked. He explained in detail the home for orphans he wanted to open. "I have a house all picked out. It's the big one behind the Kaslav's. Should hold twenty-five youngsters easily."

"What kind of staff will you have?"

"There would be one couple for each five children. They wouldn't have to be married couples, just so each five kids had both a mother and father model during the day. The women would be in charge of the youngster's daily care, and the men would have other jobs throughout the building. I'm hoping to attract someone who is a good repairman, maybe a teacher... I don't know. I haven't worked out *all* the details yet."

As Graham talked of his plans, his face became more and more animated and enthusiastic. When they sat down at the counter and ordered their banana splits, Robey had to smile to herself watching him gesture with his spoon, emphasizing his thoughts on the raising of children. She could not help but think what a wonderful father he would have made.

"Each child would have chores to do and rules to follow and they'd never really know that they were orphans, or at least they wouldn't mind because they'd be loved so much."

Robey noticed all at once that his countenance fell, and he looked dejected. "What's the matter?"

"Always get to this point in my dreams for the orphanage and then realize it's just that... a dream. Here I am begging money for repairs for the church and deep down, I know I'll never get support for the home for my motherless children."

"Why not, for goodness sake? I should think you'd get lots of support—the Willises do out on the island, don't they?"

"They are fairly self-sufficient with their cabinetmaking business and, supplemented by the State's foster program, they get along famously. Besides, they usually only have twelve kids or so. I'm thinking of over double that amount. I'd have to have everything in place with money to somehow pay help—at least for a couple of years, until sufficient donations came in to carry it on. Oh well, it's nice to daydream once in a while, and so good to have you listen to my rantings."

Banana splits arrived resplendent in fudge sauce on the chocolate scoop, strawberry on the strawberry, butterscotch on vanilla. Sprinkled with crushed nuts, it was all topped off with whipped cream crowned by a maraschino cherry.

"One of these for both of us would have been enough!" Robey gasped.

"Oh, come on, be brave. The least that can happen is we wake up tomorrow morning fifty pounds heavier!"

"It's been a long time since I've had one of these monsters. Not since Bud was born." A wistful look spread over Robey's face, and Graham reached out and covered her hand with his."

"One of the loose threads to contend with?"

"I guess, but then I suppose some of them never get really put in the past, do they?"

"Should they?" Graham asked softly.

They sat there, nibbling away at the mounds of ice cream, talking about all manner of things from her past, his past, and skirting the future until they realized they had dawdled over an hour consuming the desserts.

"We'd better head back to the church." Graham sounded sad at having to leave.

"I hope," Robey pushed herself away from the counter, "Iris doesn't have a big dinner. I think we just blew it!"

Dinner was early and as Robey passed the locked door in the downstairs hallway on her way to the kitchen, she was reminded of her intention to inquire about the rooms. Iris served ham steak, potatoes, and a broccoli casserole. Graham and Robey looked at each other like conspirators as they dished up the smallest portions they felt they could get away with without Iris being suspicious about their afternoon's satiated sweet tooth.

"Graham, I know it's none of my business..." she hesitated only a moment, her eyes darting quickly to Iris and back to Graham, "but why don't you use the downstairs bedroom, Ward's room, instead of climbing those steep steps each night?"

Iris's head snapped erect and she stared, open-mouthed, at

Robey. When no answer came immediately, Robey felt she must make some logical excuse for her meddling. "I got to thinking about it after my fall. Aren't those stairs treacherous for you on those crutches?"

"I've thought about it, Robey, but, well, for one thing, there's no bath down here and I'd hate to have to navigate those steps if I weren't wide awake."

Iris's face changed from amazed to smug as her brother offered a logical explanation for his nightly climb to the second floor.

"But there is a bath, Graham. Douglas told me that one was put in years ago before Ward had to leave."

Graham looked first at Robey, and then at his sister, who now looked at her hands, wringing them as Robey now realized she did whenever she was upset.

"Iris, is this true? You never mentioned a bath."

Instead of answering Graham, Iris stood up, towering over them both. She seemed to have gained in physical stature. "You are right, Mrs. Layne. It is none of your business. Those rooms are Ward's rooms and no one else is going to use them. You come from out of nowhere, evidently unbalanced enough to run away from what was supposed to be a loving home, butt yourself into our lives and I'm telling you, you are *not* welcome here." She almost screamed at Robey. "Do you understand?"

Robey almost broke the shocked silence by telling Graham that Iris had a night visitor who could evidently use Ward's rooms whenever he wished. But that would be vindictive. I deserved that outburst, she thought. I did tread where I knew I shouldn't. After all, Graham and I aren't married yet, and maybe we won't be.

"Iris!" Graham said, "you owe Robey an apology. She was just concerned because of her fall. But it's alright. Upstairs is fine with me. I need all the exercise I can get." He took Iris's hand, "Sit down and let's finish this good dinner." He took a second helping of the casserole, his eyes on Robey, as though he were doing penance for the banana split. Robey suppressed a small giggle.

The older woman's shoulders slumped as though all the air had gone out of her at once. She looked once more at Robey with a burning glare filled with malice, and Robey's suppressed giggle sunk in her chest as she remembered Amelia's warning to beware of Iris. Why, oh why, had she felt it her place to bring up such a subject as living arrangements for Graham? She had gotten her just desserts and on top of it, she realized, she had ruined any chance she had of winning Iris over. How stupid she had been!

The rest of the meal was accomplished in strained silence broken only by the tinkle of spoons stirring cream and sugar in the coffee cups.

Graham glanced at Robey and was interested to find her studying Iris very carefully. His eyes shifted from one to the other. Iris was pointedly keeping her eyes diverted from either of them, and he began to doubt the wisdom of having Robey here in the house. What would Iris do if they married? Since this afternoon, the idea had appealed to him more and more, but he would have to buck Iris and set up a separate household. Doubts piled high about a future that earlier had seemed so rosy and carefree.

Robey excused herself and ascended the stairs slowly. A warm leisurely bath restored her somewhat, but she wondered if her good intentions for Graham hadn't put an end to his trust in his sister. Maybe Iris was right, and she should leave. Everything was going wrong and getting so complicated.

Before dousing the light, she wrote a short letter to Lawrence. "Might as well burn a few more bridges," she said to herself softly.

Dear Lawrence,

This is strictly a business letter this time. I want to sell the house and the firm as soon as possible. Put out feelers in both New York and Vermont; we had offers from there for the business before Roger died. I want to make my assets as liquid as possible without touching my bonds, CDs and stock. I certainly don't intend running a construction firm from Knobbe Cove, and I think this is where I'll be staying. I just might go into the orphanage line of work. Pastor Hill wants to start one, and I think it is something I want to do, too.

Send a full report on the estate, too, as I intend taking charge of my finances. If needed, I'll hire someone here to help. Please send the report and information about any progress you make on the sale within the month.

I'll set up my files here, though I'll need all the papers involved in the estate—the sales, the firm, and, of course, the accident. I've given this a lot of thought. Believe me, it's not a last-minute decision. I know this will put an end to our business association, but I hope we'll always be friends.

Robey reread the letter several times before signing it and folding it into the envelope. It certainly did begin to shut the door on her past. She now felt anxious for his reply...and her fingers itched to put her signature on the sales contracts so she could get on with her plans for the future. Good old Lawrence, she mused, I'll miss being able to rely on him every time I need legal advice, but Chandor is just too far away. I know he'll understand.

After turning down the bedspread, Robey turned the lights off and stretched out, planning to spend some time thinking through Graham's plans. Instead, she found herself reflecting upon Roger, who seemed to be saying to her, "Go to it, old girl. I'm proud of you."

Sleep overtook her swiftly, but she was wakened in about an hour by a windstorm rattling shutters against the house. She quietly stepped over to the window, opened it and closed the black shutters, locking them. No sense having them bang all night. Once the window was shut, the house again fell into deep silence and Robey tried to summon sleep, but from somewhere in the house she heard water running. Her eyes scanned the bottom of her door. If anyone were in the upstairs bath or hall, or even downstairs in the kitchen, light would surely be seen, but there was none. Could it be Iris's friend was downstairs using the bath? Robey didn't want to cause any more trouble, but she felt uncomfortable having an unknown person in the house. She was certain Graham didn't know about him, and if she told him, she decided, it would start a frightful scene and probably culminate in her having to leave the house. There would be no living with Iris thereafter and that thought, in light of Graham's declaration of love, was most unwelcome. She decided to be more careful in the future and not jeopardize her position. She crawled back into bed and looked at the door, almost willing a light to be seen under it. Her head throbbed with unwelcome thoughts fleeting through, and she had to force herself to retreat to pleasant thoughts of a future life with Graham and the orphanage.

16

Iris took advantage of the early hours before either Graham or Robey awoke to write her own letter. Time was running out. It had been over four months since Robey Layne had intruded on her well-ordered existence and in spite of several occasions that should have sent her packing back to the familiar and loving arms of Lawrence LaPorte, it looked like she intended staying.

Iris reread Laporte's letter in which he declared his continuing love for Robey regardless of her absence in his life. He seemed genuinely eager to do something, anything,to get her to return to Chandor. Iris had to admit that Robey was hardly the skittish type. The attack at the graveyard was evidently long forgotten and even the bad fall she had experienced seemed to have healed in her mind, even if the bruises still showed. But now the situation was getting intolerable. Robey was pushing into areas that were dangerous and threatening to Ward, and this, Iris refused to countenance. Somehow, some way, Robey Layne had to go.

Iris outlined a plan to LaPorte and asked his help. She hoped she had impressed upon him that, if he were to have any hope of reclaiming Robey for himself, this would probably be his last chance. She had seen the glances passing between Graham and Robey and was sure she had not misinterpreted them.

Her plan was far from foolproof, she knew, but if it didn't
work, she was ready to take drastic steps she didn't even want to
think of now. But she would. Graham was getting far too fond
of Robey and that wasn't acceptable at all. 'Little boys,' she told
herself, 'especially Graham, never knew what was good for them.
He was always getting into trouble. Just look at what happened
with Amelia. He hadn't learned his lesson well, if at all.'

Grimly, she signed her name to the letter, placed it in an envelope and hid it in her purse. She'd mail it from the post office
tomorrow. With a sigh of relief, she arose from the table and set
the coffee pot on the stove burner. By this time next week Iris was
certain her troubles would be over and Robey Layne no longer a
problem.

Amelia and Robey sat across the table from each other in the
small tearoom of the hotel, crisp chef salads, small rum buns and
an iced tea comprising their lunch.

"You certainly look a lot better, Amelia," Robey smiled at her
friend.

"Gee, thanks, didn't know I looked that bad before!" Amelia
teased, knowing it had been a long time since she had reason to
really primp and preen. She had taken great pains with her appear-
ance for this lunch today, determined to start being more like the
old Amelia. Without David, she had her own life to live, and she
was going to live it.

"Didn't mean it that way, silly. It's just that you seem more
rested and relaxed. No more black rims under your eyes."

"Now that David's gone the house is quiet, and I've fallen into
a restful routine. My nerves don't jump every time I hear a car door
slam or footsteps coming up the walk."

"It must have been terrible for you," Robey sympathized.

"It was...like waiting for a beating. Did your mother ever do that to you?"

"What?" Robey was mystified at where the conversation was leading.

"Well, I remember once when I was little...do you remember when we stole the candy bar from Mr. Feldman's store?"

Robey laughed. "Oh yes, we were caught before we got out the front door, and he called our folks. Weren't we blatant failures as thieves?"

"We sure were, but Mama didn't spank me that day. She said she was busy making bread and it couldn't wait, but I'd get my spanking when she could get around to it. It took her four days before she finally plopped me across her knee and paddled me. In the meantime, for four days, every time she raised her arm or come toward me, I'd juke myself around and cover my head or jump a mile in the air. The paddling was nothing compared to those four days. I was a nervous wreck by the time I got my just punishment."

"I can imagine! How awful. Did she realize how bad it was making you feel?"

"I think so. I think she was trying to teach me that not all wrong things could be righted by a quick swat on the butt. But, getting back to the four days, it was like that with David. I just never knew when he'd show up and get verbally abusive. He only hit me that once. But I hate fights, get sick to my stomach when I see or hear someone fighting."

They ate in silence for a short while and then Robey, sensing Amelia didn't want to talk about David anymore, asked if she were going to go down to the fair and carnival.

"Not sure. I really have no one to go with, and it's no fun by yourself."

"We can go together if you want."

Amelia's face brightened but then she noticed a slight flash of regret in Robey's face, as if she were sorry she had asked. Looking hard into her friend's eyes, she knew instinctively what was up.

"Oh no, you go with Graham. I couldn't join you because of Iris, but you'll have a grand time."

"Can't hide anything from you, can I?" Robey blushed.

"Never could," Amelia agreed.

Robey became serious and lowered her voice. "Don't even know if anything will come of it, but I do know I've fallen in love with him."

"Does he know?"

"Yes, we've had a couple of talks. He puts so many obstacles in the way, and he'll have to resolve them himself. He's built so many walls around himself, the crutches, Iris. All those walls are so tall they'll be hard to tear down. I guess all I can do is wait and hope."

I'm so happy for you—at least I will be if everything works out."

"Thanks, Hon, but I still wish you could find a way to go to the celebration. We could bump into each other every so often."

"Well, maybe. I'll see." Amelia looked at her watch. "Gotta go. Dad Wentworth is coming by for a while. There're some repairs needed upstairs and he wants to see them, and he'll probably want to eat dinner at the house. You know, in some ways I hope he has news of David, and then, again, in some ways I don't."

The two walked arm-in-arm out into the bright June sun just as they used to do in what seemed another life altogether.

Amelia had been home for only a short time when her father-in-law parked his pickup in the back alley and entered the house by the kitchen door, tool chest in hand.

"Hi, Amy," he gave Amelia a quick hug and a peck on the cheek. "How's my girl holding up?"

"Okay, I guess. Just got back from a nice lunch with Robey down at the hotel."

"Good, good, glad to hear you finally decided to stop being such a hermit."

"Say, Dad. Just had a thought... now don't say 'No' for I'll feel terrible... but how's about you and me taking in the fair and carnival next week?"

Dad Wentworth smiled broadly, "When you put it like that, I can't refuse. Don't want you feeling terrible. However, it would be so nice if you'd said you just couldn't enjoy the day without my charming company!"

"I can't live without your charming company. There, I said it. Satisfied?"

In answer he put his arms around her shoulders and gave her a bear hug. Amelia looked adoringly at this man who was just an older version of David. Dark-haired still, in his late fifties, tall, muscular through hard physical work at his peanut farm, he was everything David wasn't: responsible, ambitious and, most of all, sober.

"How's David?" She asked warily.

"He's doing fine. I wanted to send him away to a private hospital to dry out, but he wouldn't go. Said it hadn't really done the job before."

"Is he with you?"

"He was for a short bit, but he decided to stay on the boat. I see him every now and then, and he does look better. Amelia, I think he's been sober for several weeks. He and Jim Parks are attending AA a couple of times a week. Pray for him, Amy."

"I'm glad for him, if he is. He was killing himself."

"He told me what happened. I was so ashamed of him. You know I never raised him to be that way," he took a screwdriver from his hip pocket and sat down at the kitchen table.

"No, you didn't, Dad, but you just never let him grow up."

"Huh? What do you mean?" He was obviously startled by Amelia's remark.

"You gave him everything. He never had to work for anything and never found out if he could succeed on his own. When he did try and failed, like we all do, he thought he was useless. He didn't know he could start all over and make it work. He felt he couldn't measure up to you or his friends."

"Come on, Amelia. Did I do that to him?"

"'Fraid so, dad. And the worst of it was when he failed me. I wouldn't say it was okay, kiss the hurt and make it better."

"Why not?"

"Because he needed to stand on his own two feet. I just didn't realize he couldn't help himself. He didn't have the experience of try and try again. With him, as a boy, it was try and if it didn't work out *you* made it alright. Or he didn't even have to try. He just asked, and with no effort of his own he had whatever it was he wanted."

"Boy, am I getting blamed for all this?" When Amelia didn't answer, he thought awhile in silence.

"Maybe you're right. I am at fault for that. But I can't change the past."

"No, you can't. I only told you this because...well, if David does pull himself out of his bottle by himself, don't you give him any rewards. He's got to know he did it for himself, by himself. He's got to respect himself or he'll go right back to drinking the first reversal he faces."

"Okay, Amy, I know you're right, but it's so hard to withhold from your only son. Maybe if his mother were still here," he sat mulling over what had just been said, then shrugged his shoulders. "I've got repairs to do, and it's getting late. We can talk more over that dinner I hope you'll cook for me."

Amelia watched him ascend the back stairs with his toolbox and then went to the refrigerator to take out a small roasting chicken. As she chopped celery and tore the bread into small bits, she thought of David, the way he used to be when they were first married. Breaking eggs, measuring, and seasoning was done automatically, with her mind down at the boat.

"We could have had so much," she muttered, "but it's all gone down the drain now." She angrily stuffed the dressing into the bird and shoved the pan into the oven. Sitting down at the table with a hot cup of coffee, she looked into the dark brown liquid as though she'd find some answers there. Funny, she thought, Robey and Graham seemed to be at a beginning, and David and I are at an end. The four of us could have been so happy as friends and neighbors. Why doesn't life ever come out even? Peace and happiness all around?

Lawrence LaPorte paced his office, occasionally stopping at his desk to pick up and re-read one or the other of the two letters he had received in the morning's mail. Both were from Knobbe Cove. They would require considerable thought and action.

Robey's letter was, he realized, a death knell to his financial security. Her orders to sell everything, the house, the business, and give a full accounting of her estate could not be ignored. Neither could it be complied with, not without disastrous results and consequences for him.

Why, he wondered, had he assumed Robey had no business sense just because she let Roger do things his way, or had she?

Looking back over the years he found many instances where an un-decided Roger one day had shown up the next adamantly insistent on just the right course of action. After he had talked it over with Robey? Obvious now. "What a fool I was," he sputtered aloud, "to think she'd come running back home after a couple of weeks on her own. She seemed so dependent, helpless, the way she just fell apart after the accident. I had to do everything for her. I guess I was never so wrong, was I?" He spoke aloud.

Gazing beyond the window which overlooked Chandor's downtown, he saw summer in full bloom. The warm weather had lulled him into a sense of well-being and Lawrence had felt he was just beginning to secure his future. Getting Robey back was all he had needed, but her letter had jarred him until his nerves jangled. When she finds out what he owes Roger's estate she could, and probably would, send him to prison and he'd be disbarred.

"Iris Hill is right. Time is running out."

Lawrence didn't like the tone of Iris's letter. The woman sound-ed slightly maniacal. Her plan might work, but if it didn't, he read a major threat to Robey's life between the lines. He would never let that happen, even if.... His thoughts jumped from the letter on the desk to a prison cell. Would he go along with murder?

He shook his head, trying to clear out what he knew were im-possible ideas put there by a devil of sorts. No, he wasn't the kind. He could never hurt Robey. But Iris could, of that he was certain. Could he, he wondered, stand by and let that happen?

17

"*I'*M GOING INTO SAVANNAH TO SHOP, BROTHER. Arnie Blake is coming by for me. He's going to see that new brooder stove he wants before he orders it. We'll be back about two."

"Hey, if you get near that new church bookstore, pick me up a catalog, will you? Save me from sending away for it. But don't go out of Arnie's way."

"If I remember rightly, the address of that place is just around the corner from the mall I'll be in. Be glad to. There's sandwich meat and gelatin salad in the icebox for lunch." To Iris all refrigerators were still iceboxes. She poked her change purse into her bag and checked to see if she had a clean handkerchief.

"I'll be glad to fix lunch," Robey began to offer but Graham interrupted.

"I won't be here either, Robey. I'm to speak at the University on the prophecy of Isaiah 5:3. Quite a deep subject to get one's teeth into, but I understand lunch is included on the menu, so I can get my teeth in that." Graham's poor attempt at levity was entirely lost on Iris, but Robey responded with a quick chuckle.

"It's okay. Leave me alone, I'll get by," Robey huffed good naturedly, ignoring Iris's obvious disapproval. An auto horn blared, and Iris stomped across the porch, leaving her brother and Robey standing in the doorway. After the car disappeared, Graham turned to face Robey.

"That was most unfortunate, the other night, especially Iris screaming at you that way. There was no reason for you not to ask about my sleeping downstairs." He gave an exasperated sigh. "I want you to be family here and there should be no secrets, but it's Iris's way. As you know, those rooms have been locked ever since I can remember, but that's not important. Iris is simply holding onto the past, and that's a problem she should be dealing with. I thought time would soften her feelings for you, and it hasn't. You've gone far out of your way to be friendly. Things seemed to be coming along pretty good for a bit. Sometimes I just don't understand her."

"I think I do, Graham. She should have been able to marry and have a family of her own to look after. She's frustrated and I also believe she senses our feelings have gone far beyond just friendship, and it frightens her."

"Come over here and sit down," Graham indicated the green striped cushioned glider on the porch. They sat down together, and the glider groaned and creaked as it began moving back and forth.

"I'll have to get Douglas to oil the hinges on this thing. I'd do it, but I don't even know where the oil can is. Do you get the idea I've let everyone else take control of my life since the accident?"

"That's understandable, especially since you have so many people around you who love you and want to do everything for you."

"Yes," he pursed his lips at her, "and make excuses for me just like you're doing."

They shifted their weight to get comfortable and the glider again protested audibly. Robey laughed and Graham reached over and took her hand, gently rubbing the back of it with his thumb.

Looking longingly at her shining face sprinkled with tiny freckles and framed by the auburn cap of hair which sparkled in the morning sun, Graham couldn't resist cupping her chin with his hand, drawing her close and kissing her lightly on her willing lips. He was aware of the delicate fragrance of her fresh scrubbed skin, which he could discern even above the roses and, running his hand up the side of her face, felt the coolness of her silky tresses. Their eyes locked for a moment and he put his arm around her, holding her close.

"The sinful thoughts I just had about you, Robey Layne me darling," he grinned.

"Like what? Should I ask?"

"You know the answer to that one without asking, I bet. But we'd be the scandal of all Georgia if I made love to you on the glider on the front porch of the manse!"

"Try me," she teased, touching his lips with her fingertips. The sensation sent flames shooting through Graham and he quickly grabbed his crutches, draped his arms over the padded foam and pushed the heels of his hands down on the crossbar. With a deft movement he stood.

"Oops," he exclaimed amusedly, "the Lodges are out on their front walk. If they saw us cuddling up, they'll tattle to Iris."

"Are you afraid of her, Graham?" Robey asked softly.

"No, not afraid. She's going to find out as soon as we decide what we're going to do. But until we finalize our own plans I don't want to upset her any more than she seems to be already."

"I guess you're right," Robey agreed. "Hey, it's getting on in time. I need to collect some of my clothes for the cleaners. Douglas said he'd take them for me if I got them out. I'll be over to the church later."

"Robey, if you'd rather, I could forgo lunch at the University.

It was just with a couple of old cronies after the lecture. We could eat downtown."

Robey almost agreed, an uneasy feeling nudged her. In her mind she paraphrased 'when the cats away' to 'when Iris is away Robey and Graham will play.' The last thing she wanted was for Iris to have more fuel for her hate fire. The time would come, and soon, when Iris would have to accept the relationship she and Graham had, but until then...

"No, I'll just have that sandwich and salad here."

"Okay, if you're sure," Graham started across the street and was surprised to find how disappointed he was.

Robey went back into the house, shut the door behind her and was enveloped by cool darkness. This was the first time she had ever been in the house alone. The quietness made her feel as though she were trespassing.

"I have every right to be here and look through," she said audibly to her reflection in the hall mirror as she stepped into Graham's office. It felt good to become familiar with things she had seen only with her eyes. She picked up pens and pencils, placing them in the old mug Graham kept on top of the desk for that purpose. She sat in his chair, rubbed her hands over the leather framed blotter, and stood up again, walking over to the library side of the room. Her slender fingers traced the titles on the book spines, "I'll no longer be a stranger in this room," she murmured quietly. "I'll feel completely comfortable here." In the few months she had lived here, Robey realized her path in the house had taken her only up to her own room, into the bath and into the kitchen for meals. Leisure time had been spent on the porch, in the yard, and only once or twice reading here while Graham finished up some phone calls for the church.

Out in the hallway the opened drawer of the dropleaf table

by the door revealed a few calling cards, some yellowed with age. The heavy oak doors to the parlor slid silently and easily into the wall pocket and Robey entered, breathing in the musty odor of a room seldom used. Several National Geographics were stacked on the shelf under a marble-topped end table and a doily, neatly embroidered and cut out, was spread over the top. Antimacassars laced the sofa back and arms. Overstuffed chairs were covered in colorful flowered chintz. Robey sat down on the divan and had an urge to stretch out and take a short morning nap. Only the prospect of a prolonged sleep betraying her and Iris finding her slumbering in her parlor squelched the inclination. Besides, she wanted to finish her exploring.

In the kitchen, the most familiar area other than her own bedroom, she opened each cabinet and drawer one at a time and became acquainted with Iris's filing system for her groceries and utensils. Iris was very efficient, Robey decided, since items were arranged to afford the least motion during preparation of a meal. Dishes were in the cupboard behind the table, pots and pans near the stove. She located the bread and sandwich meat Iris had referred to and put a jar of home canned applesauce into the refrigerator to cool.

As she passed Ward's door, she put her hand on the knob. It didn't turn, even a little. She stared hard at the defying door as though to open it with some magic word like Open Sesame, then shrugged her shoulders and went up the stairs. Standing on the landing at the top, she looked at the various doors she knew. Of course, she wouldn't go into Iris's room, that was unthinkable. She knew the linen closet would be locked, although she could not imagine why, and then her eyes rested on the fifth door, the one next to Iris's is room.

She turned to step into her own room when she realized that

door—the one usually locked, the one above Ward's room—was slightly ajar! She froze where she stood. Did she dare open the forbidden door and see what was behind it? It would be hours before Iris would return, and what if she *did* come back and find her in it? All she could do was cause a scene. Still, although Robey did not consider herself especially timid, there was a very mysterious air about the door. Mentally shaking herself, Robey walked over and resolutely put her hand on the knob. Taking a deep breath, she pushed the door open and, hearing nothing move, stepped in and positioned the door slightly ajar behind her. The room immediately became dark, just like her room before the shutters had been unnailed, and the feeling of claustrophobia swept over her. Slightly weak, she leaned against the door momentarily to steel herself and heard tumblers fall into place.

Robey turned and tried the knob. The door was locked! It wouldn't budge. "How foolish! How stupid! Why didn't I just leave the door open?" she admonished herself. Almost frantically she rattled the door, hoping it would open under her insistence. Another sound assailed her ears and she stopped deathly still, listening. Downstairs something or someone made a shuffling noise. Iris's houseguest? "This is what I get for being so nosey," she scolded. "But it's too late now, I'll just have to make myself known."

Her eyes were becoming accustomed to the dimness and she noticed a staircase leading down from the corner of the room and realized they were servant's backstairs common in old houses. Stepping rapidly across the room, her heels making a clatter on the rugless floor, she heard a door slam somewhere in the house. Her steps had brought her to the window with the missing shutter slats and she peered out through the opening just in time to see a man run past the rose garden. As he ran, he glanced back over his shoulder.

A gasp escaped Robey and her hand flew to her throat. It was the same man, with the pasty face and white hair! He was the one who had pushed her down and stolen her purse beside the cemetery! Why should he be here? Iris should know she was harboring someone capable of harm, if this was her guest. How could she tell her? Questions, unanswered, pummeled Robey's brain as she watched him disappear through the missing boards of the back fence. She forced herself away from the window, knowing she must free herself from a situation she was aware was growing into a possibly dangerous adventure.

Viewing the room with her back to the window, she noticed an unmade bed in the corner. A chifforobe disclosed, upon examination, several shirts and slacks neatly hung. An untidy pile of dog-eared picture magazines was on the floor by a well-worn upholstered chair.

Robey went to the top of the steep wooden steps and was very irritated with herself to find her knees weak as she started slowly down, trying not to make any unnecessary noise, although she was fairly certain there was now no one else in the house. Still, she didn't want to take any more chances than she had to.

On the bottom step she stopped and looked out over another room—the one behind the closed downstairs shutters. Ward's room. A linoleum top table and woven cane seat chair were in one corner and a small refrigerator stood nearby. Dishes were set out on another table covered with flaking oilcloth. At the end of the room a door stood open revealing the controversial bath. Robey walked out into the middle of the room, noting the old picture calendars that hung on every wall, some dating back several years. Looking into the dishes on the table, Robey realized the man had been ready to sit down to a breakfast of cold cereal and milk.

"He might be hungry and come right back. I'd better try to get out of here," Robey spoke aloud and then her eyes caught sight of something almost hidden behind a stack of magazines on the table. A compact, gemmed with rhinestones—her compact! She was tempted to retrieve her property but thought better of it. Maybe he would feel threatened if she took it and come after her again. Yes, much better to leave it where it was.

Sidling to the door to the inner hallway, Robey tried to turn the knob. The door was as unyielding from this side as it had been when she had tried the knob in the hall. Her toe hit something soft and she looked down to see newspapers stuffed under the bottom edge of the door. "So light won't shine out, I'll bet," she mumbled. "One thing is sure, he's not just an occasional overnight guest." Looking for how the man got out of the room, Robey could see no other door, but she *had* heard a door slam. She was certain he had not gone through the locked door and re-locked it from the hallway since the newspapers were in place on this side. Besides, he would have chanced running into Graham if he had gone into the house proper, unless he knew Graham was across town or, perhaps Graham knows about him, maybe even knew it was him at the cemetery that night. Robey felt near tears in her frustration but just then her eyes, now very used to the dimness of the room, rested on a metal handle in the floor behind and beneath the stairs. A trap door? That was what she had heard then. But where would it lead? She was almost too frightened to attempt to raise it, but if she were to get out of this fix, she felt she had better take a few more risks. After all, she couldn't just wait for her attacker to return!

Robey looked around the room for a weapon of some kind but saw nothing useful. There were spoons and forks, but no knives or anything she could use to protect herself, except possibly the pepper shaker. She screwed the top loose. If her attacker came back, Robey planned to throw the pepper in his face to give herself at least a chance to run.

Carefully she lifted the heavy door. The deep square hole opened to a ladder leading downward to a hard clay floor and light seeped from somewhere, the dim ray giving her enough courage to continue her nerve-jangling journey. Remembering the upstairs door that had locked so unfortunately behind her, repelling her into this precarious situation, she left the trap door open. If there was no way out, as a last resort she *could* break a window in the first-floor room. The musty odor that had roused her that night several weeks ago filled her nostrils and awareness swept away mental cobwebs. It must have been he, she gasped, who had been in her room that night. But how? Her door had been locked just as surely as his had been!

Looking around, Robey realized she was in the cellar where Douglas kept his gardening tools, and this is where his clothes got the musty odor. She found that the light came from the cellar doors which, she realized in relief, were never locked. They opened upward into the garden and, pushing hard over her head while standing on the couple of wood steps inside, the sunshine welcomed her to the warmth and freshness of the outside air. She quickly emerged and, thankfully, sat on the iron bench to catch her composure. She was almost afraid to look around, fearing that she would see piercing eyes peering at her through bushes or from across the fence. Steeling her shoulders, holding the topless pepper shaker at ready, she made a deliberate tour of the garden and was reassured that the pasty-faced man was nowhere around.

Uncertain of what her next step should be, she tried to put things in order. Robey now realized this was why Iris had become so upset at her invitation to Sarah and at Graham's insistence Sarah stay in Ward's old room. Recalling that conversation, Robey knew Graham was innocent of knowledge of the white-faced man and a certain amount of relief steadied her jumping nerves. In a showdown, perhaps she would have an ally in Graham, after all. Iris had a male friend and who could blame her? But Robey knew her brother would disapprove of the affair.

Robey couldn't help but wonder how Iris had been able to keep her relationship with the man a secret from Knobbe Cove, where any kind of scandal would probably spread faster than a flash flood. Maybe she should bide her time in confronting Iris with what she knew. Walking toward the front of the house, she brushed a cobweb from her skirt where it clung. The chimes of the University Clock, heard all over Knobbe Cove, rang out the hour of ten. Douglas was just leaving the church and caught sight of Robey going toward the front steps.

"Do you have your cleaning ready, Mizz Layne?" He shouted from the curb.

"Just a couple of minutes, Douglas. I almost forgot about it," she confessed, as indeed she had.

Hurrying upstairs to her room, she placed the pepper shaker on her nightstand, deciding to figure out later what to do with it. She swiftly gathered the winter clothes from the wardrobe. She was tempted to confide in Douglas of her adventure, but, after all, she had been snooping. If he mentioned it to Graham, the lid would be off, and she wasn't ready for battle with Iris yet.

Outside again, Robey instructed Douglas to have the cleaners keep her things in storage until she called for them in the fall. Douglas heaved the bundle into the back of his Jeepster. Robey had come to know the vehicle well. It usually carried plants, fishing equipment, tools, and children. The Jeep was seldom empty and never washed.

"If I cleaned it," Douglas grinned one day when Graham had asked point blank when the last time it had been washed, "kids with muddy feet and dogs wouldn't want to get in it. So, I leave it like it is."

Robey stood on the sidewalk and watched the spare tire on the back of the Jeepster disappear around the corner. Across the street, the blue uniformed postman dropped mail into the church box. Robey waited for him.

"Morning, Mrs. Layne, fine day."

"Yes, it is," Robey concurred. Didn't mailmen ever speak about anything besides the weather? He handed her two letters, touched the visor of his cap and, concentrating on the next piece of mail in his hand, entered the Lodge's yard next door. Robey knew that Mrs. Lodge was feeling poorly and decided to visit to see if there was anything she could do. She liked the Lodges and had been pleased to see a swarm of grandchildren on their lawn over Memorial Day. A pang of self-pity stabbed at her at the thought of a large family. Sally and Bud reached momentarily from beyond.

She glanced down at the letters in her hand. The top one was for her from Sarah. The second was for Iris, from, there was no return address, only the postmark Whitney. Again, it looked like Lawrence's handwriting. In fact, this time Robey was certain of it. Why would he write to Iris? Why wasn't it postmarked Chandor? Was he coming to Knobbe Cove? That was it! He wanted to surprise her and had written Iris. This solution was so comforting to Robey that all suspicion fled as the sun toasted her head and shoulders and logic took the place of doubt.

18

Robey knocked at the screen door of the Lodge home and saw the old man shuffle down the hallway. He stepped out onto the porch, his wrinkled face showing delight at her visit.

"Mother's on the sun porch doing some needlework," he explained as he led her around the outside of the porch to the garden side. The sunporch was enclosed with jalousie slats now slanting open to let in the fresh air. Mrs. Lodge started to rise, but Robey motioned her to remain seated as she slipped into a cushioned chaise beside a large jardinière containing a tall angel-wing begonia. Flowerpots and hanging baskets of fuchsia, ivy, and petunias flourished.

"What a lovely porch," Robey exclaimed. "You must enjoy it very much. So private, I can only see your garden from here."

"Yes, we do love to sit out here. Even in bad weather we can shut the slats and watch the storms come and go."

"You're home most of the time, aren't you?"

"Yes. Why?" Mrs. Lodge laid the intricate needlepoint sampler in her lap, folding her hands across it, giving Robey all her attention.

"Well, I just wondered if, perhaps, you might have seen a prowler at the Hill's house." Robey couldn't help but see a look of—was it fear?—pass between the old couple before Mrs. Lodge answered.

"No, never have. Why, was there one?"

Robey studied them both for a moment before continuing, deciding there was a definite air of secrecy in their attitudes. Cautiously, she said, "I thought I saw someone in the garden this morning and when I went out he was gone. I thought perhaps he might have run through the missing boards in the fence."

"Probably Douglas," Mr. Lodge, now rather redfaced, almost snapped.

"No, not Douglas," Robey smiled, trying to dismiss the subject. It just occurred to her that the Lodges knew about Iris's secret guest.

"Probably just my imagination. Roger, he was my husband, told me I should be a writer. I'm always finding mystery in everyday occurrences."

"Iris told us about your unfortunate state when you came here a few months ago—losing your husband and children," Mrs. Lodge sympathized. "It was enough to unbalance a person, I should think."

'Unbalance?' There was that innuendo that she was somehow disturbed and unable to cope, the same word Iris had used. Puzzlement gave way to dawning awareness that Iris had told them she was acting crazy, as she had probably written Lawrence. Poor Lawrence, he probably thought he was coming to rescue a Robey coming unglued at the edges! Fury welled within but was quickly dispelled at the sound of a door shutting somewhere inside the Lodge home. The Lodges heard it, too, for a fleeting glance between them signaled that there was, indeed, a conspiracy of sorts going on. Robey almost asked if they had a guest and decided she had been nosey enough for one day.

Bidding the couple 'good day' and thanking them for their hospitality, she left, sharply aware they had not asked her to come back. That they knew of the prowler, Robey was certain, but was the look Robey saw pass between them fear of the man, himself, or fear he might have been discovered?

While Robey was having her visit with the Lodges, Amelia had answered her phone and now stood with her hand on the receiver she had just replaced in the phone cradle. Tears stung her eyes. It had been several weeks since David had left home after that terrible scene.

"Only God knows what he's doing," she thought… "and now… and now he calls and asks to see me." She had agreed to see him, and she now heard his footsteps on the front porch. She realized he must have been across the street at the Perry's when he called.

Her heart leaped in compassion when she saw him. Thin, sallow, as though he hadn't eaten in days. 'David, oh David,' she anguished to herself, 'what have you done to yourself?' She wanted to take him in her arms and comfort him.

"Amelia," his eyes, dull from obvious distress, dropped in shame and his head bowed. "I've no right to come, none at all, but I had to, just had to."

"Sit down, David," Amelia struggled to be calm and detached for the two of them. David sat gingerly on the edge of the straight ladder-backed chair by the door. Amelia stood, looking down at the cold hearth, thinking it would be easier for David to talk if she didn't face him.

"First," David began, "let me say it has been over five weeks since I've had a drink. I know that's not long, but it's a beginning. When you deliberately try to kill yourself in a bottle of booze as I've done and you come to the realization you don't really want to die… well," he hesitated and stood up and began pacing the room. Amelia turned to face him, seeing in the set of his jaw a determination she had never seen before.

"Did your father help you come to that conclusion?"

"No, I think he knew I'd have to make the decision myself. He kind of stayed in the background to catch me, I suppose, if I went too far. No, I had to do the rescuing myself. I would have no self-respect if I hadn't. That was what was wrong the last time I tried to dry out, before I met you. *They* did it all at the rehab and when I came out I was a product of *their* efforts and I resented it."

Amelia raised her eyes to the clock on the mantlepiece and absently put the key in the hole and wound it. At long last, a contrite David. A David who had never before even admitted to her that he had a problem. But all she had read about alcoholics—and it had been volumes—told her to beware of believing contrite words.

David continued. "After I got over the DT's down on the boat, I faced some pretty awful truths, and the most terrible was what I did to you and our baby."

Amelia's whole body tensed. Then it was David at the wheel of the boat! Oh, God, no…not that. She had never believed it! Her hand came to her mouth to suppress a sob and she bit hard on her knuckles. What should I do now? Her mind spun in the dizzying revelation, David can't possibly be asking me to forgive him that, could he?

"Amelia, I wasn't in that boat. You have no reason to believe me, I know, but I wasn't." David had sensed her unasked question. "But if I had been sober, a responsible husband, you would never have been in that boat with Graham Hill and our baby would not have died."

"*Our* baby, David?" Amelia asked bitterly, "you were never quite sure of that, were you?"

"I deserve that, Amy. But I knew, I know... the baby was ours...yours and mine. I just wanted to punish you for going to work, I guess. For relying on Graham Hill, not me, when you couldn't rely on me at all. That's what makes my actions so... so..." he searched for the right word, "reprehensible and, of course unforgivable."

"What started this pilgrimage back?" Amelia sat down on the sofa, trying not to be too understanding too quickly. 'Be cool, girl, and detached. Don't be suckered by pity,' she cautioned herself.

"I've hit bottom. That's where you have to go, you know, before you can look up. And when I did, there was nothing to face but the truth. No more of Iris Hill's lies to fall back on as an excuse for another drink. I guess when I heard what was beginning to go around about Robey and Graham, a bell rang. I had heard it all before...it was repetition and... Oh, Amy, I went through hell when I began facing the glaring truths...and forced myself to face each one...one at a time...and found myself so wanting. So wrong. So wrong." His voice barely made it beyond his lips, and his head fell into his hands in humiliation and great sobs wracked him and his shoulder shook.

Amelia sat stunned. She had not been ready for any kind of confrontation this morning, and she wasn't certain she should even be listening.

"I'm not asking to come back, Amy. I have no right after the years I deliberately did everything I could to kill your love. At least I did that thoroughly. But I had to let you know I realize how wrong I was, and I'll do no more to hurt you." He stood up, squared his shoulders and dried his eyes with a handkerchief he extracted from his hip pocket.

"What will you do now?" Amelia's chin trembled and she steadied herself by leaning against the side of the fireplace.

"Dad is going to bail me out again financially. I'll work with him on the farm for a while and then…maybe another bookstore somewhere else."

An awkward pause permeated the room causing the couple to momentarily become a tableau of silence. David broke the tension by starting toward the front door.

"Goodbye, Amy. I'll keep in touch through dad. I'll not bother you anymore."

'Let him go, girl,' Amelia's mind whirled, 'let him go.'

David put his hand on the doorknob and turned it, glancing back for one last look at the small blonde woman who was still his wife in fact, if not in her heart.

'Face it,' Amelia thought, 'I still love him dearly and it's still till death do us part!' "David, don't go," she almost whispered, "don't go. I can't bear to have you walk out that door again. Don't!"

David turned in disbelief, joy animating the once ashen face. "Are you sure, Amy? Oh, Amy, are you sure?"

Not waiting for her answer, he rushed toward her as she also came open armed to him and, tears flowing, laughter choking them, they sank to the floor, their knees too weak to stand. He kissed her eyelids and cheeks and hungrily kissed her mouth as she responded as, it seemed, they had never done before, not even at the beginning when they had been so sure of themselves. This was total give in…a rebirth…a vow of renewal of trust that rose above all the reaching and grasping forces that had almost pulled him into unfathomable and lonely purgatory.

19

Saturday burst upon Knobbe Cove with warm breezes and a brilliant sun. Euphoric contentment wrapped Robey as she stretched each waking limb one by one, still under the feathery feel of the light flannel sheet. A broad smile broke across her face when she remembered the phone call she had received from Amelia just before retiring. The joy transmitted over the line permeated her now, and she felt so thankful that things would probably work out wonderfully for the Wentworths. Her friend had sounded like a bride again. A thrill of pleasure prickled Robey's whole body.

Even before sliding her feet from under the covers into the gold satin slippers waiting beside the bed, she heard sounds of gaiety drifting through the open windows. Several cars raced past the house, horns blaring and streamers flying. Robey looked at her clock. 7:30 AM! Graham had warned this yearly celebration started early, but she hadn't believed it would be quite this close to dawn. She hurried her bath and donned bright red Bermuda shorts and a flowered blouse, slipping her bare feet into white canvas ducks.

In the kitchen Graham poured maple syrup over browned French toast and speared spicy links of sausage with his fork. Iris held a mug of coffee in her hand and leaned across the sink to watch what activities she could from the side window.

"Morning, everybody," Robey greeted them.

Iris turned from her station and threw a very bright "morning, Robey," her way. The cheerful tone of her voice took both Robey and Graham by surprise and Graham raised his eyebrows and gulped some hot coffee, trying hard not to let on to Iris that he felt her warm greeting unusual.

"Do you see all those people already? Where do they come from, Iris?" Robey purposely addressed the older woman. Robey had felt a turning of the tide in their relationship in the past few days, but she hadn't decided whether it was the influence of the upcoming celebration or Lawrence's letter that had worked the wonder.

"They come from Savannah. Well, really, I guess, from all over. Soon the parents of the students will get here, too. Most will be taking their students back home with them, since graduation at the University was last night. Summer vacation officially began a day or two ago for most."

"By midmorning they're all here," Graham added, holding out his cup for Iris to fill. "The parade starts about 10:00 AM."

Robey was caught up in the excitement so favorably touching Iris. "It's been a long time since I've thought about parades. Sally and Bud used to love them. We'd go far and wide to attend even the small fire company parades."

Graham grinned, showing the lines in his cheek that probably had passed for a deep dimple as a child. "You'll see fire engines, majorettes, the school band and a few visiting bands, and maybe even some homemade floats—the whole shebang. The parade forms at the carnival grounds, circles Knobbe Cove, and ends up back where it started. The carnival came in last night and set up in the lot next to the old railroad depot."

"Everyone will have to go past here then, won't they?"

"No, not all. There's a back path leading down to Main Street behind the Catholic Church."

Iris placed a hot plate of the French toast and sausage in front of Robey who eagerly spread butter and syrup on it while inhaling the aroma of the fresh brewed coffee.

"We'll have lunch at the Cove," Graham pushed his plate away. "Iris says she'll pack it for us. Let's head down now and see the doings." He rose from his chair, anxious as a schoolboy to get going.

"This early? It's only a little past eight! Besides, I want to finish my toast first, Graham. I'm hungry and this is too good to leave, and I should help Iris with the dishes and the lunch."

"No, you go on, Robey. I'll manage better by myself."

"But aren't you coming with us?"

"No, I don't think so, not this early. I'll meet you on the school steps about twelve o'clock with the lunch. I like to sit out front and watch the people go by in the morning. The parade will come by here, and I'll have a grandstand seat."

"But they won't be giving their all until they're on Main Street, Iris," Graham protested.

"That's just fine. I'll be able to hear from the porch," Iris was adamant.

Robey downed the last of her coffee, and she and Graham joined the growing traffic toward the Cove.

"Iris likes to see people, but not be in the crowds, and she'll get to view everything anyway."

"I like crowds," Robey laughed as she was jostled by two little boys eagerly running past.

"So do I," Graham agreed, "if I don't get knocked down!" Nevertheless, he covered a remarkable amount of ground on his crutches. Robey had trouble keeping up with him and occasionally had to skip a step or two.

Cars were already parking on back streets, their occupants carrying blankets and ice coolers. When Robey and Graham reached the Cove, Robey noticed all the boats were moored to the dock. None were away from shore. She remarked on it to Graham.

"They'll stay there until after the festivities and lunch. Then they'll *all* go out for a race around the island."

"Isn't it dangerous with so many?" It looked to Robey that there were more than one hundred boats tied at the piers as, indeed, there were.

"No, only ten boats in each class race at one time. The winner of each heat then races for a grand trophy in that class."

"How many classes are there?"

"Three—small outboard, large outboard, and inboard—which takes in a couple of goodly sized yachts. It's kind of uneven, but fun, and no one really takes it too seriously."

Young couples holding hands and families carrying babes in arms herding older youngsters ahead of them all headed for the Cove. Here and there families staked out claims to the curb for the parade, spreading towels, sitting on webbed lawn chairs, and placing coolers of drinks and lunch where they intended to come back to stay. The colorful clothing and wispy scarves tied around shining faces added to the festive air. Robey could not help but think how Roger and the children would have loved this day in Knobbe Cove and a tight knot wrenched at her heart for a fleeting moment. The sound of hawkers extolling their wares jolted her attention away from the reverie. Graham tugged at her sleeve and pointed toward a juggler mesmerizing some children by the movie theater.

"Let's go watch."

They strolled to the corner, keeping on the edge of the crowd gathered around the juggler who was now throwing oranges,

apples and large lollipops into the air. From where they stood
Robey could see handcraft booths fencing the school yard, making their own lanes across the grass. Every available space on Main
Street boasted of food or craft booth, and they were already doing
a brisk business. Balloon salesmen stood on corners or wandered
through crowds, their red, green, and blue helium-filled bubbles
bobbing high over their heads. Carnival people sold plastic kewpie
dolls clothed in pink and blue feathers. Cotton candy, popcorn,
and caramel apple stands competed at the end of the path which
led back to the carnival.

Robey seemed to be constantly smiling and Graham watched
with delighted eyes. The mantle of grief and worry she had worn
ever since coming to Knobbe Cove seemed to have finally slipped
entirely from her slender shoulders and a radiant woman now joy-
fully wandered from booth to booth purchasing a few memen-
toes.

"This is for Sarah," she said, shaking out a white hand-
crocheted shawl edged with three shades of green and gold. The
vendor folded the item and pushed it into a brown paper bag.
As she accepted the package, Robey's eyes caught sight of David
and Amelia walking toward her, their faces wreathed in joy.

"Robey!" Amelia shouted, raising her hand in greeting, "Wait
up."

Robey and Graham spun around to greet them, and Amelia
and Robey hugged. Robey reached up and kissed David on the
cheek. Several people stopped to watch the exuberant reunion, but
they didn't mind. Taking David's hand in her right and Amelia's in
her left, Robey swung their arms just like a little kid.

It was David who remembered Graham standing just a few
steps away, watching the scene.

"Pastor Hill," he let go of Robey's hand, "Come on with us and let's get back to where dad is holding a choice spot for the parade. We've got a lot to talk over, don't we?"

"Yes, do come," Amelia invited, openly happy to see Graham. "It *has* been so long since we've seen each other. How wonderful it will be with the four…the five of us," she amended when she caught sight of dad Wentworth sitting amid a number of cushions, blankets, and folded sweaters marking out the spaces he was saving for them.

Dad Wentworth stood up as the group approached, extending his hand in greeting. Graham took it, giving a hearty shake and remarking on what a good job he had done picking out a viewing site. People who had come to know Robey stopped to chat and everyone seemed to feel it was their duty to give a complete program of events. Even Pop and Mom Kaslav had managed to walk down to the Cove and sat under a large umbrella scanning the sidewalks teeming with citizenry in their promenade. Many stopped to chat and shake Pop's hand and pat the misses on the shoulder, conveying a closeness Robey realized had never existed in Chandor. A nagging memory chipped away at the corner of her happiness. What was trying to come to the surface? Try as she would to recall, whatever it was kept behind the sound and scenes that closed in and jostled her from all sides.

Trumpets blared the air and bass drums marched down Church Street, making the turn toward Main. People began applauding, whistling and stretching their necks to get a first glimpse of the strutting band. Floats pulled by farm tractors chugged down the street. Horses in best saddlery pranced by and clowns threw out handfuls of candy and gum. Cheers were continually voiced for favorite bands or for marchers personally known by someone on the sidelines. Kids rode by on bicycles festooned with bright crepe paper. Robey allowed herself to laugh so hard tears came to her eyes. She spent much of the time holding one of the Lodge grandchildren on her lap and pointing out the clowns. It felt so good to hold a child again.

When the parade was over they stood to go back to the booths. Graham was the first to point out Iris in the crowd. She was standing by the walk leading to the school waiting for them to come to her. Robey couldn't believe it was already lunchtime. Having asked Graham and Robey to dinner on Tuesday afternoon and received an acceptance, Amelia, along with David and Dad Wentworth diplomatically turned away and headed toward the carnival grounds without Iris seeing them.

Iris saw Graham and Robey approaching and spread an Indian blanket on the ground. They all sat down, delving hungrily into the lunch hamper she had provided. Robey showed Iris Sarah's shawl and the handmade wooden puzzles she had purchased for Sarah's boys. She was amazed at the change in Iris, who almost bubbled into light over the gifts and seemed as though there had never been anything but sweetness and goodwill in their relationship. Robey, now totally caught up in the noise and revelry of the festival, was exultantly free from yesterday's gloom. She watched children run and play but for once did not search for Sally or Bud. Many faces, she found, were now no longer strangers. Graham gloried in their closeness and hoped it could last forever. He raised a bottle of cola and proposed a toast. Both Robey and Iris joined him, but before the bottle met his lips, forever had come to an end. Robey stopped drinking her cola, her arm still holding the bottle to her mouth, as she stared at the sight of a man approaching from the dock. He was still quite far away, but it was Lawrence, of this she was certain. That is…she hesitated…he looked like Lawrence. As he neared, she could see that it wasn't, but she knew now what had been in the back of her mind. She had been looking for Lawrence in the crowd. She became anxious now to find him.

"Iris," she blurted out, "did you get a letter from Lawrence LaPorte the other day?"

Iris nearly dropped her sandwich and flushed deeply. "Me? Get a letter from Lawrence LaPorte? He's *your* attorney, isn't he? What would he be doing writing me?"

Graham looked from one woman to the other, sensing the return of tension and an intangible current of mystery.

"Yes, but a letter came for you, and I'd swear it was his hand-writing on the envelope."

"Of course not, *No!*" Iris was emphatic. "He'd have no call to write me." Iris was visibly irritated and by the tone of her voice Robey knew the spell of the afternoon had been irrevocably broken.

Robey chastised herself. 'Why did I mention that? I've spoiled the day.' Aloud she acted disappointed. "I just thought maybe he was going to surprise me, and he had let you know, that's all."

"Iris "humphed" and picked up another sandwich, soothed a bit by Robey's explanation. Although the day continued in a friendly spirit, it never recaptured the magic shared earlier.

Noises exploded the quiet as regatta boats began to churn the saltwater, spraying the air. A brisk East wind chopped the Bay and small craft with raised prows smacked the waves, cutting across backwash from competitors. By the time the races were finished, and the last trophy presented, the sun was low on the horizon and long shadows cooled the early evening. On the dock amplifiers were set up for the country western band hired for the street dance. Churches opened their doors to serve dinners in spacious meeting halls. Both Robey and Iris spent a couple of hours serving food where chairs, set in rows by tables, were soon filled with hungry people.

Pop and Ma Kaslav entered, thumping on backs, exclaiming on the parade and events, and made their way to Iris's tables. Robey smiled at them from across the room and Pop Kaslav waved, his face shiny red with excitement.

"Now there's a real wonderful girl," he told Iris. "Wouldn't it be nice if she and the Reverend got married?"

Iris's face darkened and she nearly choked in anger. Robey, from her position several tables away, could tell Iris was distraught but couldn't hear the conversation.

"Now, now. You'll have to excuse him, Miss Hill," Ma cooed, "He's always matchmaking. Far as I know none of the couples he's paired has ever actually gotten hitched."

"Could be a first time," Mr. Kaslav persisted. Iris looked over at Robey and Robey could see the thunder in her face. Curiosity as to what had happened nagged at her, but she knew she had already pushed her limit for getting questions answered today. She turned to take some dishes back into the kitchen where she stayed, elbow deep in hot soothing suds.

After the last dinner was served and the doors closed, Iris went home to sit on the porch. Robey and Graham walked over to the carnival grounds. The tinkling music from the merry-go-round could be heard over the rumble of voices and laughter. Barkers loudly extolled the advantages of their pitch-penny booths and bingo tents. Squeals pierced the air from the funhouse where spotlights streamed illumination over millions of tiny gnats and moths dancing and swirling like dervishes in their warmth.

"Do you want to try out one of the rides, Robey?"

"No, I'd rather watch. It's more fun when you have little ones with you. Maybe after we get the orphanage we can bring them all. Wouldn't that be wonderful?"

"My, aren't we the dreamer tonight?" Graham chided. "But you're right. You really should be a kid to get a thrill out of the Whip-the -whip."

"I suppose a few oldies would give us an argument on that," Robey pointed towards the Kaslavs as they were locked into their seats on the Ferris wheel.

Graham indicated a bench facing the midway. "Let's sit over there." They sat, content to be two people sharing all within their view. The aroma of sizzling hot dogs mingled with buttered popcorn and barbecued chicken coming from the American Legion booth.

Robey's eyes, sweeping the panorama of the midway, suddenly caught sight of a man stooping to pick up something from the ground. She stiffened in shock as she looked harder, her eyes narrowing to focus upon him in the twilight.

"What's the matter?" Robey's obvious apprehension had not been lost on Graham.

"That man, see?" Robey pointed towards the funhouse where the man now stood propped against a billboard, his eyes evidently on the Ferris wheel.

Graham followed her direction and saw him, too. "The white-haired fellow?"

"Yes, well, I've seen him before...he," she hesitated, not wanting to give Iris's secret away, but still sensing the fear she felt both times she had encountered him.

"Where did you see him?" Graham prodded.

"He's the man who...attacked me at the cemetery that night."

"What? Are you sure?"

"I will never forget him, not ever."

"The Sheriff went into the bingo tent just a few minutes ago. I'll go get him." Graham started to rise, but Robey didn't move.

"Robey," Graham shook her arm, "did you hear me? The Sheriff."

"Yes, Graham, I heard. But I don't think we'd better get the Sheriff. I mean, maybe it's not that important."

"What do you mean, not important?" Graham had felt a surge of protection for Robey and was puzzled she wouldn't let him act. He sat back down beside her, looking deep into her face. "Why not?"

"Well," she hesitated, deep sigh shuddering her body, "I guess I'd better tell you." She slowly and carefully related her experience with the locked doors, the trap door, and the man who ran across the rose garden.

Graham was at first speechless and only stared toward the funhouse where the man could no longer be seen. While they had hesitated, he had disappeared. Graham's eyes searched the ground swiftly as he listened. As Robey's story came to an end, a few minutes passed while he seemed to be digesting all she had told him. Robey was grateful for the time of silence between them.

"You're saying Iris knows your attacker?" Graham sounded incre-dulous. "You must be mistaken. She wouldn't hide a felon in the house. You haven't been here long, Robey, but you should know that."

"I didn't say she knew he was my attacker, Graham, but there's no mistake." Robey bristled at Graham's doubting her story and his defense of Iris. Being disbelieved was a new sensation, and it had never occurred to her Graham wouldn't believe her. He watched her face and read her thoughts.

"Robey, I don't want to disbelieve you..."

Robey didn't give him time to finish. "You don't want to disbelieve me but, nevertheless, you do."

"What I was trying to say is, and I guess I'm doing badly trying to explain is that I want to believe you because...but," he reached out and took her hand and she left it enclosed in his strong grasp.

"After all, Iris raised me. When the boating accident happened, she nursed me back to health. When all the rumors swept Knobbe Cove about me and Amelia...oh, yes, I heard them all," he responded to a look of shock from Robey, "she stood up for me. What I would have done without her, I'll never know."

Robey listened and saw Graham in a different light. She almost told him that it was Iris who had spread those rumors to begin with, but instinctively knew he wouldn't believe that either. Here beside her, she decided, was a man tied to his sister with bonds much stronger than apron strings, ready to subject himself to her protection like a pup not yet willing to give up the teat. She stood up and started for home.

'Home', she thought to herself. 'I'd best move on. Try again somewhere else. Run, as Lawrence would call it.' Tears stung her eyes and she was so frustrated she shook. Nothing was said between them as they made their way back, Robey considerably ahead of Graham.

Graham was miserable, realizing he had put everything he wanted to say the wrong way. He loved Robey, he told himself. He loved Iris, too. Almost like a parent. What was it the Bible said? Leave your mother and father and cleave unto your wife? Perhaps Iris could clear up everything. He intended to ask.

Robey heard Graham's crutches coming up behind her and slowed to let him catch up. She didn't want Iris to think they had had a falling out, not yet. Arriving at the front walk of the house, they found Iris on the glider, her fingers busy knitting navy blue yarn into a sweater.

"Iris," Graham almost breathlessly spoke as they reached the porch steps, "Robey tells me you have had a visitor I didn't know about."

Iris's hands stopped their work but, except for an icy stare at

Robey, she didn't give any indication of guilt. Robey looked hard at Graham, trying to measure the man. At least he was trying to get the air cleared, regardless of consequences. For that she was glad.

"Mrs. Layne is mistaken, Brother." Iris quietly lied. "I've had no visitors. Just who did she say it was?" Iris spoke as though Robey were invisible, forcing Graham to reply in kind.

"She claims he is the man who tried to rob her at the cemetery." Graham sat down on the top step and Robey stood by the railing, not savoring the sound of the discussion.

"It seems to me Mrs. Layne has quite an imagination, Brother. If a man were going to go to all the trouble of stealing her purse, he surely wouldn't have left it untouched on a tombstone." Robey's heart leaped as she realized Iris was trying to throw doubt on the attack itself. Graham didn't answer but looked up at Robey as though to say there was logic to Iris's words. Robey wanted to scream at them that she was telling the truth but kept silent, her stance erect, and chin tilted upward.

After a short silence, Robey, in grim determination said, "Let's look at the rooms where he stays, then. You'll see, Graham. Someone has been living there all along, I'd say."

Iris rose slowly, deliberately taking time to stuff the sweater, yarn and needles into the tote bag beside her on the glider.

"I want you to know, Mrs. Layne, I most certainly do not appreciate you putting me in such a ridiculous position, having to prove to you, like a child…" Iris searched for further words, but Graham interrupted.

"Let's go anyway, Iris, and set this thing to rest."

Robey had a hard time masking the victory she felt as she followed the two into the house and down the hallway to the locked door next to the kitchen. Iris produced the small brass key from her pocket which had hung on a nail by the refrigerator. She hesitated at the door and looked silently at Graham as if to ask whether she really needed to continue, then, she resignedly inserted the key in the keyhole and turned the brass knob. The door swung reluctantly open and the three stepped inside. Iris, flipping the switch by the jam, flooded the room with light. Robey could barely believe her eyes. Everything was covered with dust cloths!

The refrigerator, of course, it would have food in it. She covered the width of the room in long strides and opened the door. It was empty, entirely, although it was plugged in and cold.

"I keep it running," Iris anticipated Robey's question with a smirk on her lips. "It's not good for them to stay unused. They get a sour smell. Often in the summer, when the women of the church have their picnics, things are stored there, like soft drinks."

A sinking feeling struck Robey in her stomach and she knew it was useless to insist upon going upstairs. Iris had, she was sure, sufficient time to rid the room of any sign of human habitation. She felt helpless and vulnerable and she fought back the tears that welled to her eyes. How did Iris find out that she had been there? Of course, the man had told her himself, or perhaps she had come to that conclusion on missing the pepper shaker.

Graham leaned on his crutches and swung back into the hallway, silent in his thoughts.

"It's alright, Mrs. Layne," Iris smiled solicitously, "You've been working too much. All these new people to meet and, remember, it hasn't been too long since your great loss." She put her arm around Robey's shoulder in a gesture of condolence and eased her out the door, locking it firmly behind her.

"What are you trying to say, Iris?" Robey shook herself from Iris's embrace and spoke sharply. "That I'm crazy? Is that it?"

"No, not at all. Just tired and confused. We all get that way sometimes."

"Iris is probably right, Robey. Let's go back out on the porch and forget all this for a while."

The sky was lit by carnival spotlights and shadowy clouds scudded through the deep salmon sky. They stood for a moment together and watched people streaming past the house. Robey's eyes saw, but did not completely comprehend the stuffed bears, cotton candy and taggy apples dotting the promenade with color. How joyful the world appeared outside her own troubled island.

Iris sat back down on the glider and resumed her needlework, glancing at Robey from time to time through lowered lids. Graham went across the street to the church to make sure the tables were folded, chairs stacked, and trash picked up after the dinner. Robey slumped on the porch, her legs dangling over the edge.

'No,' she shouted to herself, 'I will not accept I didn't experience or see what I saw. If there is any one solid fact to be certain of, it was that everything that has happened to me since coming to Knobbe Cove is real. What's not clear,' she mused, 'is what really happened before I came.'

Questions bombarded her. What had really occurred between Graham and Amelia? Or Amelia and David? Who did cause the accident on the Bay? Who was the white-faced man? Her thoughts reached back to what seemed so long ago but was actually only a short couple of months. Her natural caution warned her to leave, get away, but Lawrence's voice kept coming back. 'You're running away, you know that don't you, Robey? A heavy fatigue, brought on by both the day's excitement and the evening stress, made every bone of her body ache to retire to her bedroom and without even saying anything to Iris or waiting for Graham's return, she went into the house and climbed the stairs to bed.

Across the street, Graham sat looking out the window trying

to put the day's events into perspective. He felt ashamed for doubting Iris, but had so wanted to believe in Robey. He remembered a conversation he had overheard in the barbershop the other day in which he had been bluntly asked by Jolie Burgess if his new secretary were having 'nerve troubles'—as though he had taken in someone in need of mental therapy. He recalled the first day in the office. She had seemed so shaky before he had offered her the job.

"Strange," he said aloud, "all this just makes me want to protect her and help her get well. I guess it's love, after all." From the window he watched Robey get up and go into the house and saw Iris turn her head and watch her leaving. He was surprised to realize she had a smug smile on her face as though thoroughly and greatly satisfied with something she had done. His mind whirled in the predicament he found himself, and he wondered how and what he could do to make it right.

It was mid-morning before Robey walked slowly downtown. Signs of yesterday's celebration littered the streets. She did not want to go to the church first and face Graham. There was so much to think about and so many decisions to make. She headed for the Cove, certain that she could better ponder with the smell of saltwater and the loneliness of a bench along the dock. Rounding the corner at Main Street she caught a glimpse of Iris entering the hotel. Robey was startled since she was not aware Iris had left the house. She decided to investigate but waited a few minutes before following. Iris was not in the lobby or the coffee shop, so Robey walked over to the desk. The register was facing her, and she looked down. The name jumped from the page, and Robey felt a quickening of her pulse—Lawrence LaPorte. He was here. She wasn't seeing illusions, or imagining things, the letters to Iris had been from him. The hotel clerk, Bobby Ross, came into the lobby with a foam cup of coffee in his hand and saw her standing there.

"Mrs. Layne, can I help you? I didn't hear the call bell."

"I didn't ring it, Bobby. I was just looking for someone." She knew Iris shouldn't find her there. Why, she didn't know, but intuitively she felt Lawrence wouldn't like her finding out about his surprise visit ahead of time.

"Can I help?" Bobby's voice broke into her thoughts.

"No. It's alright. I've found out what I needed to know," Robey mumbled as she turned swiftly and left, as though someone were close up on her heels.

20

GLARING SUN FLASHED ON THE CAR WINDSHIELD parked in front of the hotel, and the reflection made Robey blink, temporarily blinding her as she rushed away. Speeding up Second Avenue, she rubbed her watering eyes trying to erase the effects of the sun flash. Before she realized where she had fled, she found herself at the Railroad and Second Avenue intersection. Maybe, she pondered, it would be a good thing to talk all this over with Amelia. She really felt drawn to her now, like old times. Maybe they could work out her problem by putting their heads together in a gabfest.

Transformation had taken place at the Wentworth home. Shutters lay flat against the outside walls and the windows sparkled in the morning brightness. Doors stood open welcoming fresh air, and curtains moved gracefully in the breeze. How beautiful it all looked compared to the austere face presented to Robey the first time she visited.

Amelia greeted her from the side flower bed and drew her quickly through the front door and into the living room.

"How about a cold lemonade? I just made some hoping David would come home to lunch early." Not waiting for a reply, she darted into the back of the house and returned in what seemed only seconds later laden with a tray on which a pitcher and two tall glasses reposed.

"Did I see a furrowed brow as you came in the yard?" Amelia handed a frosty drink to her friend. Robey took a quick gulp and was thankful Amelia was so perceptive. Plunging in, she related the happenings since they parted at the parade, especially how Iris kept intimating she might be imagining things.

"Do I look like I'm losing my mind?" Robey asked in exasperation.

"Of course not, you're no crazier than you usually are!" Amelia teased. Then, getting serious, she added, "Let's talk about the white-faced man. I'm certain he's the man who was piloting David's boat. There just was no other way to describe him."

"But wouldn't he change in all that time? It's been five years!"

"Not if... if," Amelia stood up, pacing the floor and pounding her fist into the palm of her hand.

"If, what?" Robey urged anxiously. "Do you have an idea who he is?"

"It might be far-fetched, but what if this man is Ward and he stays inside all the time?"

"The brother? But he's been in a mental institution all this time."

"Do you know for sure?" Amelia's eyebrows raised and her long hair swished around her face as she pivoted back across the room.

"No... no," Robey had to admit. "And Graham wouldn't know for sure, either. When he saw him at the carnival he wanted to get the Sheriff to arrest him. I wish I had let him. The mystery might be cleared up by now."

"From what I know, Graham was only about five years old when Ward was sent to the institution. Far as I know he's never seen his brother as an adult."

Robey placed her empty glass back on the tray and wandered to the window deep in thought. After a few seconds, she turned back to face Amelia, now sitting on the sofa.

"Graham described Ward as hopeless when he talked to me about him. No, I think we're way off the beam on that score but, for sure, Iris knows him. You should have seen her face!"

"What if she tried to scare you off by hiring the man to do the purse snatching?"

"Then, just leaving the bag on the tombstone would seem to fit in. He didn't really intend to steal it, only maybe to scare me enough to head home to Chandor...make me too frightened to stay. Did I tell you my compact was on the table in his room?" Robey became elated. The puzzle pieces seemed to be falling into place, only they were so melodramatic and unproven she still felt it would be a long time before she got any answers.

The back door slammed shut and David strode into the room from the kitchen. He stopped by the living room entry and when he saw Robey, came on in.

"Hi, Robey, glad to see you. How's it going?" He tossed off the greeting while snatching Amelia's glass of lemonade and upending it to his lips. "Aren't you going to have some lemonade, honey?" He grinned at his wife as he handed back an empty glass. She hurried to refill it and left to supply herself with another one.

"I want to apologize for my actions the first time you came here. They were inexcusable and I can only say it was booze talking. Didn't want to bring the subject up yesterday at the festival but it needed to be said."

"It's alright. I understand. There's been so much pressure on you both. I'm just glad to know you're back together and on the right road again."

"Really isn't fair, is it? Life, I mean. You had such a wonderful marriage with Roger and..."

"Let's not talk about that now, please?" Robey interrupted, putting her hand on David's arm, "I'm not prepared to face too many things at one time. Later, much later."

David sat down beside Amelia. "I guess I should tell you, though, there are rumors rampant in Knobbe Cove about you."

"About me? What kind?" Robey was curious and not too surprised, knowing Iris had probably started them.

"It's being noised about that you are, how should I put it, slightly," he moved a splayed hand back and forth, "unstable."

Robey, in spite of being prepared for his news, gasped and anger sparked from her eyes like fire. "I just hope people don't believe that, David. I was just beginning to feel Knobbe Cove could be my home. Oh, I don't intend to stay, not now. But it would really hurt if I thought all those people who have taken the time to make me welcome were making fun of me behind my back."

"It's Iris, of course," Amelia soothed, "and no one will really believe her, I'm sure."

"You said you weren't going to stay, Robey. Do you mean it?" David looked concerned.

Robey brought David up to date on what had been discussed including their suspicions about the white-faced mystery man.

"So, you can see, if Iris wants me out that bad I can't stay, especially with Graham's attitude. At least I cannot stay at the manse."

"Robey, about the white-faced man, I agree that he can't be Ward, but I know who you are talking about."

"You do?" Both Robey and Amelia asked in unison.

"Oh, I don't know his name. It's just that I've chased him away several times. He looked albino to me, except his eyes are not pink. I always thought albinos had pink eyes."

"I think they do. He just looked like someone who never came out into the sunlight... a night person." Robey remembered how he had darted quickly into the shadows of the garden when he left the house. "Yes, he doesn't like the sun. It was already getting dark when we saw him at the carnival last night."

"If I remember correctly," David leaned back on the sofa, his long legs sticking out into the middle of the room, "I've never seen him in the daytime, either. It was always at night."

"Well," Amelia pushed up from the sofa and walked over to the fireplace and stared into the cold ashes lying there, "Of one thing I *am* sure, Iris knows him and put him up to whatever devilment he has done trying to scare you away. She wants Graham all to herself, and she'll do anything. I warned you, Robey, he's her whole life."

"She wouldn't try to kill Graham, would she?" Robey asked.

"When was that?"

"The boat accident! Graham could have been killed. He was crippled. Iris wouldn't do that to him no matter how she hated you, Amelia. Would she?"

"No...I guess not...I guess not." David answered for Amelia, remembering whoever was in the boat that day did kill their baby. "If ever I thought..." He clenched an up raised fist in emphasis.

Robey picked up her shoulder bag. "I'd better go. I have some visiting to do, and I don't really think I can do much good here playing guessing games. It has been good to talk this out with you two. It's helped a lot."

"Don't let this get you down," David escorted her to the door. "I did, and almost ruined my life. I've made it miserable for Amy for a long time."

"She never believed you were behind the wheel of your boat, you know."

"No," he said softly and then added, "In fact, I never started coming to my senses till I heard those stories about you. I knew they couldn't be true and then I had to face up to the fact I shouldn't have believed any of the things said about Amelia and Graham, either."

"Well, at least something good came from this ill wind, didn't it?" Robey smiled up at him.

Amelia, after taking the lemonade tray back to the kitchen, joined them and put her arm through David's, looking up adoringly at him. "Liquor can make you do an awful lot of things, Robey."

"And one of them," David interrupted, "is to look for an excuse to drink. It seems Iris supplied me with plenty of them."

"I'll tell you both something. My dander is up and before I leave Knobbe Cove—*if* I go—I'm going to get to the bottom of this whole mess and hang it out to dry. Goodbye, now. Thanks for the refreshment. I'll be in touch."

David and Amelia looked at each other, almost amused by Robey's determination. "She looks like a warrior going off to battle with a cause," David quipped and then added, "bet she finds her target too."

Robey strolled down First Avenue with a lighter step than when she fled from the hotel. She went past the cemetery and stopped at the church gate, reaching down to lift the latch. Graham was on the phone when she entered the office and he motioned for her to sit down. When he finished his call, he leaned back in the chair, his fingers clasped behind his head.

"That was Willis. We need to go out there this afternoon," he began and then, when Robey didn't make any comment, he said softly, "I'm sorry for last night, Robey. I really am."

"So am I, Graham, but it's much more than last night. I understand your reluctance to believe me and I'm very sorry about that, because it makes what I thought was going to be a wonderful future, impossible." Graham took his hands from behind his head and began to protest but Robey rushed on. "I'm not imagining situations, Graham. This morning I followed Iris into the hotel.

"Are you sure it was Iris?"

"There you go again," Robey flared angrily at him, "doubting what I say. "Yes, I'm certain. Do you want me to swear on the Bible?"

"No, no, I'm sorry." he seemed genuinely regretful. "What do you suppose she was doing at the hotel?"

"When I went in I couldn't see her, not in the lobby or the tearoom. But I looked at the register and saw Lawrence Laporte's signature in it. You can check with Bobby Ross if you want," she added rather sarcastically.

Graham ignored the tone of her voice. "Your lawyer?"

"Yes, I know he has written Iris. I've seen the envelopes and don't say because they had no return address on them I'm making something out of nothing. I know his penmanship."

"Okay, I believe you, I believe you." His eyes pleaded for forgiveness. "Can you imagine why they have been corresponding?"

Robey relaxed some, realizing she had been sitting stiffly in the chair. She shifted her position, slumping a bit and resting her elbows on the chair arms. "I think she wrote him that I was emotionally unbalanced. She wants me to leave, and there are rumors zipping around town that I'm sure she started. Just like the one she began about you being the father of Amelia's expected baby!"

Graham's head fell to his chest and for a minute Robey thought perhaps he was praying. He looked up and she saw behind his eyes a heavy burden of pain and sadness, and again, disbelief!

"Iris wouldn't tell lies! Who told you that?" his voice barely audible.

"Iris told me herself."

Graham looked as though Robey had physically slapped him.

"I had only been here a couple of days and I wondered about how disloyal she could be to you disclosing such a thing to me, practically a stranger." Seeing the anguish on Graham's face, Robey quickly went on to assure him that she, for one, knew he was innocent of fathering the unborn child.

"Thank you for that, Robey." Graham swung around in the chair and stared out the window to the house across the street. "It's inevitable that I have a showdown on this with Iris. I guess it's about time."

"You can show down all you want, Graham, but I'm going back home to Chandor with Lawrence. I should never have come here in the first place nor pushed my way into other people's lives, especially yours and Iris's."

"You didn't push your way in, Robey. I invited you, remember? I wanted you... and I still want you...more than I can put into words right now. I just have to face up to the fact that my sister...who's the only mother I've ever known...will do most anything to protect me from becoming involved with a woman. She knows I'd get hurt if I loved someone enough to marry her. She was right, you know."

Robey was astounded at his blindness where Iris was concerned. "You really think that's her motive? That that's all there is to it?"

"What else? There's nothing sinister about it, just that she's obsessed with mothering me. Let it pass right now, Robey, for today. I'll try to get some more tangible evidence of her spreading the rumors and face her with it. I know a few people who will tell me the truth."

"You mean I might not?" Robey snapped. "I wanted to help you, Graham. I surely didn't want our relationship to end this way, but you know I can't stay, regardless. I have money, you know that. I've written Lawrence with instructions to sell my holdings. I was going to... I am going to... supply the funds for the orphanage."

Graham made no indication he heard her last words. He swung up onto his crutches and passed Robey where she sat and entered the hall.

"Douglas," he called impatiently. "Douglas!"

Douglas came running out of the sanctuary with the agility of a boy, shoving a polish rag into his hip pocket. "Right here, Pastor." He waved to Robey and greeted her. "Hello, Mizz Layne."

Robey smiled wanly and joined them in the hallway. Graham came direct to the point. "Have you been hearing any talk, Douglas?"

"Talk, Pastor? About what?" His look betrayed any denial he might have voiced.

"About Mrs. Layne, here. Don't act like you haven't heard, you hear everything that goes on."

"Yes, sir. I just about do... and," he hesitated, "yes, I've heard some. But don't you pay them any mind. No one is believing them, they're considering the source..." he fell silent, reluctant to continue.

"The source, Douglas?"

"Yes, sir." His eyes lowered to his hands and he looked very uncomfortable.

"Well?" Graham was impatient with Douglas for the first time in his life.

"Mizz Iris... I'm sorry, Pastor."

With a deep sigh, Graham tried to put Douglas at ease, "That's alright, old friend, I knew. Now, have you ever seen a pale, ash-faced man around the house?"

"I've seen him down at the Cove," Douglas answered truthfully, but evading the question Graham had asked. "Why do you ask about him?"

"He's the one who tried to steal Mrs. Layne's purse at the cemetery that night and he might have broken into the house one day. If you see him around, let me know."

Graham and Robey had started toward the door when Graham called Douglas back. "Just forget we had this conversation." At the hurt look on Douglas's startled face, he smiled. "I don't know why I said that. I know you never repeat what you hear in the church."

"No, sir, I don't. But I do want you both to know no one is taking these rumors as gospel, not like the Wentworths that time." Anger rimmed his last utterance and he pulled the polish cloth from his pocket and disappeared through the huge arched doors into the quiet darkness of the sanctuary, swiping almost viciously at specks of dust on the wainscoting as he went.

"There's still much to be explained, Robey," Graham pulled the office door shut and they both went out of the building into the sunlight. "We'll sleep on it, and I'll put my facts in a row. Then we'll have it out."

"Alright, Graham," Robey acquiesced, "but no later than tomorrow."

21

Lunch began under much stress and silence. If Iris had an inkling of the coming storm, she wasn't saying. Neither did she inquire about their usual quietness, for Graham and Robey were in the habit of chatting like magpies on a telephone wire. When almost five minutes passed without anyone saying anything but 'pass the butter', Graham felt he had to start a conversation just to ease the tension which hung over them like an umbrella.

"Robey and I are going over to the island this afternoon, Iris. Evelyn called to say Fred is feeling poorly, and they want to discuss the possibility of them having to give up the children."

Robey had hardly listened to what Graham said beyond his telling Iris where they were going. She wanted to shout "no" and make him stop talking about it. Fear gripped her heart when she looked into Iris's face and saw a dark shadow of determination replace her usual cool aloofness. Surely she wouldn't get the white-faced man to run Graham down again! This time David was sober, and she would have no one to blame it on. Still, Robey stared down at her bowl of homemade vegetable soup and had a difficult time trying to eat.

"Robey," Graham prodded, "you're awfully quiet. I hope you're feeling like going out."

"I'm fine, Graham. Just thinking other thoughts. I'm sorry, I should have been listening."

Graham understood and reached under the table and patted her on the knee. She smiled weakly, realizing he still didn't know Iris's involvement in the accident and, of course, she couldn't say anything since she had no solid proof. It had all been conjecture between Amelia, David, and herself. Still, knowing *that* didn't make Robey feel any easier about the boat trip across the Cove to the island, now that Iris was aware of it.

She hurried through lunch and turned to Graham. "Let's get on the way if we're going."

"I have a couple of calls to make first, but I shouldn't be long." He didn't wait for her to remark and, standing away from the table, swiftly left the kitchen, went into the office and sat at the desk phone.

'Don't be long' Robey wanted to warn him. 'Don't let Iris have time to plan an accident'. Her head spinning with unwelcome thoughts, Robey sped up the stairs to pick out a broadbrim hat to protect her face from the hot summer sun. She hunted in her bag for her sunglasses and slipped into tennis shoes, which would give her better balance in the boat. She wondered if the boat Graham would rent would be safe. In spite of Coast Guard regulations, some of the outboards tied up to the dock didn't look seaworthy enough to make the fifteen-minute trip to the island. 'Graham won't get an unsafe one', she assured herself, looking into the mirror and running a comb through the thick cap of dark auburn hair topping her freckled face.

Graham called from the foot of the steps, and she grabbed her bag and hat and scurried down to meet him.

"Wait a second while I tell Iris I'll be home for dinner after all. I was going to Amelia's, but they had a chance to go to Savannah this evening to a play. She called me earlier to ask if I minded waiting until next week."

"Iris went out right after lunch, Robey. I don't know where."

Robey thought her heart would stop beating and felt cold perspiration break out on her forehead. She wanted to renege on the trip to the island but knew Graham would go anyway. If she told him Iris would try to kill them he'd really think she were crazy. She didn't realize she had been standing at the bottom of the stairs like a statue until Graham spoke.

"Come on, I thought you were in a hurry for an afternoon on the water!"

"Sorry again...my thoughts are still on other matters."

"I know what you're thinking about, Robey, but force yourself to get off the subject and make yourself enjoy the outing, especially with all those wonderful little kids. Probably just the remedy you need. Come on." He opened the door and Robey, resigned and hopeful nothing untoward would happen, gave up her doubts with a visible shrug of her slim shoulders.

The day was busy, and Graham approached a small man under a denim cap standing on the pier unknotting a large snarl in his fishing line.

"Afternoon, Dan, got the boat ready?"

"All gassed up and seaworthy, Parson. I've already had her out this morning and she shouldn't take but a couple of pulls to get her started."

"Don't know how long we'll be. I'll pay you when we get back."

"No pay, I'll take it off my income tax as a donation." Dan grinned, squinting into the sun. "Looks as though you'll have a hot time out there. You should have brought a hat. There's not much breeze."

"Yep, I suppose, but it's too late to go back now. Evelyn and Fred are expecting us soon."

"Okay, cast off." Dan unwound the hawser and flung it into the bottom of the boat once Graham and Robey were seated. Graham expertly gave the outboard cord a quick pull and it buzzed into life without sputtering.

The Cove itself was a bit choppy with the comings and goings of many small craft, some towing water skiers on their way out to the open water of the Bay, but the water beyond the rocky outcropping at the estuary was smooth, glistening in the brilliant sunshine. Gulls dipped for fish, squawking their winged way back to settle on the rocky knob.

Apprehension built inside Robey's stomach as they neared the edge of the Cove. "So far, so good" she muttered to herself.

"You say something?" Graham asked.

"Don't you ever feel frightened when you ride across the Cove?"

He hesitated a second or two before answering. "Yes, I used to, especially the first time I came this way after the accident…but… well, I couldn't ignore the Willises just because I got chicken, could I?" he smiled and the lines in his face framed his mouth and made his eyes crinkle at the corners. His hair whipped across his head from the speed of the boat and Robey thought she had never seen him so virile and alive.

"No, I guess not," she agreed, wanting with all her being to feel the security he did.

"Besides, each time got easier and easier till now I probably wouldn't have thought about it without you mentioning it. Are you afraid?" he sensed her unspoken fear.

"Maybe a little. But then," she grinned," I *am* chicken."

Graham threw his head back and laughed but then his whole

body tensed at the sound of a large craft coming from behind the knob. Robey looked in the direction Graham had quickly strained to observe and felt the pull of centrifugal force as he tried to speed the boat into a wider arc away from the dangerous rock. She held tight to both sides of the boat to keep her seating.

A horn blare shattered the air and in a few seconds the large craft swept past them much too fast, making a backwash that cut under them, making the boat rock violently. Robey got a fast glimpse of the pilot. It was not the white-faced man, just someone recklessly entering the Cove.

"Darn fool!" Graham shouted after him. "I didn't get his registry number," he turned to Robey, "but I'll find out who he is and report him. He could kill someone with that kind of piloting." He looked at Robey for the first time since the boat began to settle down from its ride on the back wash. "Robey, you're white as a sheet. Are you Okay?"

"Yes. I'll be fine. That was quite a scare. You know, I've only been on a boat like this once before in my life. I'm a born landlubber!"

"Why didn't you say so? You could have stayed home."

"I didn't say I wanted to *stay* a landlubber. I think I could get to enjoy boating under the right circumstances. Maybe a calm sea with no other boats in sight," she laughed, relieved the incident was over and they were obviously safe, for now.

Evelyn Willis met Graham and Robey at the small tie-up pier at the bottom of some weathered wooden steps positioned flat against a small but steep cliff tufted with dark prickly reed grass. The sky was cloudless and the glare from the sun high in the heavens made Robey especially glad she had worn her sunglasses.

"Hi, I'm Evelyn," the short square shouldered woman introduced herself to Robey, who had talked to her via telephone, but had never met her personally.

"Hello," Robey smiled up at her, taking her proffered hand to help her step out of the boat. Graham was busy wrapping the hawser and knotting it securely.

"Come on up," Evelyn invited, and the two women climbed to the top of the steps. Graham then laid his crutches on the landing, sat on the pier and swung his legs out of the boat. Holding onto the railing, he picked up his crutches in one hand and hoisted himself erect. Robey, apprehensive as he maneuvered, couldn't help remarking upon his gracefulness.

"Maybe you could take up ballet one day, Graham," she laughed. The levity wasn't lost on Evelyn who examined their faces and saw the close familiarity and yes, she was sure of it, the love written there. A pleasurable warmth washed over her. 'How wonderful', she thought, 'if Graham Hill has finally fallen in love'!

Before they had walked only a few feet, children burst from around the house, running up to Graham, carefully waiting for him to reach down and caressed their tousled heads. They obviously adored him.

Evelyn began introductions. "Robey, this is Charles, my oldest. He's eighteen and headed for College in the Fall." Robey looked into the sharp green eyes twinkling from the face of a tall lanky boy holding out his hand in greeting. Shaking her hand firmly, he said "Welcome to Lighthouse Island, Ma'am." Before Robey could reply, Evelyn continued to introduce the rest of the twelve children crowding around. There were Zelda and Janet, both sixteen. Zelda was black and lithesome, her laughing brown eyes full of devilment. Janet was more serious with spectacles bridging a peeling sunburnt nose. Robert, fourteen, looked as though he had been digging in the garden and hesitated to shake hands, finally wiping them in a downward motion on his jeans legs before offering Robey a cleaner palm. Conrad, Jose and Charlene were ten and eleven-year olds, with Jose being the youngest of the three. Conrad walked with a limp and Evelyn explained he had corrective shoes. One leg was shorter than the other, but she had a hard time getting him to wear them in summer. Indeed, all three were barefoot and quickly scampered back to Graham, now seated on a stump telling stories.

"Looks like we'll have to go over there if you're to meet the rest," Evelyn giggled, and they wandered toward the small group sitting at Graham's feet. Then, Robey's heart gave a leap, as her eyes fell upon a little girl with dark red hair plaited in long pigtails which reached to her waist. When the child turned to look at her, Robey's heart almost stopped. She was a mirror image of Sally. Even her nose seemed freckled in the same way.

"Is something wrong?" Evelyn asked, concerned.

In answer, Ruby reached into her handbag and brought out a small 'brag book' of photos she always carried with her. On the second page a smiling Sally peered at Evelyn and it was her turn to gasp.

"Who is this?"

"My little girl," Robey said a bit sadly. "she's gone now… an automobile accident…but isn't the resemblance remarkable? They could have been twins."

"That's my Katie. She'll be eight next month." Evelyn explained.

"She's a bit older than my Sally would have been."

As though sensing she was being talked about, Katie turned her head toward Robey, jumped up and came skipping over. "Mother Willis, Pastor Graham is telling stories, can we have some cookies and punch, too?"

All through her little speech, Katie kept her eyes on Robey and, not waiting for Evelyn to make introductions, held out a small delicate hand. "I'm Katie. Are you Mrs. Layne? I heard Daddy Fred say Pastor Graham was bringing you."

"Yes, I'm Robey," Robey smiled and held onto the child's hand for a few moments. "Do you want to see something very interesting?" Not waiting for a reply, she stooped down and showed Katie Sally's picture. Katie kept looking back and forth between herself, her foster mother and Robey, a broad smile wrinkling her nose. "Can I take this to show the others? May I?"

"Of course. Just make sure I don't leave today without it."

Katie bounced off toward her siblings in high spirits, glad to have something to make her feel important instead of just the baby of the bunch.

Inside the screened-in porch, Graham, Robey, Evelyn, and Fred sat looking across the broad front lawn to the Bay. Birds sang, the children chattered, and an old bedraggled collie with the unlikely name of Spot lay dozing under a root gnarled Maple tree.

"As I said before, Graham," it was Fred speaking. "I've got to go in for heart by-pass surgery next week. Evelyn can get along here okay, we're not worried about that, but my energy will be at a low ebb for a long time, if it ever does get back to normal. I'm afraid we've taken in our last foster child. Had to turn the State down twice last month. It breaks our hearts, but that's it."

"Graham," Robey said softly, "don't you think you should really begin plans for the orphanage?"

"With what Robey? I told you when we first spoke about it that I would need bushels of filthy lucre to even begin."

"Uh huh, I remember, but didn't you hear me when I said you'd have it?"

Graham looked puzzled and then a nagging memory of an

earlier conversation pushed its way forward. He had been so concerned about this affair with Iris, he realized, he had given very short shrift to what Robey had said this morning.

Robey peered over the rim of her punch cup and saw the look of hope light up Grahams solemn face. He stared out over to where the children were now playing, the larger children wrestling on the ground, the little ones cheering them on.

"Graham used to be right in the middle of that mess," Evelyn smiled.

"He might be again someday," Robey picked up a cookie and took a quick nibble.

"You mean his legs are getting better?" Fred asked.

"Hey, guys, don't talk as though I'm dead and gone. I'm right here," Graham broke in.

"We thought you were out there in the middle of the yard, the way you were staring out at them. You certainly weren't with us!"

"Pipe dreaming again, I guess. Evelyn, I'll try to get someone to come out and stay with you for a few weeks while Fred gets on his feet. No need for you to be here worrying and working yourself into an attack, too."

"I'd appreciate it Graham, I really would, although that's not why I called for you to come out today. It was the matter of future homes for those who will need them. A good home, not just one where the people want the money State pays them to keep the children."

"Evelyn, I think you can put your mind to rest about that...at least in the very near future. Graham's pipe dream, as he calls it, is going to come true. Why not stop worrying right now. We'll get back to you in a couple of days...and I could come out and stay, if you want, while Fred's in the hospital. It would do me a world of good."

"Oh, would you? That takes a load off! I think all the kids took a shine to you, and the older ones all have their chores. They are a big help...usually," she qualified. "There's no school, so you won't have to be packing lunches or even leaving the island. We stocked up last week and have enough for an army, but then," she amended, "we have an army."

The air was cool on the Bay as they headed back to the mainland and Graham kept looking at Robey out of the corner of his eye, not quite ready to put his hopes into words. Robey broke the silence. "I meant it, Graham. In fact, I've already written Lawrence to sell enough holdings to finance the first two years, at least."

"How can I take your money, Robey? Especially after the way Iris has acted. I'd feel so..." he searched for words.

"It's not for you, Graham, although I cannot help but be honest with you and say I'm glad you're the one to be handling the orphanage. It's for the children."

"We'll talk later," Graham's jaw set in a grim determination to get the unpleasantness with Iris over with as soon as possible and then, he thought to himself, there will be time to set everything else to right.

"It will be dinnertime when we get back and perhaps, if we go to bed early, things will look better tomorrow."

Graham twisted the handle of the small siren on the prowl, warning boats coming from the Cove they were just beyond the knob. Neither he nor Robey had thought about the danger on the way back, their minds racing through plans and hopes and precious dreams. Robey didn't have time to ponder on Iris's treachery. For now they were safe as they approached the dock and tied up.

"Yes, honey," Graham put his hand around her waist, preparing to give her a boost up, "tomorrow is going to be a different kind of day for us both."

'Yes', Robey thought, 'tomorrow'. Tomorrow Lawrence would come, or she would go to him and she'd make arrangements to go home after Fred and Evelyn were back on solid footing on the island.

22

Robey switched off the lamp beside her bed and walked over to the window. She stood there for a while and watched the lights go out in many of the homes of First Avenue. What simple and uncluttered lives they live, she thought, no crisis beyond what to have on the dinner menu day in and day out. She could see a porch swing moving in the next block where someone was taking a leisure few minutes at the end of a busy and probably satisfying day. Robey, exhausted in body and spirit, turned wearily from the window, kicking her slippers off beside the bed. She was surprised to find the room plunged into deep blackness and glanced back at the window again. The moon was hidden by a thick layer of clouds seemingly covering the whole seaboard. A breeze began to stir the leaves of the linden, heralding a storm coming in from the ocean.

Stretching out on the bed, the pillow cool to her head, Robey thought back to the day's events. No matter what the weather tomorrow, she hoped, everything will be cleared up and regardless of what happens, she promised herself, Graham will have his children's home. Lawrence could set the machinery in motion as soon as he got back to Chandor. This afternoon she had intended to return with him, but the trip to the island had changed all that.

It was good to be needed and, Robey had to admit to herself, little Katie had a lot to do with the decision. She could hardly pull her eyes from the child all during her stay. But later, when Fred was back on his feet, she was going home. How surprised Sarah would be. Back home. It sounded secure and close, back home, back... back...she dropped off to an uneasy sleep.

How long she slept she didn't know, but she awakened with a start. What had disturbed her? There was no sound now, but something, her mind told her, a scraping noise, had pulled her from her dreams. She didn't move a muscle as they tensed under the sheets and her skin prickled with fear, her senses alert to what seemed peril, intangible peril. She ran her tongue around the edge of her teeth hunting for a drop of moisture but her mouth was cotton dry. She tried swallowing and found she could not do even that.

'Get hold of yourself, Robey, don't panic. There's no one here ...it's...it's... a mouse'. Her mind sped past reasonable explanations and she tried to relax. She had just done so enough to change her body position when someone kicked the foot of the bed.

Robey screamed and sat up in one movement. Lightning flashed, momentarily illuminating the room. At the foot of the bed was a man with a white stocking pulled over his face. Unable to comprehend, almost frozen in fright, Robey managed to roll to the further side of the bed just as the white-faced apparition vaulted the space between them and roughly grabbed her arm, pulling her back onto the bedspread face down. With a strength she didn't know she possessed, she struggled away from him, her legs kicking violently. With presence of mind, she snatched the open pepper shaker from the night table and emptied it in the air toward her assailant, putting a momentary halt to his assault. She screamed again. Her feet hit the floor, but he grabbed her again and then she heard Graham at the door. The stocking-faced man heard, too, and he gave her a brutal shove away from him. She slammed against the wall. Fortified with the thought that help was near, Robey lurched toward the door and jerked the bolt.

Graham burst into the room and, taking in the situation quickly, swung a crutch at the intruder's head, hitting his mark smartly. Without his support, Graham slipped down to the floor at the foot of the bed as the man, holding a throbbing head, ran toward the wardrobe. Graham thrust his remaining crutch between his legs, bringing him crashing down. His head hit the edge of the bureau as he fell and he lay there, barely breathing, blood seeping from a wound on his temple.

An eerie silence permeated the bedroom after so much violence.

"Are you alright, Robey?" Graham panted.

"Yes, I'm fine. Scared spitless, but okay." Her trembling belied her words as she reached for the light switch beside the door and then fell into Graham's arms. After a brief moment she crawled over to where the man still lay unconscious on the floor. Gingerly, as though any second he would wake and grab her again, she reached out and pulled the now gore-stained stocking from his head.

"Lawrence! It's Lawrence!" Robey stared in disbelief, not wanting to face the deep frustration engulfing her. She stood up momentarily and then collapsed heavily on the edge of the bed and wept openly, great sobs shaking her entire body. Graham pulled himself up to her side and nestled her head on his shoulder. Out of the corner of his eye he saw Iris peeking from behind her bedroom door which stood slightly ajar.

"Iris! Get in here at once." He was furious, certain now she had been at the bottom of this outrage. Iris obeyed him meekly, her color high, making her gray hair seem almost white. She kept wringing her hands nervously. Lawrence stirred and sat up, rubbing his head, wincing and looking at the blood that splotched his hand. He tried to stand but found his knees too weak to hold him.

"Alright, now. What is this all about?" Graham's voice seethed with authority. Robey, calmer than she thought she could be, retrieved his crutches and he held them both like clubs ready, if necessary, to swing at the hapless attorney.

"It was Miss Hill," Lawrence mumbled. "she wrote me saying you were losing your mind in grief, Robey. She thought she could frighten you into coming home."

"Why?" Robey turned to Iris.

"Because you have no business being here." Hate spewed from her words. "All I have in life is Graham and you want to take him from me. Amelia did, too, but I fixed that!"

It took a minute for her words to sink into Graham's mind and then he asked, incredulously, "You arranged the accident where I could have been killed?" Graham looked up at his sister. "You did this to me?" he motioned at his legs. Iris had no reply. She abruptly turned and started to leave.

"*Come back here and sit down!*" Graham yelled at her. Her head snapped up and for an instant Robey thought Iris would strike her brother, but suddenly she crumpled into a chair, sullenly staring at her hands in her lap. Graham continued to stare at his sister, his shoulders visibly shrunk in dejection.

Robey had gained full control of herself. "Lawrence, why would you do such a thing? Why?"

"You might as well know now since you'll investigate anyway. Your estate is missing over a hundred thousand dollars."

Robey gasped in disbelief. Her plans for the orphanage were surely in jeopardy!

"Over the years I lost it, gambling, bad investments." Lawrence hung his head, his words muffled in his chest. "Iris thought you really loved me. I told her I love you and I do, Robey, you know I do." His eyes raised to hers in a bold pleading look as though to draw Robey to him.

Robey's skin seemed to crawl as Lawrence continued his confession. "She said she had already tried to scare you by having your purse snatched at the cemetery. When that didn't work, and you survived the accident at the church, she decided on this plan, after having read most of the letters I sent you. I wasn't going to do anything to harm you, Robey. I wouldn't hurt you. You must know that."

"Even if I had gone back to Chandor, don't you think I would have found out about the money?"

Lawrence sighed and rose from the floor. Graham brandished the crutches and he sat back down again, leaning against the wall.

"I hoped you might grow to like me enough to marry me. Then you would never have known. I could have worked it all out."

For the first time, Robey noticed the wardrobe standing out from the wall. She went over to it and found that it rolled easily and almost silently on large casters beneath. Behind the massive piece of furniture was a door partially open through which she could see the shelves of the linen closet.

"So, this is how you got in, and someone else too." Her memory sped back to the night she smelled the musky odor from the cellar. It couldn't have been Lawrence. He had not arrived yet.

"Graham, make Iris tell us who the white-faced man is. She knows," Robey returned to Graham's side. He put his arms around her, bolstering her with his strength.

"You heard her, Iris. Who is he? Who is this man who evidently has been living in our home without my knowledge?"

Iris looked up at Graham and braced her shoulders. She no longer looked defeated but filled with self-righteousness and purpose. "He's your brother, Ward. Your own flesh and blood. Ward!" she almost screamed at Graham. "Do you think I would keep him forever among strangers? He escaped and I kept him home...he didn't want to go back. I was glad because when Amelia started to work for you I had to look out for you all the time. She schemed...she...," her voice shrilled. "I could not leave you to her. You thought you didn't need me anymore."

A calmness overtook Iris's words and she spoke as though in conspiracy. "Ward escaped and came home. He's been here over seven years and you never knew." She sounded proud of her achievement. "Sometimes he stays with the Lodges. They understand why I must have him home. Yes, I got him to pilot the boat. It put an end to Amelia's interference didn't it?"

"And both of us could have been killed!"

Iris's eyes were like cold steel. Robey shuddered in Graham's embrace. "No matter, no matter." Her voice dropped to a level they could barely hear, and she looked venomously at Robey. It was the last lucid emotion she had, for at that point she made fists of her hands in her lap and slowly lowered blank eyes to stare at them, having regressed into a world where no one could follow.

"Iris," Graham called but there was no answer. "Iris?" And still she sat there unhearing, unseeing and unthinking.

Graham and Robey sat stunned. What had just moments before been a vital woman ready to defend her brothers with all her being was now an empty shell unable to communicate or comprehend.

"Poor Iris," Robey's voice was full of compassion. "How tormented she has been. How tragic."

"Dearest Robey," Graham sighed, "how can you be so understanding after what she tried to do to you?"

"She was driven by demons neither you nor I could possibly know, wasn't she?"

Tears coursed down Graham's cheek and Robey took him in her arms to comfort him. "She was a good mother to you, and a good sister to Ward. Maybe she'll be alright one day. I believe there's help for her somewhere."

"Robey," Lawrence's voice came out of the corner where he still sat on the rug. "She never meant to hurt you, only frighten you away. That's why she had me come here. She said she couldn't trust Ward not to harm you if you resisted and he really got stirred up. I wouldn't have done anything more. I was ready to leave when Hill came to the door."

"Where is Ward now, Lawrence? Do you know?" Robey demanded.

"He's over next door, I think. Iris said she had to move him over there when you got so suspicious."

"Robey, go down and call the Sheriff." Graham still held the crutches threateningly. "I'll be alright here."

AFTERWORD

Amelia and David would arrive soon for dinner—perhaps their last time out before the baby came. Robey arranged pink tea roses in the gold rimmed Lenox bowl gracing the center of the dining room table. Sunshine streamed through the window and washed the room with light.

In the year she and Graham had been married she had redecorated the whole house, turning it from a shadowy, dull turn-of-the-century musty house into a bright glowing cheerful home. True, she had kept all the old furniture, but the settings were so different now from the old, that one could hardly recognize them. Heavy drapes had given way to airy lace curtains that wafted inward constantly from open windows. The old thread-worn rugs had been discarded and the new rugs cushioned one's steps. Even Graham's office had been invaded by Robey and it was no longer a mass of small tables piled high with newspapers and journals. A file cabinet of white oak now stood in the corner with clippings neatly stashed in folders. Graham had protested loudly at first and bugged Robey each time he needed a bit of information, but now he'd become used to the system and grudgingly admitted he liked it.

Robey sat down on the sofa in the living room with a glass of iced tea while waiting for her dinner guests. She thought back on the full year of litigation and the trial of Lawrence LaPorte. How small and defeated he had been, tears streaming down his face, when he had been found guilty of embezzlement and sentenced to prison. The papers carried the story of his disbarment from the State Bar Association. Robey had not filed any other charges. She could see no use in doing so. She had not been hurt, and she actually felt sorry for Lawrence.

Fortunately, more than enough money had been retained and returned in Roger's estate to fund the orphanage. In fact, Robey was still amazed at the size of her inheritance—the money Larry had stolen had been such a small amount compared to the whole. And to think Larry had risked and lost his reputation and freedom for it.

Ward had been returned to the State home, and Iris had also been committed. The court appointed Graham guardian for them both. When last they visited, Iris had still not recognized them, but Ward had been seemingly overjoyed to show them all the things he had been making out of craft kits they sent him.

Suddenly a commotion behind the house jarred Robey from her reverie and she rose from the comfortable seat to walk swiftly to the kitchen door. Looking out, she saw Douglas charge around the house, burning newspaper raised high over his head as a bumblebee threatened his graying hairs. Katie, doubled over with laughter, scooted under the cement bench as Douglas flew past.

Katie, Robey smiled, how wonderful to have her with them. Evelyn and Fred had been relieved to find a good home for her since Fred had not fared too well with his surgery. There had been so many complications, but now, with the orphanage newly opened, Graham had more or less hired Charles, Janet, and Zelda to work and stay at Hill House, as the children's home was called. Papers were in the works for their adoption of Katie. The Willises were able to cope with the rest.

"Pastor Graham's coming up the street," Katie called. Robey laughed. They were having a hard time getting her to call him Dad, or anything but Pastor.

"Pastor Graham," Robey smiled, hugging herself and leaning against the door jamb, "and Katie, my daughter, and Knobbe Cove," she added. "Home."

About the Author

PHYLLIS WOOD FRAVEL was born in Pennsylvania on December 7, 1926, but she spent her childhood in the row houses of northwestern Washington, D.C. A talented musician, her mother dreamed of her becoming a concert pianist, but World War II redirected her path. Working for the wartime federal government, she met her future husband while taking night classes. The two moved briefly to the Shenandoah Valley before settling in Woodbridge, Virginia, to raise five children.

Fravel is a lifelong artist with many interests. An accomplished pianist, she has played for a variety of northern Virginia churches from the age of twelve, while also indulging a love of watercolor and oil painting. Writing, however, has been a passion she has enjoyed her entire life. She has published numerous times, including a regular political column for the "Potomac News" in the 1960s and 1970s. *Knobbe Cove* is her second published novel. Her first novel, *Room Board and Murder* was published in 2017.